RULES OF COMBAT

PRIMARY RULES

1. The objective of Arena 13 combat is to cut flesh and spill blood. Human combatants are the targets.

2. No human combatant may wear armour or protective clothing of any kind. Leather jerkins and shorts are mandatory; flesh must be open to a blade.

3. An Arena 13 contest is won and concluded when a cut is made to one's opponent and blood is spilled. This can occur during combat or may be a ritual cut made after a fight is concluded. If it occurs during combat, hostilities must cease immediately to prevent death or serious maiming.

4. If death should occur, no guilt or blame may be attached to the victor. There shall be no redress in law. Any attempt to punish or hurt the victorious combatant outside the arena is punishable by death.

5. The right to make a ritual cut is earned by disabling one's opponent's *lac* or *lacs*.

6. The defeated combatant must accept this ritual cut to the upper arm. The substance *kransin* is used to intensify the pain of that cut.

7. An unseemly cowardly reaction to the ritual cut after combat is punishable by a three-month ban from the arena. Bravery is mandatory.

8. Simulacra, commonly known as lacs, are used in both attack and defence of the human combatants.

9. The min combatant fights behind one lac; the mag combatant fights behind three lacs.

10. For the first five minutes combatants must fight behind their lacs. Then the warning gong sounds and they must change position and fight in front of them, where they are more vulnerable to the blades of their opponent.

11. A lac is disabled when a blade is inserted in its throat-socket. This calls the wurde *endoff*; the lac collapses and becomes inert.

12. Arena 13 combatants may also fight under **Special Rules**.

SPECIAL RULES

1. **Grudge match rules**
   The objective of a grudge match is to kill one's opponent. All **Primary Rules** apply, but for the following changes:
   • If blood is spilled during combat, hostilities need not cease; the fight continues.
   • After an opponent's lac or lacs have been disabled, the opponent is slain. The throat may be slit, or the head severed from the neck – the decision belongs to the victor. The death blow is carried out by either the victorious human combatant or his lac.
   • Alternatively the victor may grant clemency in return for an apology or an agreed financial penalty.

2. **Trainee Tournament rules**

The objective of this tournament is to advance the training of first-year trainees by pitting them against their peers in Arena 13. For the protection of the trainees and to mitigate the full rigour of Arena 13 contests, there are two changes to the **Primary Rules**:
- The whole contest must be fought behind the lacs.
- Kransin is not used on blades for the ritual cut.

3. **A challenge from Hob**
- When Hob visits Arena 13 to make a challenge, a min combatant must fight him on behalf of the Wheel.
- All min combatants must assemble in the green room, where that combatant will be chosen by lottery.
- Grudge match rules apply, but for one: there is no clemency.
- The fight is to the death. If the human combatant is beaten then, alive or dead, he may be taken away by Hob. Combatants, spectators and officials must not interfere.

SECONDARY RULES

1. Blades must not be carried into the green room or the changing room.
2. No Arena 13 combatant may fight with blades outside the arena. An oath must be taken at registration to abide by that rule. Any infringement shall result in a lifetime ban from Arena 13 combat.
3. Spitting in the arena is forbidden.
4. Cursing and swearing in the arena is forbidden.
5. Abuse of one's opponent during combat is forbidden.
6. In the case of any dispute, the Chief Marshal's decision is absolute. There can be no appeal.

Also available by Joseph Delaney

THE SPOOK'S SERIES
The Spook's Apprentice
The Spook's Curse
The Spook's Secret
The Spook's Battle
The Spook's Mistake
The Spook's Sacrifice
The Spook's Nightmare
The Spook's Destiny
I Am Grimalkin
The Spook's Blood
Slither's Tale
Alice
The Spook's Revenge

The Spook's Stories: Witches
The Spook's Bestiary

The Seventh Apprentice
A New Darkness
The Dark Army

THE ARENA 13 SERIES
Arena 13
The Prey

ARENA 13
THE PREY

JOSEPH DELANEY

RED FOX

RED FOX

UK | USA | Canada | Ireland | Australia
India | New Zealand | South Africa

Red Fox is part of the Penguin Random House group of companies
whose addresses can be found at global.penguinrandomhouse.com.

www.penguin.co.uk
www.puffin.co.uk
www.ladybird.co.uk

Penguin
Random House
UK

First published 2016

002

Copyright © Joseph Delaney, 2016
Cover illustration © James Fraser, 2016

The moral right of the author has been asserted

Typeset in 11/14 pt Bell MT by Jouve (UK), Milton Keynes
Printed in Great Britain by Clays Ltd, St Ives plc

A CIP catalogue record for this book is available from the British Library

ISBN: 978–1–782–95406–4

All correspondence to:
Red Fox
Penguin Random House Children's
80 Strand, London WC2R 0RL

For Marie

The dead do dream.

They dream of the world of Nym and twist hopelessly

within its dark labyrinths,

seeking that which they can never reach.

But for a few, a very few, a wurde is called.

It is a wurde that summons them again to life.

Cursed are the twice-born.

Amabramsum: the Genthai Book of Wisdom

PROLOGUE

The combatants gather in the green room. Nobody speaks. Their faces are grim. In turn, each of them is offered the glass lottery orb. As Vitus draws a straw, he feels a sudden premonition of doom. His hands are trembling and he already knows that he will be chosen.

He is.

His straw is the shortest.

His straw means death.

He has been chosen to fight Hob in Arena 13.

Before he leaves for the arena, his mother always says the same thing:

'Come back to me. Be safe!'

'I will,' he promises.

Then they hug and part.

This time he will not be able to keep his promise.

His worst fear has finally come true.

There is not even time to say goodbye to his family. His mother never visits Arena 13 – she finds it barbaric. His father encouraged him and paid for his training, but he is dead now. His two older brothers work their large farm,

3

which is close to the city. Time after time his mother has begged him to stop fighting in Arena 13 and help his brothers, but he enjoys the challenge and needs to make his own way in the world.

He likes being a combatant, and during the two years that he's been fighting the money has been good. It pays the bills, with some left over; that is important. You can't fight for much more than fifteen years in Arena 13. You get older. You slow down. Your legs start to betray you. Vitus is only nineteen, but it is vital that he saves now. He needs to accumulate enough capital to start his *own* business. Just ten more successful years, and he could do it.

But every year Hob visits Arena 13.

Vitus always fights from the min position and is defended by a lone lac whilst his opponents, fighting from the mag position, have three lacs. It is harder to fight from the min but it offers the greater challenge and is more lucrative.

But here lies the ultimate danger faced by every min combatant. Hob fights behind a tri-glad and his challenge is always to the min combatants.

Every year there is a chance that Vitus will be chosen by the lottery to fight him.

Finally it has happened.

Now he enters the arena, his knees trembling, his mouth dry with fear, his heart pounding within his chest.

The moment he sees Hob and his three lacs his fear intensifies. Hob wears a bronze helmet, his eyes just visible through the horizontal slit, and the tri-glad is clad in ebony-black armour. Hob and his lacs are human in shape but their arms are longer. They radiate malice and move with a grace surpassing that of others who fight in this arena. They stalk like predators. Vitus knows that he is their prey.

His mind whirling, Vitus hears the big doors rumble shut. There is no blast from the trumpet that usually signals the start of a contest. They are to fight under the special rules that govern confrontations with Hob.

It is worse than just a fight to the death. If you are wounded but still alive, Hob takes you to the darkness within his lair, a thirteen-spired citadel on a hill high above the city. Nobody knows what happens there, but the human combatant is never seen again . . .

The fight begins. Hob and his tri-glad begin their advance. Their blades gleam in the light from the candelabrum above the arena. Vitus shelters behind his own lac, hoping that the code he has patterned into it will enable it to defend him against the coming onslaught. He crouches, ready to meet the imminent attack.

This year his lac has performed well. Vitus is ninth in the rankings, but most of his contests have been won in the first five minutes. It is important to achieve such early victories because after that time there is a pause in the fighting; a repositioning. Then you have to fight *in front* of your lac. That makes you much more vulnerable to the blades that seek your flesh.

To fight that way is terrifying. Combatants wear only leather shorts and a jerkin, their flesh open to blades. And now, if he manages to survive for five minutes, he will have to face Hob and fight him toe to toe, blade against blade.

He need not have worried about that. He tortured himself unnecessarily with such thoughts. He lasts barely two minutes.

There is the clash of blades; the clang of metal upon metal; the rapid dance close to the back of his lac; the steady retreat, sweat running down into his eyes. He can hardly see.

A sudden groan erupts from the gallery above, and he wonders what is wrong. To his astonishment, Vitus sees that his own lac is already down. A blade has been thrust into its throat-socket, shutting down the patterns that control it. The lac has collapsed onto the boards of the arena. Its part in the contest is over. He is alone.

Hob's lacs rush at him with their knives.

Vitus flinches, then holds up his own blades in a futile attempt to defend himself. He feels a sharp pain in his side and a stabbing in his chest. His legs turn to jelly. The world spins. He falls into darkness. For a while he knows nothing . . .

Then consciousness slowly returns. The pain seems to have faded almost to nothing. All is silent but for his own hoarse, laboured breathing.

Hob has not slit his throat.

His head remains attached to his body.

He lives.

For a moment Vitus dares to hope.

But when he opens his eyes and looks up, hope fades. Hooded figures gather around him. These are the tassels, the dreaded servants of Hob. They crouch over him and sniff at his body; they snarl and drool, their spit dribbling onto his hair and face. They are cannibals and they are hungry for his flesh.

They drag him to his feet and he is taken from the arena. As Vitus tries to walk, pain tears at his body and he hears his boots squelching. Why are they making that sound?

Outside, a wagon is waiting in the darkness. He is forced into the back and sits there, with a tassel on either side gripping his arms firmly, their saliva dripping onto his trousers. The wooden slats are closed, the interior lit by a single candle.

His eyes slowly adjust to the gloom. He looks down and sees that blood is running from his jerkin down onto his knees and dripping onto his boots. Now he understands the reason for the squelching. His boots are full of blood; his own blood.

The wagon jerks forward. He knows where they are taking him. Fear clutches at his heart. There is no hope for him now.

Come back to me. Be safe! His mother's words haunt him.

What horrors await him inside Hob's citadel? he wonders.

After a while their progress slows. The oxen pulling the wagon are labouring up a steep slope. He hears the cracking of a whip and the bellowing of the animals. They must be climbing the hill towards the dreaded citadel. When they come to a halt, the tassels pull him out roughly. He looks up and sees the high curved stone wall of Hob's lair. He is dragged to the left and moves widdershins, against the clock.

Vitus glimpses dark openings – steep muddy slopes leading down below the wall, too small for a man. There are other hooded tassels with them now. Some are small and crawl on all fours, sniffing at the ground. Others are tall, but their grey cloaks trail upon the ground. He glimpses gaunt faces and open mouths full of sharp teeth.

Vitus is pulled inside a large curved archway. He staggers and falls to his knees; they haul him roughly to his feet. They cross a flagged courtyard and descend into a dark tunnel. The tassels drag him faster, although he can now see nothing except their eyes, which glow a baleful red. Can they see in the dark?

They emerge into what appears to be a large cellar. There are torches on the far wall, but their flickering light barely reaches the place where they bring Vitus to a halt. At waist height he can see grey, globular things swaying in the darkness like flowers in a breeze. But there is no breeze. The air is still and warm. No – they are more like mushrooms. The cellar is full of them – row after row. There is a rank smell of rotting that brings bile to his throat.

Vitus is forced to his knees beside what looks like a huge anvil. Then he sees the groove in it and gasps in terror.

This is an executioner's block.

His head is forced down until his neck fits into the groove. But he sees that the tall tassel striding towards him is not carrying an axe. Across his shoulder he bears something that resembles a huge pair of scissors. They are bolt-cutters, with sharp blades – and long arms so that great force can be applied.

As Vitus looks his last upon the world, his gaze is drawn by the nearest of the flowers. Now he realizes that it is not a flower. Nor is it a fungus growth.

Now he knows his fate . . .

It is a severed human head swaying on a stem.

Why would Hob do this? It cannot be to terrorize people because nobody can see this. Nobody knows that it exists. Then what can its purpose be?

Why display dead humans in this way?

To his horror, Vitus realizes that he is wrong.

The swaying head opens its eyes and stares at him.

Somehow it lives!

He feels the cold metal of the bolt-cutters touch his lower neck, close to his body.

The horror will not end with death.

IT HAPPENS TO US ALL

Children fight with sticks; men fight with blades.
We await the child that wields both.

Amabramdata: the Genthai Book of Prophecy

I was standing at a distance from the action, my boots slowly sinking into the mud of the recreation ground. A big circle of chanting spectators hid the stick-fighters from my view. Within it, one combatant would be fighting against three. That was always the way, here in this small provincial town. The odds were against the lone combatant, so if you bet on him and he won, there'd be a good return on your money.

The crowd were cheering and whooping now, some of them leaping up and down in obvious excitement; others perhaps only to keep warm.

I was certainly shivering. It was cold, and the sun was low on the horizon, sinking towards the roofs of the squat single-storey dwellings even though it was only a couple of hours after midday.

The contest was building to a climax – though I wasn't really here to watch the stick-fighting. I never gambled any more; I didn't care who won. I was just passing through

Mypocine, heading south; this had once been my home and held lots of memories – some of them good, but others bad. Most of the former had been here in this small town, meeting my friends and taking part in the stick-fighting. The bad I preferred not to think about too much. After the death of my mother at Hob's hands, and the suicide of my father, I'd worked for a farmer who'd treated me little better than a slave.

But some habits die hard. I couldn't stop the wave of excitement that stirred within me as I pushed my way through the crowd, using my shoulders and elbows. I got a few curses and angry glares, but I kept moving forward. A few nods and smiles also came my way. It wasn't that long since I'd fought here and I was clearly remembered.

On my way through Mypocine I had hoped to find my old friend Peter. I'd just spent five months in the north of the country, being trained to fight in Arena 13, so I hadn't seen him for some time.

Peter was a stick-fighter, like me, and I had no doubt he'd be here somewhere, watching and waiting for his turn. This green just north of the city was where challengers desperate to prove themselves and move up through the rankings came each Saturday morning.

At last I glimpsed the current combatants. There were only two still on their feet and they were trading furious blows: ones to the body caused bruises and sometimes cuts, but victory resulted from a blow to an opponent's head. There were two lads on the ground holding their heads; one of them was bleeding badly.

Suddenly there was more blood – a red spurt from the nose

of the combatant facing me. It splattered the front of his white shirt and dribbled down onto his dark trousers.

The contest was over.

The winner had his back to me and I watched him bow. I'd started that convention. It was something that my father had taught me. Once Peter and I started doing it, the habit had caught on; every winner did it now.

And then I realized that I knew the winner. He was a little broader and taller now, but the lad with his back to me was Peter!

There was a loud cheer, and some groans and boos, to mark the end of the contest, and then the crowd moved away, some clutching tickets and surging towards the red-sashed tout waiting on the corner of the street. These had bet on the winner, and were now seeking the money owed them by the waiting gambling agent.

'Peter!' I shouted to catch the winner's attention.

He turned at the sound of my voice, smiled in surprise and walked towards me through the crowd. His dark hair was still shaved into a crew cut, his eyebrows were bushy, meeting in the middle, but his face seemed a little different. At first I couldn't work out what it was.

'Hi, Leif!' he called as he pushed his way towards me. 'You're back!'

Now I saw that four of his front teeth were missing – two at the top and two at the bottom.

He saw me staring. 'You're looking at this?' He grinned as he pointed into his open mouth. 'It happens to us all eventually!'

I smiled at him but I couldn't hide my shock: I had never

lost my teeth in a fight, and I hadn't expected Peter to do so either. He'd been one of the best stick-fighters in Mypocine, second only to me. And today he had looked as good as ever in combat.

'Didn't it work out in the city?' he asked.

'It worked out fine. I'm being trained in the stable of the best artificer in Gindeen. But with the season over, I've come back south for a few months.'

What I'd said was true, but I didn't mention the dark side of what I'd experienced: the terrible deaths. I made sure I didn't look too cheerful. It wouldn't do to appear boastful. Although Peter had wished me luck, I know he too would have loved the chance to go to Gindeen to be trained. But it was I who had got the winning ticket that guaranteed me a free place in a stable of combatants.

'I've kept your sticks safe for you, Leif. How about I set up a bout between you and me to see who's best these days? While you've been away, I've taken your crown as the official champion of Mypocine. Want to see if you can win it back?'

Peter had given me many a tough fight, but had never actually beaten me. I shook my head. 'Sorry to disappoint you, Peter, but I'm not allowed to fight with sticks any more. It's one of the rules laid down by Tyron, the man I work for.'

Peter's smile slipped from his face. 'You've got to be joking!' he exclaimed. 'He'd never find out. We're too far away from Gindeen. Don't be soft, Leif. I deserve a chance to beat you. Come on, what do you say?'

'Look, I'm really sorry, but I just can't risk it. Tyron has sacked me once already for stick-fighting; he wouldn't give

me a second chance. And you'd be surprised how much information finds its way back to Gindeen.'

'You're just making excuses!' Peter snapped. He seemed
angry.

I started to feel angry myself. 'It's *not* an excuse. I'm finished with stick-fighting. I won't fight you, Peter.'

'Why did you come back then?'

'I want to visit the Genthai lands and see how my father's
people live. I'm just passing through. I stopped here because
I wanted to see you. We're still friends, aren't we?'

He stared hard at me for a few moments, then his face
broke into a wide smile. 'Of course we're still friends. Shall
we go and get a drink and something to eat?'

I nodded, and he led the way across the muddy field, then
through the narrow streets of wooden buildings.

Much of Gindeen, my new home, had been a disappointment to me – its boardwalks and buildings were just as
rotten as they were here in the south – but there was one
district called Westmere, where the rich, successful people
lived; this was more impressive than anywhere I'd ever been
in my life. There was a big plaza with cafés and shops where
you could sit outside when the weather permitted.

Here, our destination was a café that looked ramshackle
but was full to bursting: we had to wait before a table became
free. We both had the same – eggs and beans on toast
followed by a glass of fruit juice.

At first the conversation flowed easily. I asked questions
about the lads I remembered. For many of them, things
hadn't changed, but a few had drifted away; one had even got
married and his new wife wouldn't let him fight any more.

It was five months since I'd left and there had been changes, but that was only to be expected. Stick-fighting was usually something teenagers did. Then they moved on, got married or found jobs on farms. And when Peter started talking about people I'd never heard of, I realized that if I came back to Mypocine regularly, we'd have less in common each year. I would become more and more of a stranger. I tried telling Peter about my new life in Gindeen, but I saw that he wasn't really interested; he changed the subject whenever he could.

I began to wonder if he was jealous of me: after all, I'd got away and become an Arena 13 trainee; I belonged in Gindeen now. I liked being trained by Tyron and living with Deinon, another of his trainees, and the rest of his family. Kwin, Tyron's youngest daughter, came suddenly into my mind – her hair deliberately cut shorter on one side to display the scar on her cheek; the scar she'd got after activating one of her father's lacs and fighting it, blade against blade. I missed Kwin, but I still wasn't sure how she really felt about me.

I came out of my daydream to see Peter staring at me, a strange expression on his face. 'I'd best be off,' I said. 'I'd like to be well clear of the town before nightfall.'

'Do you know any of the Genthai?' he asked with a frown.

'I met one of them briefly a while back. So I thought I would visit.'

'Well, you should be all right,' Peter said, 'being half Genthai yourself. But most of the ones left in this town beg or steal and drink themselves unconscious each night. And those living in the tribal grounds think they're better than us. They've never been that friendly—'

'It's their right to keep themselves to themselves,' I

interrupted. I was trying to stay calm, but it annoyed me when people criticized the Genthai and complained about them.

'No offence, Leif. I'm just trying to tell you that things have got worse in recent months. Town folk who've ventured into the forest have been forced back. One group of hunters resisted and made a real fight of it. They were beaten bloody, then bound and dumped on the outskirts of town. The tribal Genthai were always territorial, you know that, but now they think the forest belongs to them. I'm just trying to warn you – that's all.'

I smiled and nodded, but what he'd said disturbed me. Maybe it wouldn't be so easy to visit my father's people after all. I'd assumed that I'd be welcome, but now I was dubious about my reception.

'Thanks for the warning, Peter,' I said, 'but I'll be fine. I'll tell you all about it when I pass through here on my way back.'

Soon I was leaving the city behind, but Peter's warning had worried me. Konnit, the Genthai leader I'd met, had told me that they were on a war footing. They might have no time for me now. Perhaps, even though I'd come all this way, I would be turned back too . . .

HALF-BLOOD

The moon shall dim as the sun grows bright.
Amabramsum: the Genthai Book of Wisdom

That night, as I lay amongst the tall conifers at the edge of the forest, looking up at the stars, I thought again about Peter's warning. I decided that if I was stopped, I would explain why I was making this visit and ask permission to proceed. But if they still barred my way, I would turn back. After all, the forest was part of the Genthai domain.

From time to time I was disturbed by the forest creatures – though nothing large enough to make me feel nervous. I lay there, thinking. I remembered what Konnit had said to me on the slope below Hob's citadel after his warriors had rescued me from some tassels:

First we must take back this land from the traitor who calls himself the Protector, and cleanse it of abominations such as Hob. That done, we will ride forward beyond the Barrier to defeat those who confined us here.

I wasn't sure I agreed about the last bit. It seemed extremely reckless. We didn't know how powerful the opposition beyond the Barrier would be. However, I certainly wanted to destroy Hob.

In a great war, centuries earlier, mankind had been defeated by powerful djinn who had turned against their human creators. This world was all any of us had ever known. How could the Genthai expect to change things? Although I had no love for the Protector and his men, I feared that overthrowing someone who'd been placed here to rule us and keep us in submission would bring down immediate and terrible retribution. After all the Protector was the ruler of Midgard and he enforced order using his guards. And, even if they defeated and removed him, how could the Genthai hope to pass through the Barrier that enclosed our land – that wall of mist and terror that drove men mad.

I'd never ventured anywhere near it. It was foolish to do so, as some had found out to their cost: they returned jabbering with terror, their minds fragmented.

Perhaps the Genthai had become more territorial because they didn't want outsiders to discover their preparations for war.

My musings were interrupted by the hoot of an owl and the shriek of a bird I couldn't identify. There were little rustlings, but I knew that the forest was home to large black bears and wolves. Now I heard howls in the distance – along with a cry that I couldn't identify; something that wasn't a wolf.

I finally drifted into a broken sleep. A couple of hours before dawn I heard something moving through the nearby trees. I came up onto my knees and gripped the dagger I had brought with me. I listened hard, thinking that it sounded as if it was walking on two legs rather than four. Black bears could be dangerous, but they didn't attack unless provoked or threatened. The unseen creature soon moved away, and I slept again.

By late the following afternoon I knew that I was being followed. There were at least three of them. They made no noise, but out of the corner of my eye I caught occasional glimpses of shadows slipping between the trees. They had to be Genthai.

It seemed that they were getting closer. How long would it be before they confronted me?

There was a clearing directly ahead, but before I was half-way across the open space a figure stepped out to block my path. I glanced over my shoulder and saw that my pursuers were in the open now, directly behind me; there were five of them.

The mounted Genthai warriors who'd rescued me from the tassels had had facial tattoos. Although these armed men had none, they were clearly Genthai. Dressed in leather and furs, they had swords in shoulder scabbards and daggers at their hips; all carried axes. I was fifteen and big for my age, but as I came to a halt and they closed in, I realized that all were at least a head taller; the one who confronted me was nearly seven feet tall.

The giant balanced his axe across his broad shoulder, gripping it with his right hand. 'You're not welcome here,' he told me, his words rumbling up from deep inside him.

I looked straight back into his eyes and paused before replying to give him a chance to take in the colour of my skin, which was almost as dark as his. I wanted these people to see that I had Genthai blood.

'I've come to visit the land of my father's people,' I told him. 'My name is Leif. My father fought in Arena 13 under the name Mathias, though most folk shortened it to Math. His Genthai name was Lasar.'

The big warrior raised his eyebrows in surprise and then looked me up and down. 'Your father might have been Genthai, but your mother was not of our people,' he said, his voice full of disdain. 'You're a half-blood.'

Back in the city of Gindeen, I'd occasionally encountered prejudice because of my darker skin and Genthai appearance, but I'd never thought for a moment that I would find it here. A truth suddenly struck me – something that I'd never even considered before. I belonged neither to the Genthai nor to the city dwellers. I would always be somewhere in between; always an outsider.

'I was invited here by Konnit,' I said, suppressing my emotions.

'Konnit? Which Konnit do you speak of? There are several families who go by that name.'

I glanced quickly at the men surrounding me. All were clean-shaven – unlike Konnit.

'That was the only name he gave me. He had facial tattoos and a moustache that obscured most of his mouth. He rode a big horse and wielded two swords,' I said. 'He said that he would one day become the leader of the Genthai.'

The warrior glared at me and clenched his left fist, and for a moment I thought that he was about to strike me. It took all my willpower not to flinch. 'If you prove to be a liar, half-blood, we will beat you to within an inch of your life. You speak of Hemi Konnit, who is indeed our leader now. Tie his hands!' he snapped at the men behind me.

They snatched my bag from me, then bound my hands behind my back roughly, tying the rope so tightly that it cut into my wrists. For the first time I began to feel afraid. If Konnit didn't remember our meeting I would be in for a terrible beating. The big warrior probably didn't care whether I lived or died.

Then I was blindfolded and pushed hard in the back. I staggered and almost fell, but I was dragged forward by my arms, and we set off at a furious pace.

We continued in this way for about an hour, changing direction three times. Twice we stopped and I was spun round on the spot with some force – round and round, until I became dizzy and almost fell. I guessed that the idea was to make it impossible for me to remember the way to the Genthai camp. My captors laughed, but not once did they speak to me. I was completely in their power.

At last I heard other voices, and suddenly I sensed a change in the air and smelled the stink of urine and sawdust. I realized that we were indoors. The blindfold was ripped from my eyes and somebody at my back began to untie my hands.

I found myself in a small windowless room with an earthen floor, furnished with only a chair, a bed and a small table with a jug on it. In one corner there was a post in the ground, with manacles attached. It was a cell for holding prisoners.

'You'll spend the night here while we find out if you're a liar as well as a half-blood,' the big man said. 'Don't try to escape. The door will be locked and there are guards outside.

There's water on the table and a pot for your piss in the corner.'

With that, my Genthai captors went outside and I heard a key being turned in the lock.

Grateful that I hadn't been chained, I sipped the water to slake my thirst. Since leaving Gindeen at the end of the season I'd been living off the land, snaring rabbits and hares. I remembered that there were some strips of dried meat, cheese and oatcakes in the bag I'd bought in Mypocine, but the Genthai hadn't returned it, so I was going to go hungry.

It seemed a long night. I pushed away images of the terrible deaths I'd seen in the arena, along with my visit to Hob's citadel, and concentrated on Kwin.

She was wild, fierce and unpredictable. She wanted to fight in Arena 13 – although that was impossible; a dream that could never come true. Only men and boys could fight there.

I liked the rebel in her, and remembered her challenging me to a stick-fight. She'd been very fast and skilful, and I'd probably only won because she'd slipped on a bone in the circle we'd cleared in the slaughterhouse. Right from the start I'd been drawn to her and was desolate when I found out that she had a boyfriend called Jon. But then they had broken up and my hopes had started to revive.

A vivid memory of that stick-fight came into my mind: I'd just won the second of three bouts, catching her on the forehead; blood was trickling down into her eye, but she wasn't angry. She smiled. Her face was illuminated by a shaft of moonlight, transfigured into something otherworldly and beautiful. It was the face of an angel.

I could see it now. It was something I'd never forget.

Holding onto that image, I drifted off to sleep.

Finally the door was opened again, allowing in the morning light. One of my captors poked his head through the doorway and beckoned me outside. He set off towards an open fire; some kind of animal was roasting over it on a spit. The other warriors sat around it sipping from metal mugs.

I followed, glancing back at my prison – a single small oblong hut with a sloping roof. I could see other larger buildings set amongst the trees. I wondered if the Genthai kept other prisoners here. If so, what sort of crimes would they have committed? My father had told me a little about Genthai rules and values, but I'd still much to learn.

The warrior pointed to the ground so I sat down. Nobody spoke, but a mug was thrust towards me and I took it in both hands and sipped. The liquid was very hot and spicy, with a hint of peppermint. Soon the meat was being carved. I was the last to be served but I was grateful. It was venison and it was delicious.

'We decided to feed you rather than beat you, half-blood,' the big man growled, staring at me hard. 'We sent word to Konnit and his reply has just come back. Lucky for you he remembers your meeting. So you'll be seeing him again later.'

We set off within the hour. This time they didn't blindfold me or bind my hands. My bag was also returned to me – though the men were no friendlier.

I saw more and more wooden buildings set amongst the trees and realized that this was a kind of town, spread over a large area – two hours later we were still crossing it – but much less densely populated than Gindeen. There were trees and areas of green space between the clusters of wooden dwellings.

When we finally reached the far side, we came to a huge wooden building, oblong in shape like the others. It wasn't anywhere near the size of the Wheel or the slaughterhouse in Gindeen, but it was still truly massive. I'd have expected to find something like this at the centre of the Genthai dwellings, but not here at the edge, with just the forest beyond.

There were steps leading up to a veranda and a pair of large double doors, which stood wide open. Three prominent carvings of muscular men decorated that entrance. One was high above the door; the other two on either side. All three had two features in common: the first was the Genthai facial tattoos I'd seen on Konnit; the second were their open mouths, from which protruded very long tongues, reaching well below the jaws. Each figure held a weapon – the ones on either side of the doors wielded huge clubs, the one above, a curved sword. They were clearly warriors making some kind of threatening challenge.

There was a queue of Genthai sitting outside on the grass, waiting in silence. They were all barefoot.

'You'll have to wait your turn,' the big man told me. 'It could take an hour or more. Konnit likes to give everyone a fair and thorough hearing.'

A line of white stones marked the edge of the grass, and when we reached it, the big man came to a halt and glared at me.

'Take off your boots before you cross the line!' he

commanded. 'This area is called the marae – it's a sacred assembly ground.'

We both took off our boots.

'Leave your bag there as well. Nobody will touch it,' he instructed. I obeyed, and we moved forward to join the queue.

Before sitting down, I glanced over the heads of those waiting in front of me. In the gloom inside the building, I could make out two figures sitting face to face on the floor, engaged in conversation.

The big Genthai waited beside me, not uttering another word until it was my turn. Then he gestured towards the open door, gave a grunt and walked beside me towards the seated man, who was facing us, arms folded.

I noted that although the building was constructed of wood, there were three large stone fireplaces set into one wall. I looked up and saw hundreds of faces carved into all four walls. They seemed to watch me as I passed by.

As I got nearer, I recognized Konnit. He still had the moustache drooping over his upper lip and the whorls of fierce-looking tattoos on his face.

'This is the youth, lord. His name is Leif,' said the warrior.

'I remember him well, Garrett. He fought a tassel on the hill below Hob's citadel. He fought and won, but did not have the courage to deliver the killing blow.'

I felt dismay at Konnit's words. He made my victory seem like nothing. Was he calling me a coward? I wondered. Perhaps I'd been a fool to come here.

Konnit gestured at the wooden floor, and we sat facing each other. Garrett stood nearby, silently staring into the fireplaces. They were filled with grey ashes and the air was chilly – even colder than outside.

I noticed another huge door at Konnit's back. It could surely open only onto the closely packed trees of the forest.

'Welcome to the meeting hall of the Genthai, Leif, son of Mathias,' Konnit said with a smile. 'This is the centre of our culture and our laws. Now, tell me, have you come to join us?'

I knew that his invitation had been for me to take part in the coming battles, not to visit merely out of curiosity. But I screwed up my courage and told him the truth.

'My training in the city is not yet completed,' I explained. 'I wish to fight in Arena 13 and must return before the next combat season starts. But I'm here to learn what I can of my father's people – if you will allow me to stay for a while.'

Konnit frowned. He looked far from pleased. 'First you will address me as "lord" and give me the respect due as leader of the tribe!' he said, raising his voice slightly.

'Yes, lord,' I replied, 'but what of the Obutayer? Does she no longer rule here?'

My father had told me that the tribe had always been matriarchal. The Obutayer had been the leader and mother of all.

Konnit stared at me hard. 'There are lines from the Amabramdata, our Book of Prophecy, which address this. Listen well.'

He closed his eyes and began to recite from memory:

'*This is the time of waiting. This is the time when women rule. But soon it will be over. The moon shall dim as the sun grows bright. Then Thangandar shall return to lead us to victory over the cursed djinn* . . . Are you familiar with these lines?'

'No, lord.'

'Then I will alleviate your ignorance. The sun, of course, is symbolic and refers to the ascent of male leadership. The moon is the matriarch who has yielded power to me. The time of waiting and subjection to the will of the djinn is now over. We are preparing for war. When victory has been achieved, I will yield to the Obutayer and she will rule our people once more. We will speak again of this, and I will answer any questions you have, but now I have business with others. You may stay, Leif, but you must work hard for your meat and bread. Garrett!' he called, and the big man stepped closer. 'I place Leif in your charge. Train him as a forester and report back to me regarding his progress.'

'Yes, lord,' Garrett said, bowing.

With those words I was dismissed, and after giving a bow towards Konnit I followed Garrett out of the hall, full of misgivings. I tried to shrug them off. It was only fair that I work for my keep, but I didn't like the idea of being supervised by a man such as Garrett. He had been hard on me, but even worse was the way he referred to me as 'half-blood', which I found insulting.

After crossing the sacred ground, we tugged on our boots and I picked up my bag. Garrett grunted and pointed. Instead of heading back the way we'd come, he led me in a different direction – I wondered if he was taking me straight to work. But as we passed the end of the long meeting house and walked in among the trees, I saw the other end of the huge structure. Here there was no veranda, the ground sloping down to meet the bottom of the closed doors.

And there was something else that caught my eye: four

parallel paths sloped down through the trees towards those doors. Who would come out of the forest and use those when they could come through the front door, as we'd done? Perhaps they weren't allowed to cross the sacred ground? Perhaps the paths were used by hunters or others who brought food to the meeting hall? It seemed strange to use four narrow paths when one broader one would have served better.

Suddenly, in the distance, far off amongst the trees, I heard a strange howl. Garrett didn't react, but it sent a shiver down my spine. It reminded me of the cry of a wolf, but it sounded eerily human.

THE WOLF WHEEL

There are Wheels within Wheels.

Amabramsum: the Genthai Book of Wisdom

After Tyron had dismissed me for fighting with sticks, I'd spent several miserable weeks working in the Gindeen slaughterhouse. My memory of it was still vivid. It had been stinky, back-breaking work, but in many ways forestry among the Genthai was worse. My misery wasn't caused by the work, hard though it was, but by the person who was supervising my training.

No, it wasn't just my aching muscles, blistered hands and lack of skill in swinging an axe; it was Garrett. I could do nothing right, and after a week he moved on from cursing and swearing to violence. Several times he cuffed me hard across the back of the head, then progressed to the odd kick to the backside or boot in the shins. Tyron always treated his trainees with respect, and Garrett's bullying was more than I could stomach.

Part of me wanted to return to Gindeen early, or perhaps spend some time in Mypocine, but my pride wouldn't let me.

Garrett was a bully, and I would not allow him to drive me away.

One day I snapped and whirled round to face him, my fists raised. He was twice my size, but I didn't care. I knew I was fast enough to land a few blows. It would be worth it.

I balanced myself on my toes and waited for him to attack. It would be better if he made the first move. He was big – I was sure that if he rushed me, I could step aside and get at least one blow into the side of his head.

I took a step nearer and balanced myself again. 'Come on!' I challenged him. 'You like dealing out blows from behind. Why don't you try it face to face?'

Garrett just stared at me, and then smiled. 'So you do have a bit of spirit, half-blood. I'd almost given up on you!'

My blood was up and I took another step towards him. Then I came up onto my toes again, my heart thumping, ready to launch an attack.

His grin widened. 'You still have all your teeth. That's unusual in a stick-fighter – even for the champion stick-fighter of Mypocine. But I'll tell you one thing, Leif: come at me with those fists and you'll lose your front teeth for sure. Now get back to work!'

His comment took me completely by surprise, but before I could respond, he turned his back on me and walked away. Slowly my anger dissipated; I didn't go after him. Instead I picked up my axe and went back to my inexpert chopping at the tree I was supposed to fell. But after this he never cuffed or kicked me again, and maybe he even swore at me a little less than before.

Later, my mind kept returning to his remark about me being the best stick-fighter in Mypocine. How did he know that? I'd never told any of the Genthai about that part of my life. Had they been checking up on me? I wondered.

The weeks dragged by. I slowly got better at felling trees, but I was unhappy and ready to go back to Gindeen earlier than I'd planned.

I was aware of intense activity all around me; things that didn't include me. The older men were hunting and trapping far and wide, gathering food that seemed to be considerably in excess of the tribe's current needs. Slowly I began to realize that the majority of the meat was being salted and stored against some future eventuality.

Was this part of their preparations for war?

Every morning the young men left early, before dawn, and set off into the forest in groups and didn't return until dusk. I suspected that they *were* training for war, but when they left the communal shelters they didn't carry weapons. Eventually I realized that there must be training camps deep within the forest.

Then, late one morning when I was working alone as usual, I saw part of the Genthai army. I was near the top of a hill and there was a track at its foot that wound through the trees. The only warning of their approach was the thunder of hooves. A column of horsemen came into view. They rode three abreast at a canter.

Dressed in chain mail, two great swords were attached to the saddle of each warrior. They rode fine thoroughbreds, made for speed. Some carried spears and others had bows strung across their shoulders. They must have been aware of me but all looked ahead; not one even glanced in my direction.

The column passed me by for almost an hour. That meant a lot of warriors. But I kept thinking of the weapons they wielded. They might pose a real threat to the Protector's guards. But could swords, spears and bows be effective against the might of the djinn that dwelt beyond the Barrier?

There was a great sense of comradeship amongst the Genthai, but I was excluded. Hardly anybody spoke to me. Nobody befriended me at work. Nobody shared a joke with me. *I* was the joke. They whispered and laughed at me behind my back.

At night, when we ate in one of the communal shelters, the women avoided my eyes and the children kept their distance. I was a half-blood – not even a person, in their eyes. But they seemed happy together – affectionate and warm; only I was excluded.

About a month after I'd arrived, I was chopping down a tree chosen by Garrett. Later I was to measure it carefully and cut it into lengths. It would form part of the foundations of a new dwelling.

Chips of wood were flying and I was almost a third of the way through the trunk. I'd finally developed the right muscles for the work, and I was getting into the rhythm and controlling the weight and swing of the axe. It had started to snow, and the ground was covered in a thin white blanket. I became aware of someone standing behind me and lowered my axe. I thought it was Garrett, but to my surprise Konnit was standing there, a slight smile on his face.

'Leave that for now, Leif. Let's walk for a while.'

I put down my axe and followed him, feeling somewhat nervous. Had Garrett complained about me? I wondered.

Immediately I was put at ease.

'Garrett speaks well of you,' he told me. 'He thinks you've made real progress.'

I was surprised, and was struggling to find the words to reply when Konnit asked me a question.

'Are you happy here?'

I decided to tell the partial truth. I didn't want to reveal how miserable I was. 'I am content, lord, but not happy. I'm not of full Genthai blood – I feel that I'll never be accepted here.'

'Sometimes acceptance can come suddenly. Were you to train as a warrior and fight with us, it would quickly come. But you prefer to follow in your father's footsteps.'

He was staring at me as we walked. I couldn't meet his eyes, so I just nodded.

'Your father defeated Hob in the arena fifteen times, but it all came to nothing. Hob murdered your mother, and then your father drove you away before taking his own life.'

'How do you know about that?' I asked in astonishment.

'Remember my title, Leif! A Genthai warrior would not forget!'

'Sorry, lord,' I said.

'I made it my business to find out what I could about you. You showed promise fighting that tassel. Your speed was truly something to behold. It will be wasted in the arena; your talent could be put to better use as a warrior, fighting with others who will liberate this land from the yoke of the djinn. But let's speak of other things.'

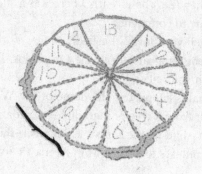

He came to a halt and turned to face me. Then he picked up a stick and drew a rough circle in the snow. Quickly he divided the circle into thirteen segments, one significantly larger than the others. Then he numbered each segment.

'Do you know what that represents, Leif?' he asked.

It seemed obvious to me. 'It's the Wheel in Gindeen, seen from above, lord, with the dome cut away,' I answered. 'It's a bird's-eye view showing the arenas.'

'It could be, but it's not. This is something much larger. The Wheel in the city which houses Arena 13 is merely a physical representation of this far larger, invisible wheel. It has thirteen spokes and turns by one increment each year. We call it the Wolf Wheel – it divides the whole of Midgard into thirteen segments.'

I listened to him, trying to keep the disbelief from my face. I had never heard of this before, and it came as a complete surprise. It seemed too fantastic to be true, but I didn't want to offend him. Was this some part of Genthai religion or a myth? Did they *really* believe it? There was a silence. Was he waiting for me to comment?

'It turns each year, lord?' I asked.

'Yes, its geographical hub is the Omphalos, like the huge centre post in your city's Wheel.'

The Omphalos supported the dome of the Wheel; it must have been cut from a tree of incredible height and girth – I'd never seen its like in the forest. Each week the Lists – the schedule of contests to be fought in Arena 13 – were fastened to it.

'As I told you,' Konnit continued, 'our invisible Wheel revolves at the rate of one segment every year. The outer portion of each segment, close to the rim, is inhabited by a different species of wolf. Twelve of these are just ordinary wolves. When that invisible Wheel turns, the wolves migrate with its movement; each year a different species hunts through the Genthai lands. But the thirteenth year brings the worst of all: wolves that are more than wolves. On thirteen nights, beginning on the night of the full moon, Genthai warriors fight them in ritual combat.

'We fasten a young child to a stake – always a girl. She is the bait, the prey, and is chosen by lottery. The wolves come out of the darkness and try to snatch the child, who is defended by a single warrior armed with blades. There are four of them – a deadly quartet known as a werewight. Three of them run on four legs and look like ordinary wolves. The fourth is a beast with the head of a wolf that walks upright on two legs, driving the three before it like lacs. It is believed that the four of them share one mind.'

I was astonished by what he was describing. It had some

similarity to combat in Arena 13, but it was like something out of a nightmare. How could they be so cruel as to tie a child to a stake like that to face such a horrific death?

'Why is the child always female, lord?' I asked.

'Only one in four new births is female, so this inflicts the greatest damage on the tribe. Girl children are precious. The intention is to cull the tribe.'

'Do many warriors win, lord?' I asked.

Konnit shook his head. 'It is very difficult to defeat four adversaries while protecting a child.'

'So the child and the warrior die?'

'They die and are devoured.'

It was snowing harder now. The circle, with its segments, was gradually fading from view, like a bad dream fading in the dawn light.

'Why, lord?' I asked. 'Why is it done? Why fight in that way at the cost of so much life? Why sacrifice children and warriors?'

Konnit frowned and his mouth tightened into a thin horizontal line. When he answered, I could hear the bitterness in his words. 'The ritual only has one positive aspect for us – it is a test of bravery and combat skills, the ultimate test of a warrior. However, it is not something that we choose to do. It is the price we Genthai pay for being allowed to live our lives *within* the Barrier – it is the price of our continued survival. City people are ruled by the Protector, who has been placed in authority over them by the djinn who defeated mankind. That Protector turns a blind eye to Hob, who terrorizes the city. We Genthai bear a different burden. Our bravest and best are culled by the ritual. It is a deliberate strategy to weaken our military strength. If we did not take part, we believe that the djinn would exterminate us.

'This was once a land of birds – but for the humans who lived here there were no mammals. To sustain, support and challenge us, bears, deer, pigs, horses, oxen and wolves were placed here by the djinn. Obviously the Wolf Wheel did not evolve naturally. It is a construct, a matrix of patterns, also created by the djinn. We live freely within the forest, hidden from the jurisdiction of the Protector, but we must submit to this ritual combat that culls the tribe. That is what the djinn set in place for us. We are the prey of the werewights.'

I nodded. It seemed to me that combat in Arena 13 might have evolved from this cruel Genthai ritual.

'I have a reason for telling you this now, Leif,' Konnit said with a grim smile. 'You see, this *is* the worst of all years. We have just entered the thirteenth segment of the Wolf Wheel. Three more nights will bring us to the full moon. Then the combat ritual will begin. You want to learn about your father's people? Here is your chance to see something that no outsider knows about. You are invited to watch the ritual, along with a select band of warriors – those who will fight, those who are kin to the combatants. Each warrior will defend his own daughter. All but one! This year there is one child who is an orphan, but the lottery has still chosen her to be bound to the stake. This happens only rarely, but now a member of the tribe must volunteer to defend that child. You want acceptance, Leif? You want to be a true warrior of this tribe, with all the honour and respect that will bring? *Do* you?'

I nodded. 'Yes, lord.'

'Well, there is a way. An opportunity presents itself . . . but will you take it? Would *you* be prepared to defend that orphan child?'

'You want *me* to defend her, lord?' I asked in astonishment. 'Why should it be me?'

'Oh, it need not be you, Leif. There will be many volunteers, each eager for a chance to prove himself brave, skilful and fast, but if you wish to grasp this opportunity, it is my gift to you. The orphan girl will be tied to the stake on the third night – you will have plenty of time to see werewights in action and decide how to achieve victory. You have the speed, but do you have the tactical ability to win and save the child? Do you have the guts to do what is necessary? I watched you fight the tassel, but you did not slay it as a true warrior would. This time you would have to use your blade to slay the werewight. You will need to kill all four of its selves.'

'My blade, lord? I have taken an oath not to use blades outside Arena 13.'

Konnit sighed. 'That oath is taken by city people to meet the needs of the city. Here we are in the forest, in the Genthai domain, and different rules apply. Do not make excuses, Leif!'

Then he nodded to me curtly and walked away through the whirling snowflakes, his eyes cold.

I returned to my tree and picked up my axe, contradictory thoughts spinning inside my head. I did not want to lose my place in Tyron's combat stable; I wanted to fight in Arena 13. Despite what Konnit said, if anyone in Gindeen found out that I had broken that oath, I would be dismissed and never allowed to fight in the arena again.

Had Konnit told me that I was the only one who *could* defend the orphan, it would have been different. But that wasn't the case. There were young Genthai warriors eager to take the role that had been offered to me. Whatever I decided, the child would be defended.

Yet I also wanted to prove myself; to be accepted by the Genthai. I wanted to show Konnit what I could do. He probably thought me a coward for not slaying the tassel. If I fought, I would have to slay the werewight. Killing wolves would be easier than slaying something that looked human and walked upon two legs – surely I could do it.

What should I say?

Undecided, I attacked the tree trunk once again.

LEIF, SON OF MATTHIAS

*Combat in Arena 13 and the werewight ritual are
but shadows of a more terrible conflict.*
Amabramsum: the Genthai Book of Wisdom

The meeting hall of the Genthai impressed me again the next time I saw it. It was spectacular, with its high roof supported by heavy beams lost in shadows, its three stone fireplaces, the myriad faces carved into the walls. But the huge double doors that gave direct access to the forest were closed.

I watched the torches being taken down from the walls and extinguished. My mouth was dry, a sign of nervousness about what I was about to witness.

At a signal from Konnit, I moved back with the Genthai warriors, retreating to the fading warmth and light of the fires, leaving a wide empty space in the middle of the great hall. This was where the fights between the warriors and the werewights would take place.

Beyond it, from a large wooden throne set back against the far wall, Konnit watched the proceedings impassively.

A deep rumble shuddered through the floor as the large

wooden double doors were dragged open to admit the night. The full moon was visible through the trees, low in the sky, casting its brilliant white light directly into the hall. It illuminated the stake, projecting its thin shadow far across the floor.

The first Genthai defender strode towards the stake, a child in his arms; he placed her gently on the floor, fumbling with the chain as he tried to bind her to the stake. She gave a small plaintive cry, and I saw that the man's hands were shaking. A metallic rattle set my teeth on edge.

A cold wind blew through the open doors; suddenly I saw a dark silhouette against the moon and a long grotesque shadow cast before it. A stark figure entered the hall, walking on two legs. This was the leading self of the werewight, and it was preceded by three others; three lean, black-furred wolves which wove to and fro before their grim shepherd in rapidly changing patterns.

The Genthai defender strode forward and positioned himself between the child and his adversaries. As he lifted his two short daggers, their blades gleamed in the moonlight. The action was instantly copied by the werewight leader, which also wielded blades.

The mouths of the wolves lolled open as they advanced, saliva dripping. Their breath steamed in the moonlight.

Somewhere to my right, a child started to cry and was hushed into silence. Did she realize that it would soon be her turn? The girl bound to the stake made no sound at all. In fact, considering what was about to take place, the whole meeting house was astonishingly silent. There were no mothers in the room — only the fathers, who were no doubt expected to be strong, stoic and silent.

The warrior must be in torment, I thought. I had heard Konnit's explanation, but now as the action was about to unfold I saw the problem clearly. It would be difficult to win, as the werewight's selves could approach the child from any angle. While the man tried to fend off one wolf, another would attack simultaneously. And he himself would be vulnerable. He could be attacked from behind. He had to defend himself and the child. And if he lost, not only would his own life be forfeit. His daughter, whom he no doubt loved very much, would die. Judging by what I'd seen so far, the Genthai were devoted parents. The father wouldn't want this fight. He wouldn't want to risk his daughter's life, but he had no choice. From Konnit I'd learned that all female children over the age of three were entered into the lottery.

Ninety-one were chosen.

Most of them died.

The wolves padded deeper into the hall now. For almost five centuries the Genthai had played out this same grim ritual once every thirteen years. They believed that these creatures they fought shared a soul – that the werewight was one being with four selves. If that was the case, I reflected, perhaps they were similar to Hob. He had one mind and many selves. Perhaps these creatures were a type of djinni?

The wolves were fast and attacked from all sides. The man was also fast and he fought bravely. He was the first to draw blood, cutting one of the wolves on the shoulder. As the blood sprayed upwards, all four of his enemies screamed in pain and rage.

They all felt the pain – they had reacted like one being!

And now they attacked together; they were fluent, fast and deadly.

The warrior did his utmost to protect his daughter, who was now screaming with terror. But things very quickly went wrong. Three wolves came at him together, one from behind. His legs were pinned and he was dragged to the floor. Then he too was screaming as the wolves ripped and tore his flesh – and then that of the girl. She stopped screaming first.

I watched, sick to my stomach. The wolves were feeding, tearing flesh from the body of the warrior, which was lying in a pool of blood. The man-wolf was also on all fours; mercifully its face was still in darkness, but the moonlight gleamed on the dark fur of its back and shoulders. It was more wolf than man.

All that could be heard now was a snuffling and growling and the frantic rattling of the chain as the man-wolf shook its prey. I glanced across at Konnit. His face was expressionless; it could have been carved from stone.

For a moment I turned my face away, but no one else in the meeting hall moved. The Genthai were like statues enduring the horror in silence.

Soon the four selves of the werewight padded back into the darkness, leaving the remains of their victims behind. Warriors dashed forward to clear away the fragments of flesh and bone and to scatter sawdust to soak up the blood. There was a lot of blood.

I witnessed six more contests that terrible night. There was only one human victory; only one child was saved from the jaws of the werewight.

On the second night, all the children died.

Then it was the third night, when the orphan girl would be tied to the stake. I had no idea which of the seven she was. Konnit had not spoken to me since our meeting in the forest, and I had still not decided what to do. With each loss I grew more tense, and sweat began to run down my neck and shoulders.

When it was time for the sixth contest, a lone warrior came forward carrying a child who seemed bigger than the previous victims; old enough to be fully aware of what was about to happen.

He knelt and began fixing her to the stake. I noticed that his hands were steady: he seemed calmer than the other warriors. Was he more confident of victory?

As he bound her, the girl sat up and stared at us. She had large, almond-shaped eyes that glittered with intelligence, but her face was expressionless. She showed no sign of fear.

Then I noticed that the warrior was carrying no blades, and realized that this was the orphan.

The man turned to face us and spoke, his voice echoing from the dark shadowed beams of the ceiling.

'This girl is an orphan. The lottery has chosen her, and with no father to defend her, she must nevertheless be fastened to the stake. Who is prepared to fight for her?'

Nobody replied. The hall was filled with silence. I sat there, frozen. Was it my imagination, or was the warrior staring straight at me? Beyond him, Konnit seemed to be staring in my direction too.

Of course they were! They expected me to respond.

Again and again I had gone over the reasons for either

accepting the role or rejecting it. Although news of stick-fighting in Mypocine might have got back to Tyron, this probably wouldn't. What went on here in the depths of the Genthai domain would remain hidden from the outside world.

And Konnit was right to point out that the oath I'd taken was intended to keep murder off the streets of Gindeen; it was to prevent skilled Arena 13 combatants being tempted to use their blades in quarrels. Here it was a different world.

But could I use my blades to draw blood? Could I kill? I asked myself.

I had still not decided what to do.

Some believe that there is no free will. Ancient philosophers have argued that our conscious selves are not truly in control of our actions; that something deep within our brains, unknown and invisible to us, makes our decisions for us.

That's what seemed to happen to me now.

Before I realized what I was doing, I'd clambered to my feet. My mouth was dry and I had to swallow twice before I was able to speak.

'I will defend her!' I cried, my whole body shaking with nerves.

'What is your name?' the warrior demanded as everyone stared at me.

I gave him my answer: 'My name is Leif, son of Mathias.'

I turned and saw that Konnit was smiling.

I turned my back on the girl and faced the light of the full moon. Holding the daggers, I took three rapid steps towards the huge double doors, then flexed my knees experimentally, shifting my weight onto each foot in turn.

My eyes searched the gloom until I picked out the figures approaching along the four paths through the trees, crossing the hard-packed snow. One strode on two legs; the other three loped towards me in the shape of wolves.

I was the sixth to fight tonight – the sequence of combatants was determined by the order in which the children were drawn in the lottery. But I wondered how the werewights chose their combatants ... And how many waited out there within the darkness of the trees ...

At last they reached the hall, moving onto the wooden floor, the three wolves crossing and re-crossing before their leader. I moved forward to meet them, reading their elaborate movements, patterns quickly forming in my own mind. The combat training I'd received from Tyron could prove very useful here. I was getting better at reading the movements and feints of adversaries.

They were so close now that I could smell their stench; a rank animal sweat masked the underlying sweetness of blood that still tainted the air. The eyes of the wolves glittered in the darkness that seemed to move before them, blocking out the light of the moon.

I wasn't afraid for myself, but I was afraid for the child. If I put a foot wrong, one of the selves of the werewight would race past me and kill her. At the same time I was excited, the adrenalin pumping hard through my body.

I had fought in the Arena 13 Trainee Tournament, but that had been but a shadow of the real thing. This was what it would feel like fighting in the Arena 13 under the full rules. There, after five minutes of combat a gong would sound and I'd have to fight to the fore of my lac, facing my human opponent and his three lacs, who would try to cut my flesh in order to claim victory. I would be that much closer to danger. One false step might result in my death. It was the same here.

I made myself focus on the task. How would they attack? I wondered. Each werewight had launched a different first assault, its intent hidden. The key was the man-wolf. Slay that, and the co-ordination of the others might collapse. The wolves might be easier to deal with. However, I knew that I probably wouldn't be able to choose which I attacked. I was outnumbered four to one. All I'd be able to do was react. Only my speed could bring victory and save the child.

I shuffled two steps to the left and two steps to the right, then began to move backwards at an angle, as if in retreat, my feet drumming rhythmically upon the boards. Instinctively I was using the sound-code Ulum, even though I had no lac to direct. It gave me confidence, and drew a murmur from the crowd, which usually remained absolutely silent. It was the same move I'd have made in Arena 13. It allowed for flexibility of response.

By the time the wolves surged forward, as if encouraged by my seeming retreat, I'd already reversed direction.

A wolf bounded past on my left, making for the throat of the child. It took all my self-control not to go after it.

The girl started to scream, but I maintained my position.

As I deliberately let the first wolf pass, I raised my daggers against the other two. They attacked together, but instinctively I'd already stepped into a different place – the space between spaces – and with both arms outstretched, my blades arced, slitting their bellies wide open to spill their intestines.

Behind me I could hear the child shrieking frantically.

The two wolves were dead, but before their dying bodies had even thumped onto the boards, I'd already turned and was racing back towards the stake.

When it was barely a hand's span from the terrified child, I pinned the neck of the third wolf to the floor.

Then I turned to face the man-wolf; I took a step towards it, raising my daggers as I approached. Konnit had questioned whether I had the guts to kill it. Now I knew the answer. This beast would have taken the girl's life without a thought. My anger had slowly grown as I witnessed death after death. Now I had no scruples.

The creature was fast; possibly as fast and skilful as any lac in Arena 13. I didn't underestimate the danger: on its hind legs, it was a full head taller than I was, with formidable strength and uncanny reflexes. It snarled, pulling back its bestial lips to reveal its fangs, then slashed with the blade in its right hand; slashed at the place where I'd stood but a fraction of a second earlier.

We circled each other warily. I moved to the left, then feinted with my right blade, watching the response. The creature began to retreat, but I was already in very close, ducking beneath its arcing knife to strike home twice, left and right.

Both hands were jarred as my blades encountered ribs, and I was forced to retreat, keeping my arms relaxed at my sides as I danced backwards, watching the eyes of the creature carefully, reading its intent. I sensed its uncertainty and moved in fast, stepping inside its defences, burying my right blade to the hilt beneath its ribs, then slashed my other blade across its throat.

It screamed, then dropped to its knees, blood gushing onto the boards. It twitched a few times, then sprawled forward, dead.

The Genthai warriors came to their feet and began to applaud what I had done. The sobbing child was released from the chain and carried away; the daggers were taken from me. Someone led me back to my place. As I sat down, the warriors did the same.

I felt no sense of elation, but I had saved the child. The werewight had been cheated of its prey. I watched the corpses being carried away and sawdust being thrown down.

Then, to my dismay and horror, another child was tied to the stake, the seventh that night. My victory had changed nothing. The contests would go on.

I felt like standing up and crying out that it should stop. But I did nothing; simply endured in dumb misery as another father and daughter died.

I felt numb. I wished I was back in Gindeen.

SOME UNKNOWN SCRIBE

From face to foot he was a thing of blood.
The Compendium of Ancient Tales and Ballads

Late the following afternoon I was summoned by Konnit. Once more I had to wait my turn outside the hall. The snow had changed to drizzle, and I sat there on the grass getting soaked to the skin. I noticed that the other Genthai waiting beside me kept glancing in my direction. One actually nodded and smiled at me.

When bidden, I sat down cross-legged to face Konnit, water dripping from the end of my nose.

'You did well, Leif. I knew you had the speed to be successful, and in taking the life of the werewight you showed the true heart of a Genthai warrior. All present in the meeting house were witness to what you accomplished. You have earned their respect.'

'Thank you, lord, but I only did what needed to be done. But how can this go on? All those deaths . . .'

Konnit frowned and sighed heavily. When he replied, he sounded exasperated. 'It will go on for ten more nights, Leif, and I expect you to be there to witness it. We cannot put an end to it yet lest those beyond the Barrier recognize our intent before we are ready. But we are almost ready. There will be no more years such as this, I do promise you that. Our submission to the djinn is almost over, but we must give them no early warning of that. We need to take them by surprise.'

'Yes, lord,' I agreed, dipping my head. But inside I considered the enormity of what the Genthai intended. How could they hope to win? What would happen to the remaining inhabitants of Midgard when they were defeated? Surely there would be terrible reprisals.

Or was there something I didn't know? Was there some secret reason for their confidence?

'Do you know what a Genthai warrior should be – how he should fight?' demanded Konnit.

'He needs to be brave, fast and skilful,' I answered.

He nodded. 'There is a line from *The Compendium of Ancient Tales and Ballads* which for me sums up the idea.' He closed his eyes, then recited slowly and with passion:

'*From face to foot he was a thing of blood whose every move was timed with dying cries!*'

I saw the image of the warrior in my mind's eye. It was terrible yet powerful.

'Those lines were written centuries ago by some unknown scribe. We have forgotten so much. The history of humans is in fragments; but the words are still inspirational. That is what we Genthai must become in order to defeat our powerful enemies.' With a sigh, Konnit dismissed me from his presence.

So it was that I endured ten more nights of slaughter.

The only compensation was that now I seemed to have been partially accepted by the tribe. Nobody engaged me in conversation, but at least they no longer kept their distance. Children came close and stared at my face, and some women even smiled at me as I passed. The men too nodded in greeting, and Garrett stopped swearing at me.

At the end of that period of bloody combat, only four more human warriors had been victorious. Each one of us was offered an honour which we were free to accept or reject.

It was to receive the Genthai facial tattoo.

From Mokson, the man who was to carry out this work, I learned what the tattoos represented and why not all Genthai warriors displayed them.

'We have many brave warriors, but displays of courage are not enough to earn facial tattoos,' he explained as I knelt cross-legged on the floor of his hut. He was old and wizened, but he circled me with slow, delicate steps, like a bird preparing to peck at a worm. The weather had turned cold again and the door was wide open. Our breath steamed.

'Only a warrior who slays a werewight and saves a child may receive that honour,' he continued.

It explained a lot. That was why Konnit had the tattoos but not Garrett.

'The tattoo I will create on your face is called a moko,' he told me. 'The process will take many weeks because time must be allowed for healing. But we have a problem. Your ancestry will be inscribed upon your face. The left side will show the ancestry of your father, whose true Genthai name was Lasar. The right side should represent your mother's lineage. But you had no mother . . .'

I felt myself flush with anger as I remembered my mother and the terrible way she had died at the hands of Hob. I remembered seeing her body lying in the grass, drained of blood.

Mokson patted me on the shoulder. 'I mean no disrespect. I merely mean that you had no *Genthai* mother. The woman who gave birth to you had no Genthai lineage, so I must leave the right side of your face blank.'

I felt bitter. How could this be an honour? My status would be clear for all to see. I would only be half a Genthai warrior. But then I took a deep breath and allowed that feeling to pass. Why should I deny what was clearly true? I *was* only half Genthai. Why not accept and declare that fact to the world?

'Do you still wish me to go ahead?' the old man asked.

I nodded. 'Yes, do the left side of my face.'

'It will hurt,' he said. 'The pain will be severe. You must be brave.'

His warning proved correct. He gripped me firmly by the hair and tilted my head back, his thin, sharp-bladed knife approaching my left cheek. Then he quickly began to cut, and the stinging pain came in waves as he worked. My eyes filled with tears, but I tried not to flinch; not one tear leaked from my eyes.

At last he stopped, and wiped away the blood from my face with a rag. I thought he was finished for the day, but worse was to come. The cutting was nothing compared to the pain of the second part of the process. He took a small sharp chisel and dipped it into a basin of dark dye.

'Now I must manoeuvre this into the cuts,' he explained, 'in order to force the dye deep within the skin.'

Mokson used the heel of his hand to drive the chisel into the cuts. Each blow was little more than a tap, but the resulting pain was like a burn and it seemed that he was cutting through to the bone. Every few seconds he dipped the chisel into the dye and then started again.

Afterwards he applied an ointment and sent me back to work. Yes, I was to chop down trees for the rest of the day – Garrett's orders. It proved to be a good idea. The heavy work took my mind off the pain and I attacked the trees with a fury.

My second appointment with the old man was scheduled for the following day, and that proved to be even more painful. This part of the tattoo was above and below my mouth. The swelling was terrible. Afterwards I couldn't open my mouth properly to eat. This time I had to rest, lying on my back while they fed me soft, almost liquid, food through a wooden funnel.

After that I had a week's rest from the process, but when it continued, I started to have nightmares about my visits to the old tattooist: in my dreams he started to bite into my face with his teeth, tearing pieces of my flesh away.

Five weeks later it was over, and gradually the swelling went down. When I touched it, the tattooed side of my face was no longer smooth. It was grooved where the lines had been scored.

At last I looked into a mirror. When I turned my right cheek towards it, I was Leif, a trainee Arena 13 combatant; when I turned my left cheek, I was a stranger – a Genthai warrior.

I felt satisfaction at having endured the process and coped with the pain. Then gradually there was something else: pride.

The time when Tyron expected me back for pre-season training was approaching. What would Kwin think about my tattoos? I wondered. Maybe she would think them ugly and I'd have lost my chance to be with her.

That night, just before I headed for the corner of the communal hut where I usually slept, Garrett approached me, smiled and put a hand upon my shoulder.

What he said came as a complete surprise.

'We need to talk, Leif,' he said, using my name for the first time. 'I want to tell you about your father.'

We walked into a clearing in the trees and sat on a grassy bank. The night was cold, the sky clear and filled with stars.

'I'll start by telling you what you've endured,' he began. 'We call the process Edos.'

'You mean the tattooing?'

'It's more than that,' Garrett replied. 'For you that was only the final stage of the process. Few get that far. City life does not not agree with our people. Many drink too much, beg, fall into decline and forget what they once were. Their children continue in that same downward spiral . . . But some are curious. They want to know where their families come from and they seek us out, as you did. So we put them to that test, which we call Edos. We work them hard and shun them. You see, Leif, to become a full member of our tribe, you have to be strong, both mentally and physically. The weak give up and go home; the strong, such as you, endure and become one of us. They become Genthai. They become warriors.'

'So ever since I arrived you've been testing me?'

'Yes, and you passed every step – though you're the only one who ever raised his fists against his teacher and meant to carry it through,' Garrett said with a smile. 'That I did not expect. And you are the only outsider who has ever arrived in the thirteenth year and fought and defeated a werewight. Most decline the invitation to defend an orphan child. The few who agreed fought and died. You are truly your father's son.'

'You said you had things to tell me about him.'

'Your father was born here and brought up as a Genthai. He had a sister who was chosen by the lottery. As a boy, Lasar watched his sister and his father being slain by a werewight. Later he showed great promise with the sword. He had your speed, Leif, and was destined to become a great warrior. He was even better with short blades. Thirteen years after the death of his father and sister, he defended an orphan just as you did – it's strange how history repeats itself,' Garrett said, shaking his head.

'Your father won, but he refused the facial tattoos. He declared that he was sickened by the ritual combat and left to seek his fortune in Gindeen. They say that at first he made his living fighting with sticks, but then was taken into the stables of a trainer called Gunter.'

'That much I do know,' I interrupted. 'As an artificer, Gunter was the best of the best, and they called him "the Great". I know something of the history of their partnership and how my father went on to defeat Hob fifteen times.'

'And after that?' Garrett prompted.

'After being badly hurt in that final fight, he was forced to retire from Arena 13 combat. He married my mother and became a farmer . . .'

'Well, there is something you probably don't know. Between retiring and meeting your mother there was a gap of five years. During that time he worked for the Trader.'

Lacs fought alongside humans in Arena 13, and the Trader was our only source of them. He came from beyond the Barrier, and somehow managed to sail his ship through without harm to himself or his crew. Where he came from nobody knew.

I looked at Garrett, hardly able to believe what he'd just said. 'What sort of work?' I asked.

'Of that I have no idea, but he accompanied the Trader on his voyages to and from Gindeen.'

'He travelled beyond the Barrier into the land of the djinn?'

Garrett nodded. 'We must assume so. But he never came back to visit the tribe so we know nothing of that time.'

'Was my father well thought of by the tribe?'

'He was a true warrior, and was held in great esteem. But many were disappointed when he rejected the facial tattoos. Some thought he had wasted his life fighting in the city arena; others liked the idea of a Genthai rising to supremacy in combat against city dwellers, and were glad to see him defeat Hob so many times. What about you, Leif? You have proved your courage and skill and have accepted the facial tattoos. Will you not put aside your ambition in the arena and stay to fight with the tribe? It will not be long now before we take up arms against our enemies.'

I shook my head. 'I'm sorry, Garrett, but I've not changed my mind. Two weeks at the most and I must return. I want to complete my training and fight in Arena 13.'

I was really looking forward to returning to Tyron's house, which I now considered my home. I was eager to begin training with Deinon. But most of all I wanted to see Kwin again.

'It's your decision, Leif, but let me do one thing for you before you leave us. Have you ever fought with a sword?'

I shook my head.

'Well, the skills are very different to those required when using short blades. Tomorrow you'll chop down fewer trees and spend a little time working with me. I can't do much in a couple of weeks, but I can give you the basic skills.'

Garrett was as good as his word. Soon after dawn I faced him in a forest clearing, frozen leaves crunching underfoot. I was shivering. It had been a cold night.

We held our swords in a two-handed grip. He took a step towards me.

'Right, Leif, let's see what you can do!' he challenged. 'Attack and press me hard. Don't worry – you won't be able to do me any damage.'

I did as he instructed, and immediately sensed the difference between this and fighting with a dagger. For a start, the sword was a far heavier weapon. I swung at Garrett and he evaded my blow with ease. After failing to make contact with anything solid, the sword continued to move, carrying me with it, and I almost overbalanced.

Garrett could have chopped me down like a tree. For a moment I was totally vulnerable.

He grinned. 'It has *some* things in common with swinging an axe, Leif. You need to use the weight of the sword. Go with it. You will miss opponents, so you need to swing it upwards, then reverse, allowing the weight of the weapon to add strength to your blow.'

It was easier said than done, and after five minutes I was exhausted. My breath rasped in my throat and my shoulders and arms felt like lead.

I rested for a while, and then Garrett adjusted my stance and grip. The second bout I found a little easier. But when I finally managed to land a blow, Garrett blocked it with his own sword, and the clash of blades was so hard that it jarred both my shoulders and I almost dropped my weapon.

At the end of the two weeks I was much improved, but it was just a start. I probably wouldn't have lasted more than a minute against any of the Genthai warriors. However, I had the basics, and I thanked Garrett for his help. I was really starting to like him now. A few more months and I might have felt that I belonged with the Genthai.

But now it was time to go home.

A WORRYING DEVELOPMENT

He that depends upon your favours
Swims with fins of lead.

The Compendium of Ancient Tales and Ballads

Tyron had asked me to return three months before the Arena 13 season began so that I could start to train early. That meant leaving the Genthai lands before the winter was properly over. This time I had no lift on a wagon to make the journey easier. I would have to walk all the way back to Gindeen.

Before leaving, I had one final meeting with Konnit. He led me into the forest until at last we reached a long hut the like of which I'd never seen before. A deep stream ran close by, and in the water was a huge wooden wheel set within a stone base. The wheel was being turned by the fierce flow of the current.

There were dozens of armed Genthai surrounding it. Did the hut contain something valuable? I wondered. I could hear a strange hum coming from inside the building.

Konnit unlocked and opened the door, and we stepped into darkness. The humming grew louder.

Then there was a sudden click, and the interior was flooded with light. I looked up at the source in amazement: a glass sphere hanging from a cord. The light radiating from within it was almost too bright to look at.

'The source of that light is called electricity,' Konnit explained. 'The ancients lit whole cities in this way. The stream outside turns the waterwheel, which creates electricity from a machine called a generator.'

I was astonished. City people looked down on the Genthai, considering them to be primitive. Yet they relied on torches and candles, while the Genthai employed the technology that had been used by humans before the victory of the djinn and our imprisonment behind the Barrier.

'But this is not what I have brought you to see, Leif. Electricity provides light but can do much more. Follow me!'

Konnit turned and lifted a trap door in the floor, flinging it open to reveal steps leading downwards. He stepped back and clicked something on the wall, and the steps were flooded with light. He led the way down until we reached a small cellar. Here the hum was louder than ever.

On a bench by the far wall lay thirteen long fat metal cylinders, each connected to the wall by a thin tube.

'Electricity charges them with energy, but they use a far more advanced technology to deal out death. These are weapons, Leif. They are called the gramagandar, which means the Breath of the Wolf. We have thousands of warriors, many of them on horseback, which might be able to overthrow the Protector – but against the djinn beyond the Barrier, well . . .' Konnit shrugged. 'These weapons will make our victory possible. They destroy false flesh. The bodies of the djinn will melt before their withering fire. Yet they present no danger to normal human flesh.'

'Lord, could they be used to destroy Hob?' I asked, the thought making my heart lurch with excitement.

Konnit stared at me hard. 'They *could*, but that would betray our secret. When we fight the djinn for the first time, we need the element of surprise. We would both like to see Hob destroyed, but we must find another way. So you must not speak of this to anyone else. Speak neither of the gramagandar nor the ritual combat against the werewights. Do you understand? These are Genthai secrets – not for outsiders.'

When it was finally time to leave, Garrett walked me to the edge of the Genthai lands.

'Good luck, Leif. Take care in that arena,' he said, clapping me on the shoulder.

'Thanks for the training,' I said, smiling up at him. 'Not only can I chop down trees, I've built up my body strength. That should help me when I fight.'

Garrett waved as he walked away. I wondered if I'd ever see him again. But my thoughts were now directed towards home.

Most of the snow had melted, but the ground was soggy, and once I'd left the forest, I had to struggle through mud and circle dangerous areas of swamp. Although I'd said that I might see Peter on my way back, I avoided Mypocine.

After all that had happened, I wasn't in the mood to talk, and he would ask me a lot of questions which I'd be unable to answer.

It was almost two weeks before I saw Gindeen in the distance. The first thing that came into view was Hob's thirteen-spired citadel. The sun was setting, casting its threatening shadow over the city. The shadows of those spires were like talons slowly extending towards the copper dome of the Wheel.

Nowhere in Midgard was safe from Hob, but he concentrated on the city from which he took the majority of his victims. I was glad to see the Wheel, but the sight of those threatening shadows sent shivers down my spine.

I didn't want to walk through Gindeen's streets after dark – Hob might be hunting for victims – so I spent one more night outdoors, some distance away. The cold weather had returned, and there was a severe frost that night. My blanket proved inadequate and I hardly slept at all. I was only too glad to start moving again, and I was already approaching the city soon after dawn.

Soon I could see the huge block of the slaughterhouse, with a flock of vultures wheeling above it in long slow spirals. At dusk they tended to circle above the Wheel. It was probably just to take advantage of the thermal currents rising up from the dome, but many believed the flock gathered there before a death in Arena 13.

Of course, it was just superstition. Apart from grudge matches and visits from Hob, deaths in the arena were rare, though I'd already seen one combatant killed in a grudge match, and then witnessed Hob's defeat of Kern.

That night Tyron and I had visited Hob's citadel and Tyron had bought back Kern's remains – his severed but living head in a box.

I knew that tassels ate the bodies, but why did Hob keep the heads of his victims? What did he want them for?

These were dark memories, but more recently I'd witnessed thirteen nights of werewight combat in the meeting house of the Genthai. I'd seen too much death. I was sickened by it. Perhaps that was one thing I had in common with my father. He too had been sickened by what he'd witnessed there – though he hadn't accepted the facial tattoos.

At last I was striding through the narrow streets, keeping to the wooden walkways that ran along in front of the houses and trying to avoid the worst of the mud – though some of the planks had rotted away. Then I climbed the slope towards the area where the wealthier citizens lived. Here there were stone flags instead of boards, cinders in the roads and even some avenues of trees – still leafless, though spring wasn't far away.

Being the most successful artificer in Gindeen, Tyron had a big house; there were four storeys above the street and a deep cellar.

I walked through the yard and knocked on the back door. I was looking forward to seeing Kwin again, but very nervous too. Again I worried what she would think of my tattoos. I certainly hoped I'd have time to wash and tidy up before we came face to face.

It was Tyron who came to the door. He opened it wide and stared at my face for a long while, making me anxious about what he was going to say. Then he shook his head and whistled through his teeth. 'Leave your muddy boots and bag here and go up to my study, boy,' he growled. 'I'll be with you in five minutes.'

As he turned and walked back into the house, I tugged off my boots and left them with my bag. Then, in my stocking feet, I made my way up to the top of the house. I was sure that I was in trouble because of my tattoos but, despite that, it was really good to be back. I had missed living in Tyron's house.

The study door was open, so I went in and sat down facing the desk. I knew I was in for a real telling off, and there was nothing I could say to defend myself.

I glanced around the room. Nothing had changed since I'd last been here. It was the study of a wealthy man. The walls had mahogany panels and the chairs were upholstered with leather; white wolf furs were spread out upon the floor. I looked at the sealed glass bookcase that had caught my eye on my first visit. There was a row of no more than seven volumes, supported at each end by a wooden bookend carved into the shape of a wolf. That image sent a shiver down my spine. It brought back memories of the werewights and the slaughter I'd witnessed.

I went over and peered through the glass. The first book was entitled *The Manual of Nym*; the second was *The Manual of Trigladius Combat*. But it was the third one that caught my eye and sent my pulse racing. Its title was *The Testimony of Math*.

Had my father written that book? What was it about – an account of his contests in Arena 13? It was something I'd love to read, but I couldn't mention it to Tyron without admitting that I'd been prying.

I heard him climbing the stairs, so I quickly returned to my seat.

He came in, closed the door behind him and sat down facing me. 'Why?' he asked. 'Why on earth did you do it?'

He was staring at my face, examining the tattoos that now covered the left-hand side – the jaw, cheek and temple. Dark lines and whorls followed every contour. I wanted to tell him that the tattoos had been earned by my defeat of the were-wight; that only the bravest of warriors were entitled to them. I wanted to explain that it was a great honour that marked you out as someone who had cheated a werewight of its prey, saved the life of a child . . . But I had to remain silent. I'd been bound to secrecy. I couldn't break my word to Konnit.

Nor could I admit to using blades. Strictly speaking, some might consider it to be breaking the oath, though my conscience was clear. That was a rule designed to keep peace in the city; the demands of life in the forest were very different.

'I didn't fit in with the Genthai. At first I felt like an outsider. Getting the tattoos helped,' I said by way of explanation. Strictly speaking, I hadn't lied.

'Well, it won't help here, boy. As you well know, even your father never wore tattoos like that. Those facial markings will make you an outsider. They will draw attention. Don't you see that? The Protector's Guard won't like it, either. It could cause you all sorts of trouble.'

Tyron was right. The guard didn't like outsiders. My skin was darker than that of city dwellers – a small patrol had once beaten me for that and driven me out. The tattoos would draw even more attention. I'd been worried about Kwin, but the reaction of the Guard had hardly crossed my mind.

I looked at Tyron. He was stocky and muscular, with a

ruddy complexion topped by his stubble of grey hair. He looked a little older, even though only a few months had passed since I last saw him. He had more fine lines around the eyes, and the furrow that divided his brow was deeper. No doubt it was due to the death of his son-in-law, Kern, and the terrible effect this had on his elder daughter, Teena.

'I'm sorry,' I told him. 'I don't want to cause any bother.'

Tyron sighed. 'Well, what's done is done. We'll just have to make the best of it. Anyway, on Friday the Trader will call at the Sea Gate. I intend to go there and buy some lacs. I think it would be useful for you to see that, so you'll be coming with me.'

'One of the Genthai told me that after retiring from the arena my father worked for the Trader for five years. Did you know that?' I asked. 'He probably saw what it's like beyond the Barrier.'

'Yes, he probably did. He was sometimes there when I visited the Sea Gate. We never got a chance to speak alone, but he always greeted me warmly.'

'Maybe the Trader will be able to tell me more about my father.'

Tyron frowned. 'No, boy – nobody asks questions of the Trader unless it's relevant to what's being bought. It's just not done. I'll introduce you simply as Leif, my trainee. I can't tell him that you're the son of Math – we want to keep that a secret for now. So hold your peace. We'll be setting off before dawn – that's if you can manage to get up,' he continued. 'You look exhausted. Did you walk all the way back?'

I nodded. 'It's taken me almost three weeks. What's the winter been like here?'

Judging from the look in his eyes, Tyron knew what I meant. Hob preyed on the city after dark. I was wondering how bad it had been during the long dark winter nights.

'It's been a cold winter here, and Hob hasn't confined himself to taking people from the streets. He's broken into houses and snatched over twenty people from their beds, most of them women. He seems to be targeting the families of those who work at the Wheel. The wife of a patterner was taken, and the daughters of two Arena 13 combatants. That's new and disturbing. He's usually left people with links to the Wheel alone – except in Arena 13. Maybe we're all Hob's prey now.'

'Has nothing been done?'

'Aye, the usual. We've petitioned the Protector, who's promised to put more guards on the streets after dark. But relying on him to help is like trying to swim wearing lead boots. Everyone's being vigilant. This house is better fortified than most, so we should be safe. But I don't want you out after dark – especially not on your own. Now we walk in twos and threes once the sun's gone down – Hob tends to snatch lone victims. Well, life goes on, doesn't it? I think you've grown a couple of inches and you've certainly put on more muscle. That'll help in the arena, providing you still have your speed. What have you been up to?'

'Mostly chopping down trees.'

Tyron smiled, but he seemed weary, a tired man trying to put a brave face on things. 'Well, now it's back to chopping down lacs! Go down to the kitchen and get some breakfast. Then go to bed. You're in no fit state to start training yet. Deinon isn't back till the end of the week, so we'll start then.'

'I thought he'd have been back already.'

'He's had a few problems at home. It caused a bit of a delay, that's all.'

Kwin was eating breakfast at the kitchen table. She looked as beautiful as ever, and my heart leaped in my chest at the sight of her. How I'd missed her!

The scar was there, on the side of her face where her hair was cut shorter. She'd done that to draw attention to it; it was something she was proud of. It didn't detract from her beauty one jot.

She looked up at me and my heart began to pound.

'Leif!' she said, starting to smile. 'Good to see you back . . .'

Then her expression changed and her eyes widened as she saw my face. I couldn't read her expression and my stomach turned over as I waited for her reaction. I had almost refused the honour of the tattoos, worried that she might think me ugly.

She got to her feet and came over. To my relief, she smiled up at me and touched my left cheek with her forefinger, tracing the contour of one of the lines.

'That suits you, Leif,' she said. 'It makes you look fierce. Maybe I should get it done too!'

'I don't think your father would like that,' I told her.

'You look taller,' she said, studying me, 'and broader. That's good, but don't take those muscles too far. Speed is more important than strength.'

I suddenly felt a twinge of anxiety. Perhaps chopping down trees was the wrong type of activity for fighting in Arena 13. Maybe the muscles would take the edge off my speed? I tried to dismiss this thought. After all, hadn't I managed to defeat the werewight? Hadn't I allowed the first wolf past me, and then, after slaying the other two, caught it before it reached the child?

However, my doubts wouldn't go away.

The following day I rested, as Tyron had advised, but the day before the visit to the Trader I spoke to him.

'I feel much better today,' I said. 'Could I try a workout against a lac?'

'Itching to get started, Leif? That's good. I can spare an hour this afternoon. Meet me on the training floor at two.'

Tyron had constructed the best training floor in the city. It was a replica of the one in Arena 13: fifty feet long and twenty-five wide. I was down there fifteen minutes before two. Immediately memories came flooding back. I remembered how, before Hob slew him in the arena, Kern used to train us here. A wave of sadness washed over me. I still missed him. How much worse it must be for his widow, Teena. It made me all the more determined to destroy the djinni that had brought so much horror and misery to this land.

I lit the wall torches and swept the wooden floor.

I was nervous. Would I still be as fast? I wondered.

Tyron came in and nodded to me, then walked across to where the armoured lac stood, inert. It was the one with the dented armour that we used for training; the one that had been modified for my use, its speed increased for the Trainee Tournament.

'Awake!' Tyron commanded, and the lac raised its head,

eyes flickering behind the horizontal slit in the face armour. It was nothing like the four selves of the werewight that I'd confronted, blade, tooth and claw seeking my life, but it seemed to be staring at me; as usual, it made me slightly nervous.

'What do you want to do? Some warm-ups dancing behind it?' Tyron said, turning back to face me.

'I'd like to try the game – the one where the lac uses a leather ball.'

Tyron nodded. 'Yes, let's do that. It's a good test of speed and reactions.'

He went over to the weapons that hung on the wall and drew a short-bladed Trig knife from its leather scabbard. Handing it to me, he went back to the lac.

'Selfcheck,' Tyron commanded. Now the lac would be checking its internal systems, sifting through its patterns of Nym code.

A few moments later he barked out a new command: 'Report!'

'*Ready*,' answered the lac in its harsh, guttural voice.

'Stand!' Tyron said. 'Combat stance! Training mode!'

The lac went into a crouch. By calling the wurdes 'training mode', Tyron had reduced its speed and reactions to make my task easier. He picked up a leather ball about the size of a human head and handed it to the lac. It had a strip of leather attached to it, designed for a hand to slip inside.

The lac would attempt to clout me with the ball; I would do my best to insert my blade into its throat-socket. If I did that, it would silently call the wurde 'endoff' and collapse inert on the floor. I would have won.

'Are you ready, Leif?' Tyron asked.

I nodded, gripping my blade firmly, taking up my position facing the lac, my heart beginning to speed up. The lac's eyes flickered behind the horizontal black slit in the face armour. It was watching me.

I stared back, took a deep breath and moved into the initial pattern of the dance. Two steps to the left. Two steps to the right. As the lac came towards me, I began to retreat diagonally to the right. It was a textbook opening manoeuvre.

The lac advanced rapidly, starting to swing the leather ball. I reversed suddenly, my bare feet slapping hard against the boards. I was moving in, aiming for the throat-socket.

I ducked.

But I wasn't fast enough.

The ball struck me hard on the back of the head, knocking me to the floor. I stayed down, stunned, with a ringing in my ears and my head spinning. Then I clambered to my feet.

Before the end of last season I'd been able to win the game two out of three times. I was disappointed now, but my determination grew. It was good to be back on the training floor. This time I *would* succeed!

Shaking my head, I took up position to try again.

'Are you ready?' Tyron asked me.

I nodded and began the dance again. The next thing I remember was another blow to the head, and then I was sitting on my bottom.

'Perhaps we should call it a day,' Tyron suggested.

'Please, just one more try,' I said.

The result was the same. By now I had a throbbing headache.

'You're still tired after your journey,' Tyron said, patting me on the back. 'It's best not to force things. Wait till next week when Deinon's here. You'll be back to your usual form then.'

I nodded and forced a smile onto my face, but I was far from happy – though the prospect of seeing Deinon cheered me up a little.

THE TRADER

'Why do you love? Why do you breathe? Why do
    you fight?' demanded Soutane, the Lord of all
    Daemons.
'Because nobody told me,' she answered.
'Nobody told me that I was dead.'
    The Compendium of Ancient Tales and Ballads

Life settled down as I worked on my Nym patterning, but it
wouldn't return to normal until Deinon arrived and full
pre-season training began.

As promised, three days later Tyron took me with him to deal
with the Trader on the first of his two visits to the Sea Gate.

Just before dawn, I followed him out of the small wooden
depot on the outskirts of the city and prepared to board the
barge that would take us down the Western Canal on the
slow, sedate journey north to the Sea Gate.

At the front of the barge a fresh team of eight horses was
being harnessed, restlessly stamping their big hooves. Despite their size and power, they were quiet and obedient to the
soft commands of their handlers. Their breath dissipated
upwards in white clouds, while darker smoke from a nearby

smithy rose towards the pale stars before curling eastwards across the city.

Beyond the dilapidated depot the huge bulk of the slaughterhouse rose square and uncompromising, a stark black cube above which the vultures already wheeled. About two dozen men, clutching leather cases and shivering in the cold air, waited with us on the canal bank. Each had his own private errand, but would join the same queue to haggle with the Trader.

Tyron had paid a large sum of money to be first in that queue. He'd also told me it was likely that one of those men was an agent of Hob, here to buy from the Trader under the djinni's instructions, seeking to improve his lacs. But what he bought wouldn't be delivered in the usual manner; it was said that tassels visited the Sea Gate at the dead of night to collect his purchases.

Although he was a djinni, even Hob was cut off from the technology that must exist beyond the Barrier. The djinn had defeated humans, so they must now have the technology once possessed by us. And they'd had over five hundred years to develop it further.

'Why would someone buy on Hob's behalf?' I asked.

'It's more likely to be out of fear than choice,' Tyron replied, 'or perhaps in the hope of gain. Hob often meddles in the affairs of this city. And think about the business he generates. He buys oxen each year – that means big contracts for the beef suppliers. He hires smiths and armourers, and provides work for masons. Think of the influence and dependency that results from all that.'

As we clambered aboard the vessel, Tyron nodded to the

barge master. 'That's Kepler,' he said. 'He's a good man and very useful to know.'

I looked back and sized him up. Kepler had an aura of strength and carried himself very upright, as if to shrug off the advancing years that had already stolen the colour from his hair.

The barge was divided into compartments; ours was right at the front. We quickly took our places and made ourselves comfortable as best we could on the narrow seats.

The sun was just above the horizon when, with a sudden jerk, the barge started forward and began to gather momentum. Once underway, our progress was smooth and we eased slowly out of the city and through a patchwork of farms that quickly yielded to uncultivated grassland.

This was the first time Tyron had taken me with him on business like this. Before the death of Kern, no doubt he'd have taken him. I was looking forward to the trip and intrigued as to what the Trader would be like. But what Tyron had already told me was disturbing.

A man entered our compartment and shook hands, first with Tyron and then with me, before taking his seat opposite us.

'This is my trainee, Leif,' Tyron said by way of introduction. 'Leif, this is Wode. We go back a long way.'

I saw Wode staring at the left side of my face before quickly looking away. I wondered if Tyron had mentioned my Genthai blood to him.

Tyron had already told me a lot about Wode: although he was Tyron's rival, he was also a friend and a respected colleague. They'd trained together under Gunter, and after a number of years fighting in the arena had started their own stables of combatants. Tyron had told me that in those early days they'd often collaborated by pooling their resources.

Wode had never quite matched Tyron's success, either in Arena 13 or out of it. He'd been retired prematurely by a serious leg wound that had left him with a permanent limp – but his stable of mag combatants was ranked highly. The demand for his services as an artificer had once been second only to Tyron's, but in recent years things had gone downhill.

They weren't in direct competition when they visited the Trader. Tyron had come to buy wurdes and lacs, while Wode had come to buy the soul of a long-dead artificer, which would be reborn into false flesh. He hoped to purchase a highly skilled patterner with knowledge of Nym that had been lost to Midgard.

It was something I hadn't thought possible. When Tyron told me this, it had filled me with astonishment. How could the dead be returned to life? But that amazement quickly changed to revulsion. It was like buying a slave who would be given no choice as to whether they wished to be born again and live a second life.

I had already told Tyron that I didn't like the idea.

'I don't think the boy's too happy with you,' Tyron said, smiling at Wode. 'He thinks a bit less of me too because of my involvement.'

Wode shrugged, clutching his case to his chest. He was a tall, graceless man with gangly limbs – too easy a target, I thought, to have done well in Arena 13, even fighting behind three competent lacs.

'Many people depend on me for their livelihoods,' he said.

'And to give someone back their life – what's wrong with that? I don't see the harm in it.'

'But it won't be the same life,' I said. 'Everybody he ever knew will be dead. I mean, there's no way for you to find out how he feels. Perhaps he'd prefer to remain the way he is? And I don't like the idea of owning someone. He'll be your slave!'

Wode laughed. 'After two years they get their freedom, whatever happens. If things are amicable, it happens much sooner. What's wrong with that?'

I gave up arguing and leaned back uneasily against the cool leather of the seat, peering through the vents that served to admit light while deterring the wind and weather.

The grassy plain was now slowly being replaced by trees, but rather than the conifers of the forested slopes, these were squat deciduous giants, their leaves still confined within tight green buds.

'How would an artificer end up dead and available for sale?' I asked, directing my question to Tyron.

'Things were different before the fall of the Human Empire and the erection of the Barrier. Dissent was dangerous when your employer was the Imperial Military. Then again, there were accidents. Accidents have always happened. If nothing could be done for the body, then sometimes the soul could be preserved,' Tyron answered.

Although Wode was hoping to buy himself an artificer from the Trader's Index, a lot would depend on the price. Tyron had told me that he was prepared to help financially, because Wode had offered him a share in any new knowledge that came out of it.

There was an Index of wares for sale, but the information supplied about each item was very limited and selections were always hazardous. If Wode and Tyron got lucky, they might even buy someone capable of patterning sentience into a lac. That was the dream. Alternatively, they could end up with someone with experience so narrow and specialized that he would be of no more use than a first-year trainee. In either case it would be very expensive.

The Terminus was a disappointment, nothing more than a goods depot of dilapidated wooden sheds, their rotting walls leaning at impossible angles, ready for demolition by the next gale.

In the company of the other passengers, we strolled across the grassy bank, left the canal behind and entered the trees. People kept glancing at my face. It would be hard to get used to that. Tyron was right; it was going to make my life more difficult. We were escorted by two members of the Protector's Guard, surly men in dark blue uniforms who were already sweating in the morning sun, their hands never far from the projectile weapons they wore casually across their right shoulders. In Midgard, only the Protector's Guard were allowed weapons other than blades, and the metal stars they catapulted could break a bone, sever an artery or penetrate a skull.

I noticed that they were giving me hostile glances. I avoided eye-contact. They wouldn't be happy that I had Genthai blood, and no doubt the tattoos made it worse. But I consoled myself with the knowledge that I was safe enough with Tyron. They could do nothing as long as I was his trainee.

Now I could hear the sound of waves breaking against

rocks, and was peering through the trees, trying to catch a glimpse of the ocean, when suddenly I saw the Sea Gate directly ahead.

It was far smaller than I'd expected. It consisted of a small harbour beyond which extended short protective headlands, like arms curved towards each other, leaving just the narrowest of gaps for the passage of vessels.

Not far from it was a dark stone tower, which appeared to be deserted. Nearby stood a huge gong suspended between two tall stone pillars, and leaning against the furthest pillar was a big hammer. I wondered what it was for. Did it have some sort of ceremonial purpose? Did they strike the gong to welcome the Trader?

The green water in the harbour was choppy, but nothing compared to the white turmoil visible beyond the bare rocky arms of land that enclosed it. The wind was freshening, and behind us the sun was rising above the hills to the east. Despite that, far out to sea, the encircling wall of mist lay undisturbed. The distance between the Barrier and the shore varied; on certain days, it was said, it was even too close to allow fishing from the small vessels now at anchor in the harbour.

'I thought the Trader's ship would already be here,' I said to Tyron.

'His vessel never lingers in the harbour, boy. It'll be back for him later,' he said gruffly. 'That's where we're headed . . .' He pointed towards the stone tower just south of the harbour.

But I soon realized that we weren't actually heading for the tower. A large green canvas tent came into view. It was well-camouflaged in all but one respect: above it, a flag fluttered in the freshening wind from the sea. It was the blue of a summer sky, and upon it was the silver outline of a leaping wolf. As the flag rippled in the wind, it seemed that the wolf leaped again and again towards the sky.

'Listen carefully, Leif. Leave the talking to Wode and me. Time is money here, and we can't afford to waste it on either questions or pleasantries. And remember what I said about not questioning the Trader directly. Don't even think of it! There are protocols to be observed. Watch and learn, and ask me questions when we're back on the barge. We aren't permitted to browse through a list of commodities. Nor will there be inert lacs on display. We can only try to specify what we want. If it happens to be in the Index, a limited amount of information, including the price, will be given, and we have to accept any item at the stated terms. There is no haggling.

'The Trader is vital to the economy of the city. He's our only source of lacs. Without him the Wheel and its arenas wouldn't exist. He has a phenomenal mind – he remembers everything,' Tyron continued. 'The Index is inside his head, and our credit-worthiness, including the funds we have immediately available, have already been cleared through the Protector's Executive in anticipation of his visit. We have extensive documentation confirming this, stamped with the Protector's seal, and we'll present it to the Trader for verification before negotiations begin. Our payment is authorized immediately on our return to the city; the following day, goods are delivered by barge to the depot on the edge of Gindeen for us to collect. Now, watch and learn.'

I nodded and followed Tyron and Wode into the tent.

I'd not expected to actually meet the Trader, thinking that we'd be greeted by underlings, but to my surprise I saw a circle of wooden chairs set out in the tent. Seated in one was the Trader, a large red-haired and red-bearded man whose face was covered by a silver mask.

The Trader who'd given me the blue ticket had looked very similar. He'd visited Mypocine and asked to watch some stick-fighting. I'd won, and that prize – the ticket – had won me the right to be trained for Arena 13.

Could it be the same man? I wondered. It was impossible to tell because of the mask, but it seemed likely.

'This is Wode, and this is Leif, my trainee,' said Tyron, introducing us both.

He quickly got down to business; Wode and I were silent spectators. Tyron had told me that he wanted better quality items than those he'd bought previously – particularly new wurdes of Nym to develop sentience in a lac. But the Trader didn't offer any advice. It seemed a strange way to do business; the conversation between him and Tyron was very complex and difficult to understand.

Wurdes were each capable of being combined with other wurdes, and included primitives embedded deep within them – units of syntax that had been developed long ago by the pioneers who created the art of patterning.

Tyron's theory was that the wurdes so far supplied to Midgard lacked the language primitives that formed the building blocks of sentience; primitives that he'd been labouring for years to develop himself. The whole dialogue took a form not unlike the opening moves of combat in Arena 13. Each participant was seeking an advantage, tentatively probing the defences of his opponent. But then, after a while, I saw it in another way.

It was not what Tyron took away with him that was truly important here, it was what he was *learning* from the lips of the Trader. For, in the course of this complex conversation, Tyron, the master artificer, was being taught by an even greater master of the patterning art of Nym.

It was true that a number of wurdes would later be written down and despatched to Tyron, but that was merely for form's sake. The true substance was being exchanged now, and it was for this that gold would be paid.

After an hour of this arcane dialogue, Tyron bought a dozen lacs, none of them viewed in advance. It was then that I realized something else: there was great trust between the Trader and Tyron; my master was clearly a very privileged customer. It seemed that different rules applied to the dialogue between Wode and the Trader. What they said was also much easier to understand.

'I wish to buy the soul incarnate of a patterner,' Wode said.

'Five are available from the Index today,' replied the Trader, his eyes glinting through the slits in his metal mask. 'The first four are male, and we shall refer to them by their designated numbers: #3671; #2587; #2004 and #1805. The fifth is a female, and her designation is #0001.'

They were catalogued according to the length of time their souls had spent in Containment. The Trader then went on to state their price, starting with the most expensive, which was the female, #0001.

Wode gasped at the sum, and Tyron raised his eyebrows.

'Did I hear you correctly?' Wode asked. 'That price is

astounding. It would take two years' profits from the Wheel and all its associated gambling houses to buy that female.'

'You certainly did,' replied the Trader, his voice muffled by the mask. 'The female in question died almost eight hundred years ago at the height of imperial power.'

I gasped. That was an incredible length of time.

'What about the other four patterners? I trust that they will be somewhat cheaper?'

But the remaining four were also way beyond Wode's means. He glanced at Tyron, who shook his head to indicate that he would not spend such huge sums.

So Wode left without making a purchase.

It was a very disappointing end to the day's business, though I saw that Tyron had a satisfied expression on his face. Wode, however, seemed very down in the dumps.

On the way back I asked Tyron about the female Nym patterner.

'That price was ridiculous,' I said. 'Who'd ever be able to pay that?'

'The price is linked to the length of time each soul has been held in Containment,' Tyron answered. 'But it's not storage costs that affect the price. That's determined by the potential knowledge being bought. That female artificer practised her craft at a time when imperial power had reached its zenith. If you *could* afford it, you'd be buying someone who knows how to pattern sentience into a lac. It's as simple as that.'

'But why does the Trader price her so highly?' I asked. 'He'll never make a sale.'

'He has his reasons,' said Tyron. 'Some believe there are

islands where small pockets of humanity like ours still live out their lives beyond the Barrier. Maybe some of them are wealthy and can afford such a high price. Then again, you never know with the Trader. He plays his own strange games. I've seen him drop his prices very suddenly for no apparent reason. Let's just say this, because I'm pretty sure it's going to happen – at some point in the future, that artificer will become affordable. I just hope I'm still around when she does.'

THE JOURNEYMAN PATTERNER

Peek is a basic Nym wurde-tool.
It is used to read elements of patterns and how they
are linked.

The Manual of Nym

Back at the city there was soon astonishing news. Although Wode had failed to buy a soul incarnate, somebody else had been successful.

'Despite making it impossible for Wode and my father to buy one, the Trader *did* supply a soul,' Kwin whispered in my ear at breakfast on the second morning after our return.

'How do you know?' I asked, glancing at the door and listening for Tyron's footsteps while I buttered my toast.

'There are always lots of curious witnesses to deliveries from the Sea Gate, and now it's the talk of the town,' she replied. 'Everybody in the admin building is gossiping about it. A sealed body-shaped casket was delivered to the wharf by barge. My father is going to be so angry. But he shouldn't let it bother him. Such purchases are usually a waste of money.'

Then, with a smile that melted my heart, Kwin left the kitchen. I went off to my study before Tyron arrived. I knew he'd be in a bad mood.

The next morning I was disappointed when Kwin didn't appear at breakfast – it was usually the only time I could talk to her in private. I was just finishing a second bacon sandwich when Tyron strode into the room, his face full of fury. He shook his head.

'That fool of a girl!' he cried. 'I swear, if you put your finger in the fire, she'd do the same!' Then, without a word of explanation, he left.

I spent the rest of the day wondering what Kwin had done. It was late afternoon when I next saw her. She was just back from working at Tyron's office in the admin building. Immediately I realized why her father had been angry. She'd got a tattoo of her own, right in the middle of her forehead, just above her nose. It was identical to the clasp on Tyron's broad leather belt.

'So what do you think of it?' Kwin asked, her eyes flashing.

'Your father's not best pleased!' I told her with a grin. 'He thinks it's my fault! But it suits you. Looks great!'

'He'll get over it! I've been meaning to get one for a long

time and you getting yours gave me the nudge,' Kwin said, stroking my tattoo with the tip of her forefinger. 'Do you know that, years ago, all Arena 13 combatants had this tattoo on their foreheads?'

I nodded. 'Yes, your father told me that, but I guess he never thought you'd get one!'

'He's angry with me, but it's nothing to the rage he feels about what the Trader did. He feels let down because he and Wode weren't able to buy the soul they're all talking about.'

'Somebody with lots of money must have bought it,' I said. 'The Trader offered Wode five souls from the Index, and the cost of even the cheapest would have made your eyes water.'

'You're wrong there.' Kwin smiled. 'The man who bought it is called Tallus and he's a journeyman patterner – very ordinary. He only has one lac and has had mixed results entering it at the Wheel's lower combat levels. I don't think it's fought any higher than Arena 5. He can't have paid that much.'

'Maybe he saved up,' I suggested.

'More likely the Trader dropped his price. My father's raging about that because he thinks that he and Wode should have been given first refusal. Do you know what's made him *really* livid?'

I raised my eyebrows.

'The soul is that of a woman. It could even be the artificer who died eight hundred years ago – the one who should know how to pattern sentience into a lac. Father feels that if the Trader dropped his price, *he* should have been the one to benefit. After all, he paid a lot to be the first in line and is one of the Trader's best customers.'

*

Tyron didn't like his trainees to work with lacs unsupervised, so apart from studying Nym and trying to commit some of its basic wurdes to memory, I'd had a lazy Sunday, ending with a stroll around the city. I was making the best of it because I knew that Tyron would work us hard once Deinon got back.

Since Kern's death, the atmosphere in the house had become silent and sad, and Teena stayed in her room most of the time. Tyron had told me that her child had been sent away from the city to be cared for by an aunt. She visited her young son but didn't feel able to care for him on a day-to-day basis.

At supper neither of Tyron's daughters put in an appearance. I was both surprised and disappointed not to see Kwin.

I realized that when the season began, it would be a year since I'd begun my training. Usually Tyron's second-year trainees were based in quarters at the Wheel. It would be interesting to meet new young people, but my anticipation was tempered by the realization that I'd rarely see Kwin any more.

Tyron was away somewhere on business, and at the end of the previous season Palm had left for his new quarters in the Wheel, so I dined alone. I tucked in eagerly.

I was looking forward to seeing Deinon. I needed some company. Fortunately he appeared soon after supper on the Sunday evening.

'Hi, Leif – it's good to see you!' he said, clapping me on the shoulder.

'Good to see you too. It seems ages since the end of the season.'

'I like those tattoos! They're Genthai, aren't they?'

'They are. They show your ancestry. But if you think this is good, wait until you see Kwin's! She's got a number thirteen tattooed on her forehead. Tyron went berserk!'

'Can't wait to see it!' Deinon laughed.

I'd have liked to tell him about everything that had happened to me in the forest, but I was bound by my promise to Konnit.

Deinon was friendly enough, though I thought he seemed a little subdued. We sat on our beds and chatted for a while before going to sleep.

'How was it back home?' I asked. Deinon had gone back to help on his father's farm.

'It was good to see my family again, but my father worked me really hard. Things are quieter in winter, but that's when we do routine maintenance like repairing fences and patching up the barn. I had to do a lot more than my brothers – but I can't complain, can I? I'm away here while they have to do all the hard work in summer.'

'Tyron said there was some problem that stopped you from coming back earlier. You can't believe how glad I am to see you. It's been so quiet here. Another week and I'd have gone crazy.'

'It was to do with money, Leif,' he answered glumly. 'My father was struggling to pay Tyron for my training, but it's all sorted out now.'

Deinon's father could only afford to send one of his sons to train for Arena 13. I guessed that this might have made things uncomfortable for him at home.

'What about you, Leif? Did you get to stay with your people?'

'Yes!' I said with a smile. 'But they worked me hard too. I spent the winter chopping down trees. It'll be good to get back into training.'

'I've decided to concentrate on patterning,' Deinon said, his face suddenly becoming serious. 'Tyron thinks I'm good enough to make a living from it, and I don't think I'll ever be good enough to fight in the arena.'

'Someone with two left feet like you is lucky to get across a room without stumbling,' I laughed. We were good friends now and I knew he wouldn't take offence. 'But he'll still make you practise dancing behind a lac,' I continued. 'Tyron once told me that even if a trainee specializes in patterning, he needs to keep in touch with what's required.'

'I don't mind that – I won't have to fight in Arena 13. It's not for me. Imagine fighting to the death in a grudge match. And you can get badly hurt in an ordinary contest. They don't all end with a ritual cut. If you stumble and get separated from your lac, the others come at you with their blades, and they aren't fussy how they cut you.'

I didn't want to contradict Deinon. He had a right to his opinions. But I didn't agree. I liked the danger. I loved the idea of pitting my skill against another combatant and his lacs.

'Speaking of Arena 13, would you dream of entering the Lists without being trained by an artificer like Tyron?'

I shook my head. It would be madness.

'Well, the wagon driver who brought me into Gindeen was full of the news that's sweeping through the city – that somebody is going to do exactly that. Tallus, the man who bought the dead artificer from the Trader, has applied to enter the Arena 13 Lists. What do you think of that?'

'The start of the season is less than three months away,' I said. 'He's had no training. He'll never be ready in time. It just isn't possible.'

'It'll be interesting if he manages to win!' exclaimed Deinon. 'That might be worth a bet. You'd get very good odds.'

'Yes!' I said with a laugh. 'It's a pity neither of us bets!'

It was true. I'd bet only once – forced into it because of my rivalry with Palm. But it wouldn't happen again. Deinon and I had discussed this at length. Although a punter might win sometimes, in the long run his losses always outweighed his gains. The gambling houses knew exactly what they were doing and had made a fine art of calculating odds.

However, it seemed to me that although Tallus might not be ready in time, his lac would be. The artificer he'd bought would be patterning it for him.

'I wonder what it's like for her,' I mused. 'Imagine dying at a time when humans ruled the whole world and waking up to find yourself a slave in muddy Midgard.'

'It'll be a shock all right,' Deinon agreed. 'I hope nobody tells her about the others that were bought from the Trader and what happened to them. That would make her feel really bad.'

'What did happen to them?' I asked.

'A couple just disappeared,' Deinon told me. 'Maybe they were taken by Hob.'

'Why would Hob want them?'

'For their knowledge of Nym – they were all patterners, after all,' Deinon explained. 'Another one committed suicide. And one went raving mad and had to be locked away until he died.

'They were all men except one,' he continued. 'What happened to the woman was terrible. She aged rapidly. They say that when she was first bought, she looked no more than thirty. One year later she was a wrinkled old woman. She broke her hip in a fall and died of pneumonia.'

For a while neither of us spoke. No doubt we were both thinking of this woman artificer's situation. She too was no better than a slave. However, I was intrigued and excited. I wanted to be there when Tallus fought. Would we be shocked and amazed by the changes she could bring about in a lac? I wondered.

'I miss Kern,' Deinon said suddenly, changing the subject.

'It's not the same without him,' I agreed.

On that sad note we climbed into our beds. That night I dreamed of Kern. Not of his defeat in the arena, although that would have been bad enough. I saw his eyes looking at me from the box where his severed head had been placed, pleading for a help that I was unable to give.

Then another pair of eyes stared at me. Fear gripped me and I began to tremble, but trapped in the nightmare, I couldn't look away.

They were the pitiless, inhuman eyes of Hob.

HISTORY IN THE MAKING

Slim Nym is the shortened Core Dictionary of a
language which will never cease growing.

The Manual of Nym

The following day Tyron supervised our first training session.
He worked us very hard at dancing behind the practice lac.
I knew that we would end the session with the game with
the ball and was determined to do better this time.

Deinon went first, and received a blow to the head that
sent him reeling to the floor. He looked up and gave a rueful
smile. It didn't matter that much to him, but to me speed and
precision were everything. I needed to prove that I could still
do it.

My mouth was dry and I was desperate to win. I moved in
fast, just managing to avoid the leather ball, and lunged
towards the lac's throat-socket. My blade struck close to the
target, but not close enough. It made that metallic noise that
everyone in Arena 13 is familiar with – the sound that indi-
cates a near miss.

I circled and attacked again. This time the blade hit
home, the shock travelling all the way up to my shoulder.

The wurde endoff was called, and down went the lac, following the patterning in its mind.

Only when I'd managed to win twice more did my anxiety evaporate. I was back. From now on I would get better and better.

After that Tyron concentrated on theory. I groaned inside, but hid my feelings. I much preferred to work on the training floor, although I knew that Deinon would love this.

'I would like you to write a simple wurde to direct a min combatant's lac to first feint, making a false attack, then to step forward and aim for the throat-socket of the central lac of the opposing tri-glad. As components of your new wurde, use existing wurdes from *The Nym Dictionary*. Each wurde must be clearly explained using comments. Is that clear?'

We both nodded, and retired to work alone in our small studies. Experienced Nym patterners held the basic Nym wurdes in their memories, but, as trainees, we were each allowed a printed version of *Slim Nym*, which was the shortened Core Dictionary of the language.

I decided to call my new wurde 'Gambit'; after all, making a false attack was a ruse before making the real attack. It took me about twenty minutes to find the wurdes I needed and then to combine them within 'Gambit'. Calling that wurde would begin the sequence of actions. I was also careful to use / and add my comment, an explanation of what each section did:

:*Gambit* –/ this is the name of the wurde to be compiled and then called

BeReceptive*/ this alerts the lac to await target instruction

CentralLac*/ lac directed to attack central lac of opposing tri-glad

Feint*/ lac directed to make mock attack

BeClumsy*/ and seem over-extended

StepB2*/ two steps backwards

StepF1*/ one step forward

TargetSocket*/ thrust blade at lac's throat-socket

Retreat;/ move backwards

I was quite pleased with what I'd achieved. Of course, the next step would be to create the Ulum sound-code linked to that wurde. Once completed, drumming that on the boards of the arena would call up the wurde in the mind of the lac and it would follow the instructions.

We took our written solutions to Tyron, who was waiting on the training floor. He nodded and read our wurdes.

'That's good, Leif,' he said with a smile. 'That would definitely work.'

Then he stared down at Deinon's effort and whistled through his teeth. He was clearly impressed. 'That's excellent, Deinon. I'd like to discuss this with you after our practical workout. I think I can suggest a couple of improvements.'

Then I caught a glimpse of what Deinon had produced. It was three times the length of my code, and contained numbers and symbols I had no knowledge of. Compared with Deinon's code, mine was the crude scratchings of a child using chalk on a slate tablet. For a moment I felt envious, but pushed it aside. Deinon was good at patterning. He had a flair for it and that would be his future. My forte was actually fighting in Arena 13.

I was again surprised and disappointed to find that Kwin was not there at supper. I hadn't seen her all day.

After we'd eaten, Tyron dismissed Deinon but asked me to stay behind. I felt nervous. What was this all about? Was I in trouble again?

He closed the door and turned to face me. 'Yesterday I went to see a man called Tallus,' he said. 'The name that's on every gossip's lips because he's the one who bought that female artificer. She's the very one that the Trader offered to Wode. There's no doubt about it. She will have far greater knowledge of Nym than we have. No doubt she'll have the skill to pattern a sentient lac.

'I think we should share that knowledge, and you know why, boy. It would enable us to defeat Hob. So I offered to buy some of her time. I offered a lot of money – more than Tallus would normally earn in a year – but he refused point blank. I can't really blame him. He sees me as a rival who's trying to steal some of his advantage. He believes he's going to earn big money.'

'Did you see the artificer?' I asked.

Tyron nodded. 'Yes, but I got precious little chance to speak to her. She has a strange accent and it's hard to understand what she says. Language, especially its pronunciation, will have changed a lot since her day. But Tallus told me she's making good progress and is improving rapidly. She told me her name and why it was given to her – that was all.

'She's Tallus's property and has to hold her tongue, but

what I saw impressed me. The false flesh she's been reborn into is that of an attractive woman no older than thirty. But it's her eyes that tell you she's something very special. They shine with intelligence and spirit. She's a proud and wilful woman – one glance told me that. Her name is Ada. She says she was named after the first ever human patterner, who was also a woman.'

'What will you do now?' I asked.

'There's little more that I *can* do, but I did have one stroke of luck. Well, in truth, it was more than luck,' Tyron said with a satisfied smile. 'I was canny enough to let Kwin accompany me when I visited Tallus. Ada took a shine to her, and Kwin liked Ada too. No doubt they have things in common, including their attitude – though even if they were opposites, she'd welcome Kwin. The woman is alone in an unfamiliar world and slave to a stranger, and a man at that. I suggested that Kwin might provide a bit of female companionship. Tallus was suspicious at first, but he soon realized that Ada would work better with Kwin to talk to. So she's staying with them for a while.'

I tried not to let my disappointment show. I would miss her. I'd been hoping to get closer to her and felt a twinge of loss.

'So Kwin will be able to learn from Ada?' I asked. 'She'll be able to find out about Nym and pass it on to you?'

Tyron smiled and shook his head. 'She's a clever girl, is Kwin – make no mistake about it. And she knows the basics of the language. But that doesn't mean that she'll be able to work out what that artificer is doing. Still, we've got one foot in the door. There's a chance that Tallus might change his mind. That's if he doesn't get himself killed first. He's already scheduled to fight in the first week of the season and he's been drawn against Brandon, a skilled veteran. Normally I wouldn't expect a novice like him to last two minutes, but with Ada patterning his lac, it should be interesting.'

'I'd like to see that!' I said.

'And so you shall,' Tyron replied. 'The gallery is bound to be full to capacity, so I'll book seats. It's something we should all watch. It could be history in the making – the first sentient lac to fight in Arena 13. Of course, it could be a complete fiasco. Tallus may not stay on his feet for more than twenty seconds.'

Creating a sentient lac was of great importance to Tyron. Such a lac would be fully aware and able to take the initiative, forming a better partnership with the human combatant. Tyron also believed that a number of such lacs might enter Hob's lair and destroy every last one of his selves.

It struck me that lacs armed with the gramagandar would find the task even easier, but Konnit had his own plans for those weapons.

At the end of the first week of training we had our usual Saturday off. Deinon and I spent the afternoon at the Westmere Plaza. The sky was blue and cloudless, but there was little warmth in the sun and the deciduous trees were still not out – there were no conifers allowed in the city because their roots could not gain sufficient purchase on the slopes; they blew over in winter gales and were a hazard to property and people.

We sat outside our usual café. Despite our heavy coats, we were both shivering in the cold air. I could hear Deinon's teeth chattering.

'Are you happy that we're to stay on in Tyron's house?' he asked before taking a sip of his drink.

We had just been given the good news. Usually, at the end of the first year, Tyron's trainees moved to accommodation in the Wheel. I'd expected that, like Palm, we'd both be moving just before the start of the season. But then Tyron had told us that we wouldn't be going after all. He wouldn't be taking on any new trainees this year so there'd be room for us to stay.

'It suits me,' I said with a grin. 'That way I'll see more of Kwin!'

'Seriously, Leif, don't build up your hopes too much. The other day I was near the Wheel and I saw her talking to Jon.'

I shrugged and smiled, trying to put a brave face on things, although I felt hurt. I thought they had broken up.

'I'm not,' I said, trying to avoid Deinon's eyes.

'I was looking forward to working at the Wheel and getting to know the other trainees,' he said, 'but Tyron is right – it's better if I stay at the house. There'll be more peace and quiet to work on my patterning.'

Tyron clearly believed that Deinon could become a first-rate patterner of lacs, so he'd be concentrating on that now, although he'd still need to work with lacs. That way he'd have a better grasp of what he was trying to achieve. But Tyron had different reasons to keep me there.

He thought that if Hob still intended to hurt me, he would be less likely to do if I remained at his house. At the Wheel Hob had spies and agents; it would be easier to attack me there.

Suddenly I saw Kwin walking across the plaza towards the café – my heart lurched and began to beat more quickly.

She was with a group of lads, and I soon recognized the tall muscular one walking next to her as Jon. Were they back together again? I wondered in despair.

Kwin smiled and waved at us and we returned the greeting. Jon waved too, but only Kwin came over to our table.

Last season Jon had lost a fight with a tassel on the slopes above the city. Persuaded by Kwin, I'd helped fight it, hoping to earn his freedom. It had been dangerous; but for the intervention of Konnit and other Genthai, all three of us would have been taken to Hob's citadel. I wondered why Jon hadn't mentioned the incident, but perhaps he was embarrassed and just wanted to forget it.

'Hey!' Kwin said, dragging up a chair and joining us. 'Glad we met up. I've a proposition for you two – we don't get much chance to speak at the house without being overheard.'

'We're all ears,' I said with a smile, doing my best to hide my misery.

'You ever been down to the Commonality, Deinon?' she asked, fixing her gaze on him.

Deinon shook his head.

'Well, Leif has, but only because I took him to see it. Neither of you two good boys would go down there just to explore!' she joked.

I let the comment go. It was probably true. Last year Kwin had got me in all sorts of trouble: against my better judgement I'd fought her with sticks – and nearly lost my place as a trainee because of it. Then I'd faced a tassel and almost got killed. I didn't regret any of it, but left alone, I'd not have got involved in any of those things.

'I showed Leif the illegal combats between lacs down in

the Commonality,' said Kwin. 'They are forced to face each other in an arena ringed with blades. They fight without armour, almost naked, and get cut to ribbons. Lots of them die. It's wrong! Cyro, who's supposed to be in charge of the Commonality, turns a blind eye because the gambling houses make a lot of money and give him a cut. We're planning to do something about it. Tomorrow night a group of us are going down there to protest – to make our feelings known by occupying the arena and halting the contests! Want to come? Jon's organizing it. It was his idea to ask you two.'

For a moment Deinon looked doubtful, but then he spoke up. 'I do think something should be done. They shouldn't be allowed to get away with it!'

'What about your father?' I said, raising my eyebrows. This was clearly something Kwin didn't want Tyron to know about.

She shrugged. 'He wouldn't want us to go, Leif, that's true enough. But he never allows his lacs to fight down there. He's against it. I'm sure there wouldn't be any serious consequences if he found out.'

The protest was worth making, I thought. 'OK! See you tomorrow night,' I said. 'Where shall we meet up?'

'At the back entrance of the Wheel at six-thirty, just before sunset.'

'We'll see you there,' said Deinon, grinning from ear to ear. I could tell he was looking forward to it.

On our way back we passed the shop selling Trig equipment and paraphernalia. I carried on walking, but I knew what would happen.

Deinon came to a halt and pointed at the window. 'The red boots – they're gone! I wonder if Palm bought them for Kwin.'

Palm was soft on Kwin, and had intended to buy the boots for her. He'd bet that I wouldn't win a single contest in the Trainee Tournament. I'd won the bet and used some of the money to buy those boots.

But now Deinon was staring at me, and I saw his expression change as understanding dawned. 'No, Leif! Tell me you didn't . . .'

I shrugged. 'I bought them for Kwin.'

'You shouldn't have. You needed that money. It could have bought you a first-class lac!'

'I didn't spend it all,' I told him.

'You shouldn't have spent *any* of it. Tyron's rolling in money. He'd have bought them for Kwin eventually. I hope she thanked you!'

'At the time, she seemed very angry, but really I think she was embarrassed. Later, she admitted that she did like the boots, and they were the best present anyone had ever bought her! I don't regret buying them one bit.'

'How grateful was she?' Deinon said, giving me an evil grin.

'She kissed me on the cheek!' I joked as we moved away from the window. 'It was a very sisterly kiss!'

A TRAVESTY OF ARENA COMBAT

Anything which bleeds can feel pain,
But not everything which thinks bleeds.

Amabramsum: the Genthai Book of Wisdom

When Deinon and I arrived at the back gate, there were already about a dozen young people gathered at the Wheel – a roughly even mix of girls and boys. I recognized a few as trainees from other stables. Because we were living in Tyron's house rather than at the Wheel, we didn't know any well enough to talk to, but we exchanged a few friendly nods.

I couldn't see any sign of Jon. Was he with Kwin? I wondered. No doubt they'd arrive together.

I glanced up at the huge copper dome reflecting the light of the setting sun. The vultures were already starting their slow spirals above it, riding the air currents.

'There's something strange about that dome,' Deinon said, following my gaze.

'What do you mean?'

'Look at the colour of it. What do you see, Leif?'

'It's copper, so they say. It's a sort of browny-gold,' I replied. 'I like the way it reflects the sun.'

'Yes, but copper open to the elements doesn't usually look like that. It turns a sort of green. Something called verdigris forms on it. We have a well on our farm. It's got a round wooden lid which is coated with copper riveted to the wood. That lid is green. My father says that the dome of the Wheel must be made out of a very special kind of copper.'

'I wonder who built it,' I mused. It was one more mystery to add to the many others about the origins of Midgard – though nothing compared to the Wolf Wheel that Konnit had described. Just how much of our land had been shaped by the djinn? We patterned lacs, but they had patterned Midgard.

Ten minutes later Kwin and Jon arrived. They weren't arm in arm, but their shoulders were almost touching, and immediately I felt jealous. Kwin hardly seemed to notice us; she went straight to the front of the group with Jon, and they led the way through the narrow gate into the Wheel. We followed behind, and I did a quick head count. I was surprised to find that there were only nineteen of us. I'd expected more.

There were few people about in the Wheel because it was still early. Contests didn't start until eight in the evening. We went down the stone steps that led to the Commonality. They led downwards in a tight spiral. Nobody spoke, and all that could be heard was the echo of our footsteps.

Soon we were moving along a series of tunnels. At one intersection I saw a cluster of pale fungal growths dangling from the ceiling. Kwin had told me about them on our previous visit, and now I noticed the poison dripping from it. Deinon was heading directly towards it, and there was no time to call out a warning; I leaped forward and pushed him roughly out of the way. A drop of skeip just missed his left shoulder.

He looked back at me angrily.

'Sorry about the push, but that's skeip fungus,' I said, pointing it out to him. 'It's deadly. You should never stand underneath it because it drips a deadly poison. It almost hit you!'

As we watched, it began to drip again, each globule of poison splattering on the tunnel floor.

Deinon looked at me with wide eyes and said, 'Thanks.'

We moved on. The tunnels were lit by torches, but there were gloomy sections that could have concealed any number of dangers. After passing through a curved stone archway, we reached a matrix of straw-lined stone containers where hundreds of lacs were stored; row after row extending up into the darkness until they were lost to view.

The lacs were in the deep sleep – a type of hibernation in which they required little food and expended hardly any energy. For their owners it made good economic sense; renting the cots cost little. Until awakened for combat by a wurde, they would stay in that somnolent state.

Deinon knew that such places existed in the Commonality, but he'd never seen such a big storage area before. His eyes went everywhere as he registered what he was seeing.

'Who'd have thought there'd be so many lacs here – it's huge!' he exclaimed.

'Those were exactly my thoughts when I first saw it,' I told him.

There was something strange and scary about the sight of so many shaven heads and yellow-soled feet – and the pink-lipped throat-slits without the armoured throat-socket.

There was a hiss of breathing; some slack-faced lacs were snoring too. It sounded like the drone of angry bees or a wind gathering to storm-force. The atmosphere was compounded by the unpleasant stink of damp, urine-soaked straw.

I was glad when we'd passed through the far exit and were walking along the tunnels again. Finally we reached a rusty iron grille set into the wall. Beyond it, steps led downwards, descending into utter darkness.

'That's to keep the feral lacs out of the main area of the Commonality,' I told Deinon as we passed it.

He came to a halt and stared at the grille. I stood beside him, peering into the darkness.

'There really are wild lacs down there?' he asked. 'I thought that was just a story to scare children.'

'Well, Cyro takes it seriously enough to keep those gates well-maintained. At least, that's what Kwin told me,' I said with a grin. 'It's said that they eat rats, and sometimes each other.'

'You mean they're cannibals like the tassels?'

'That's what Kwin believes!'

'How do they get down there?'

'They escape from their owners. Maybe something goes wrong with their patterning and they wake up out of the deep sleep. They're more than capable of ripping a gate like this off its hinges.'

We suddenly realized that the others had moved on without us and we ran to catch up. Kwin had told me about the danger of getting lost down in the Commonality. It was best to keep to well-lit tunnels.

When we emerged onto a high ledge, I realized that we

were looking down on the amphitheatre, which was ringed with torches. From my last visit I recognized the circle of two-foot-high sharp blades that marked the perimeter of the combat area, which was covered with sand to soak up the blood. A contest between two lacs was already underway.

There was a fair-sized crowd in the elevated seating around the arena. They would gather here to bet and enjoy the brutal spectacle, and then go up to Arena 13 to watch the contests there.

One of our group was about to set off along the winding path that led down to the arena when Jon halted him with a gesture.

'Best to wait until the contest is over. Then we'll take them by surprise.'

Nobody argued, so we watched in silence as the two lacs fought it out below, whirling and slashing, their oiled bodies glistening in the torchlight. Unlike Arena 13 lacs, they had no armour. Apart from the metal bands that held the throat-sockets in place, all they wore were loincloths; white and black in this case, to make it easier to tell them apart. We watched in silence, listening to the occasional gasps or cheers from the excited audience. Once again, I was impressed by the agility and speed of the long-armed lacs.

The last time I'd watched one of those contests, it had ended bloodily. One of the lacs had been forced back into the ring of blades; its legs were cut to ribbons as its opponent delivered the killing blow.

This contest finished with the endoff, much like one in Arena 13. Victory was achieved when the black-clothed lac slotted its blade into its opponent's throat-socket. The lac in the white loincloth collapsed on the floor. Not one drop of blood had been spilled. The lac would live to fight again. But how many times could it fight in this way without receiving some serious injury?

The audience were quiet. They'd been denied the gory end that many of them craved.

'Right!' said Jon. 'Let's do it!'

He ran down the path with Kwin at his shoulder. Once again Deinon and I were at the back. By the time we reached the arena, the blades had been retracted into the ground and the lacs removed. Without hesitation, Jon led the way to the centre of the arena.

The spectators stared at us, puzzled or angry expressions on their faces. They began to murmur, many clearly resenting this intrusion.

Jon raised his arms for silence – and got it. Then he spoke in a loud, clear voice.

'We are here to protest against these barbaric contests where lac is pitted against lac without armour. It is illegal for lacs to fight in this way. Lacs may only enter combat in the thirteen arenas of the Wheel or in training sessions that prepare them to fight there. That is the law.'

'Get out of here!' shouted a voice from high up in the banked seats. 'What do you know about it, you stupid, ignorant lout. You're still wet behind the ears!'

I glanced up and saw that the red-faced man who'd spoken had risen to his feet. To my astonishment, I saw Palm sitting next to him. What was he doing here? I wondered. Trainees didn't come to watch this travesty of arena combat. It was generally held in disgust and contempt.

'I'm an Arena 13 trainee combatant, as are others in our group,' replied Jon. 'We know this business very well. We know what's permitted and what is not. These practices disgust us. The blades that encircle this arena during combat are designed to cut lacs who do not wear armour. Why is that? I ask you. Why aren't they provided with armour? It is because you *want* to see them bleed!'

'They're just animals!' the voice called back. 'I'm a farmer and I work hard to put meat on your table and keep your bellies full. Do you worry when cattle are cut to pieces in the slaughterhouse? What's the difference?'

It suddenly struck me that the man was probably Palm's father. He was a rich farmer who ensured that Palm had the best of everything – including lacs for fighting in Arena 13.

Jon opened his mouth to reply, but then Cyro waddled out of the shadows, his belly overhanging his broad belt. Last season I'd only seen him from the ledge high above. Now, closer to, I saw that it was muscle, not fat, that bulked out his huge body.

A couple of dozen guards followed behind him, thick-set, thuggish men with broad shoulders and short, fat necks. They gripped wooden clubs, tapping them into the palms of their hands and grinning, clearly enjoying their work. A club like that wielded with force could easily break a limb or cave in a skull, I thought.

'Well, children,' said Cyro, his voice heavy with sarcasm. 'You've had your few minutes of fun. But now it's time to go home. Go in peace, or stay and take the consequences. Time is money, and every second you stay makes me a little angrier.'

'What you're doing is illegal!' Jon shouted, moving across to face him.

'Illegal, is it?' Cyro smiled. 'This is my domain and you haven't been invited. So according to the law, you're trespassing, and I'm going to evict you. If a few heads get broken in the process, well, that's a pity, but I'll still sleep well tonight. So what is it to be, sonny?'

'We're staying,' Jon replied, but he sounded slightly less confident.

Now Kwin stepped forward. 'Yes, we *are* staying! We're staying until everyone leaves and we're sure that none of this butchery will continue!' she cried, her voice full of fury.

Cyro smiled and very deliberately looked her up and down. With her lips painted in that distinctive fashion, red and black, and the 13 tattooed upon her forehead, she would be easy to identify. But it seemed that he knew her already:

'You're Tyron's daughter, aren't you? You work in the admin building.'

Kwin didn't reply.

'I thought so,' he said. 'I wonder how your father will react when he knows what you've been up to!'

'He doesn't agree with what goes on down here either. None of his lacs ever take part.'

'What your father does best is minding his own business. He minds his and I mind mine. I'll be in touch with him tomorrow. We'll have words about you. He needs to keep you under control.'

'It's *you* who are out of control!' Kwin snapped back. 'You think you're beyond the law!'

Had I been closer to Kwin, I'd have warned her not to

antagonize Cyro. But I saw the anger in her expression. She wouldn't have listened anyway.

Cyro stared at her, his face now flushed with anger. 'I really hate lippy women,' he said, his voice low but clear. 'And lippy young girls like you are the worst of all.' He gave an exaggerated sigh, then turned and began to walk away. I couldn't believe it. Had he given up? But then he gave a gesture – a sudden downward thrust of his left thumb.

Immediately his men started running towards us, their clubs raised.

Everything happened very quickly. Perhaps they'd expected us to run, but we didn't. We stood our ground. I watched Jon duck under a blow aimed at his head. The club missed; Jon's fist didn't. It connected with the jaw of his assailant, who went down. Others were racing to attack, and Kwin was in their path. I ran forward, attempting to get in front of her.

Then I was ducking and punching, and we were suddenly moving forward in a line, driving our opponents back. I glanced to my right and saw Kwin fighting alongside me. She now had one of the clubs in her right hand and was swinging it with deadly accuracy. I suddenly thought we might actually win.

Cyro had expected us to run for it; in any case we surely had no chance against his armed thugs. But we were either trainee Arena 13 combatants or stick-fighters. We were young and fast, more than able to cope with the clumsy attacks of Cyro's muscle-bound men. The girls were also fighting back; with her club, Kwin was a force to be reckoned with.

Then Deinon pushed through to my other side, also wielding a club. As our eyes met, he gave me a grin.

But my initial optimism was shattered when I saw Cyro summoning reinforcements. Outnumbered, we fought on for another minute, but then they were all around us. Suddenly our line broke. People were fleeing in all directions. I was reluctant to run, but I saw Kwin sprinting away and tried to follow her.

Then I felt a tremendous blow to the back of my head and knew no more.

I opened my eyes and looked up to see Cyro frowning down at me. I was hauled roughly to my feet. A dozen or more of his thugs surrounded me.

A quick glance about told me that I was no longer in the amphitheatre. We were in one of the tunnels – the dark ones. The only light here came from torches carried by Cyro's men.

'I don't think Genthai should be allowed to fight in the arena,' Cyro said. 'You're animals, just like the lacs. You belong with the ferals down there.'

He gestured, and a cold shiver ran down my spine as I guessed what he intended to do. He was pointing towards a metal grille in the wall of the tunnel. Beyond it were steps leading down into the darkness.

This wasn't the grille I'd passed with the others, but it served the same purpose: to prevent feral lacs from getting into the Commonality. I noticed that the metal here wasn't rusty, and it was larger and sturdier, with hinges and a lock. It was really a door. It could be opened . . .

It was open now.

They dragged me to the doorway and pushed me through.

I almost fell down the steps. Before I could regain my balance the grille clanged shut behind me.

Cyro grinned at me through the bars. 'You won't be missed and your absence will be easily explained. They certainly won't dare point the finger at me. Every year people go missing in these tunnels, never to be seen again. But your disappearance will deter others from intruding into my domain again. A few broken heads and a missing trainee – that should do it. It could have been any one of you, but I'm glad it's a Genthai scumbag. You won't starve to death, sonny, because you won't have time. The feral lacs are very hungry. They'll soon smell your warm flesh; the stink of your fear!'

Cyro turned his back on me and walked away, his men following behind. I wasn't sorry to see the back of him, but they took the torches with them. Soon I was plunged into absolute darkness.

FULL OF MENACE

Sycoda is the category of djinni to which Hob
  belongs.
Spying and torture are its main functions.

The Manual of Nym

I stayed crouching by the grille as I sank into despair. Kwin had told me to keep to the illuminated tunnels of the Commonality; they were used regularly, and if you got lost, someone would find you.

Nobody with any sense ever ventured into the dark. No doubt Cyro had chosen a particularly remote tunnel. My chances of being found were about zero.

My head was throbbing, and when I put my hand to the back, I found a lump as big as an egg. It made me feel nauseous. After a while my eyes adjusted to the dark; I could just make out the shape of the grille and, looking the other way, the first two steps leading down. So there had to be some light in the tunnel . . . or maybe it was reflected up the steps.

Would the feral lacs find me? I wondered. Could they really smell my flesh? It seemed likely. What would I do when they arrived? It would be good to have a club or a blade to defend myself with, but I'd nothing but my bare hands.

Despite that, I was determined to fight. Lacs were stronger and generally faster than humans, but I was fast too. I'd make sure I got a few blows in before they overwhelmed me. I turned away from the metal grille and sat down on the top step with my back against it.

I would be ready for them when they came to get me. After a while I thought I heard sounds from below – a cough and then a snuffling. I listened carefully, my whole body tense, but there was no further indication that lacs might be climbing the steps. Then I realized that their approach would be hard to detect. They might not be wearing boots, and their bare feet would make little noise.

When I did finally hear a noise, it wasn't from the steps. It came from the tunnel behind me.

I heard the sound of boots approaching, the steps slow and heavy, suggesting someone large.

Who could be walking down the tunnel – one of Cyro's men on patrol? Or maybe it was an escaped lac. But I was filled with terror when I suddenly realized there was another possibility.

It might be Hob.

The djinni preyed upon the city after dark, but it was said that he also roamed the lower levels of the Wheel and the Commonality. People went missing down here. Some blamed the feral lacs, but others pointed the finger at Hob.

I froze, hardly daring to breathe as the steps drew closer.

A bulky figure appeared through the gloom. For a moment I hoped it was a guard who would just continue past. But there was no question of that. The figure came right up to the grille as if that had been his intention all along.

At last I saw the huge head and abnormally long arms. It could have been a feral lac, but now the creature's forehead was almost touching the bars, and I remembered the large hooked nose from our last encounter.

I was face to face with Hob.

I knew that I wasn't safe behind these bars, even though they were thicker and tougher than the other grilles. He could easily rip them away to get at me. My knees began to tremble and I took a deep breath to steady myself.

'Do you remember our first meeting, boy?' Hob boomed.

I tried to say yes, but my mouth was dry and I couldn't speak.

'Well, I remember how you threatened me. I remember how you dared to draw a blade in my presence. But I didn't realize who you were then. I do now. You are the son of Mathias, whom I fought in the arena.'

'Yes, the Math who defeated you fifteen times!' I snapped back, anger and hatred suddenly filling me with hot, reckless courage.

'In the end I defeated *him*. I had your mother in thrall to me. Each night I summoned her to the river bank and sipped a little of her blood. I did that for a reason. I wanted your father to come in her place. I wanted to fight him blade against blade one more time. But he never did. His courage failed him.'

'My mother wouldn't allow him to go in her place. You'd threatened to kill me. She was trying to protect both me and him. He was brave to the end.'

'Do you know the *real* reason why she wouldn't allow him to take her place?'

Again I didn't reply. I was standing close to the bars, aware that Hob might reach through at any time or tear them away. One part of me wanted to retreat, but my pride wouldn't let me.

'She *wanted* to meet me by the river, boy . . . When I drain the blood of a human female, it gives her intense pleasure. She was addicted to it. That's why she wouldn't let Mathias take her place.'

'No!' I cried, stepping closer. 'That isn't true!'

Faster than I could have imagined, Hob's arms shot towards me. I had no time to move. He grabbed me by the shoulders and pulled me hard against the grille so that the metal dug into my face and shoulder.

'Tell me why I shouldn't kill you now.' It was hardly more than a whisper. The djinni's eyes were cold; I couldn't discern any emotion in them.

Our faces were inches apart and I was staring into those eyes – the whites unusually large, each small dark iris just a pinprick. I was conscious of the power emanating from him and my legs turned to jelly. Hob released me, but I was no longer able to move. Those eyes were staring hard into mine, and I was completely in thrall to him.

However, my hatred and desire for revenge soon returned, and I broke free, staggering backwards. Then, instead of retreating, I rushed back towards the bars.

'In the arena!' I shouted, almost spitting in his face. 'We'll fight in the arena. That'll be your chance to kill me – that's if *you've* got the courage! That's if you've got the speed and the skill!'

For a moment Hob just stared at me. Then his hands came through the bars and he grasped my shoulders again, his grip tightening. I sensed his great strength: his huge hands were capable of crushing my shoulders. My courage was replaced by terror. I was about to die or be maimed so that I'd never be able to fight in the arena again.

Then, suddenly, he released me. I fell back onto the steps and rolled down three or four before I managed to stop myself. Trembling, I came up onto my knees and stared at the figure behind the grille.

'Have you learned to love yet, boy?' Hob asked, his voice full of menace.

He'd asked me this before, when I'd gone with Tyron to buy back Kern's remains. Angered by what he'd done, I'd drawn a blade and Tyron had been forced to beg for my life.

Then Hob had asked that strange question:

'Whom do you love, boy?'

My answer had been that I loved nobody. After all, my parents were dead and I'd had no close friends.

He'd then threatened that when I *did* care for someone, he'd kill them before he killed me so that I would suffer the pain of their death first.

Once again I didn't reply, keeping my distance so that he couldn't reach me.

Was he just playing games with my mind? I wondered.

'I can see that you have changed since we first met,' Hob said, holding me in thrall once more. 'I sense that you *do* care for someone. The object of your love is female – I am certain of it. Perhaps I will take her soul. Or maybe I will wait until we have fought in the arena. I could take you both into my citadel. I would enjoy that. You could watch her cease to be fully human. There are worse things than death – as you will discover one day.'

Without another word, he turned and strode off into the darkness, in the direction from which he had come.

I crouched on the steps for a long time, thinking over what he'd said. I was terribly afraid for Kwin. What I felt for her . . . was that *love*? How could you really love somebody if your love wasn't reciprocated? Was Hob's threat really directed at Kwin, or was he just bluffing?

But, I reflected, anyone Hob *thought* I loved might be in danger . . .

These questions whirled around my head, but I had no answers.

I tried to sleep, but it was very uncomfortable on the steps and Hob's words tormented me. Finally, utterly exhausted, I drifted off.

I was awoken by harsh laughter and the sound of a key turning in the lock.

The metal grille was opened and I was dragged roughly to my feet.

Before me I saw four of Cyro's men: two to grip my arms and two to hold torches to light the way. They marched me along the tunnels.

I wondered where I was being taken. The answer came quickly enough, as we emerged into the amphitheatre. The arena was empty, the blades marking its perimeter invisible.

Cyro was waiting there, legs apart and arms folded. They brought me to a halt in front of him, still gripping my arms tightly.

'Did you have a comfortable night?' he asked with a grin.

I remained silent.

'Were you brave enough to go down the steps and explore?'

Again I said nothing. I suspected that anything I said would be used against me in some way. My captors were chuckling at each of Cyro's questions. I was the only one who didn't get the joke.

'You stayed at the top of the steps. I can tell from your face. Well, if you had been brave enough to go down them, you wouldn't have found any ravenous lacs waiting to eat you. The feral lacs *can* be reached down steps such as those, but they are contained by fixed grilles. Down those steps you'd have found a storeroom, that's all. You were never in any danger.'

I thought of mentioning Hob's visit, but what purpose would that have served?

'I'm not a murderer, Leif – and yes, I know your name, just as I know that you're also one of Tyron's trainees. In this city, knowledge is power. I've no intention of killing anybody, but don't force my hand. I will defend what's mine with everything I've got. Take that message back to your friends.'

Suddenly he pointed to the arena. I could see dark patches in the sand. Was that blood?

'After Tyron dismisses you, as I'm sure he will – he's a shrewd businessman and knows what he needs to do in order to keep profits rolling in – I might have a role for you here. Once you lose your place as a trainee, you could always turn to stick-fighting. And soon I intend to pit human combatants against lacs in that arena, one against one, without armour. What do you say? I was hard on you before because I wanted to teach you a lesson. But it's come to my notice that you have great potential as a fighter. We could work together.'

I shook my head. 'That's not for me. In any case, I've taken the oath not to use blades outside the arena.'

Even as I spoke I remembered I'd already broken my oath by fighting the werewight. But then I was struck by what Cyro had said. It was as if my future was already sealed. Would Tyron dismiss me because of this? Would he yield to Cyro?

'You're not listening carefully, Leif. I said *after* Tyron dismisses you. You will no longer be an Arena 13 combatant and the oath won't apply. Think about it. We all have to make a crust somehow. Take him away!' Cyro commanded, and his thugs marched me away up the steep path.

I could hardly believe that I was being released – though what Cyro had said disturbed me. How much pressure could he bring to bear upon Tyron? Could he persuade him to sack me?

It was daylight when I left the Wheel – late morning, judging by the position of the sun. I hurried back to Tyron's house. When I entered the yard, Kwin ran out to greet me. I was surprised to see her there. She was supposed to be staying with Tallus and Ada.

'Are you all right?' she asked, her face full with concern.

Before I could reply she ran forward and threw her arms around me, pressing her face against my neck. Then she gave a sob, took a step backwards and looked at me. To my astonishment I saw that her eyes were brimming with tears. Did she care about me after all?

'Yes, I'm all right now, but last night was pretty scary,' I replied. 'They locked me behind a gate and left me in the dark. I thought the steps below me led to the domain of the feral lacs, but it was all a trick to scare me. To be honest, it worked. What worries me now is that Cyro said he was going to get your father to stop training me.'

'I thought you'd been killed by his thugs – until we got a message from him late last night. I thought I'd never see you again, Leif. Don't worry about being kicked out again – that won't happen.'

'What was in Cyro's message?' I asked, watching Kwin wipe away her tears with the back of her hand.

'Cyro complained about our part in the protest. He said he was going to hold you overnight to cool your heels. My father went to the admin building soon after first light for a meeting with him. He's due back any time now. Come and have some breakfast while we wait.'

'Where's Deinon?' I asked. 'Is he all right? And what about the others?'

'There were a few cuts and bruises, but everybody got back safely. Deinon's working in his study. He got a big ticking off from my father – though nothing worse than we'll get.'

'You two don't wait for trouble,' Tyron said. 'You go looking for it.'

I was sitting at the table opposite Kwin. Tyron sat down beside his daughter.

'I'm sorry,' I said lamely.

'We're both sorry,' Kwin said. 'But not sorry for protesting. Terrible things go on down in the Commonality and they must be stopped. No, we're just sorry for causing you trouble. By the way, Palm was down there watching the lacs fight. He was with a big man with red cheeks. Was that his father?'

Tyron nodded. 'His name is Jefferson – he's one of the main supporters of those contests. As well as being a rich and successful farmer, he owns many of the lacs that fight down there. He was at the meeting I've just had with Cyro. He had the cheek to threaten me. He said that if I didn't get rid of Leif, he'd withdraw his son from my stables. I told him to go ahead, but he won't do it. Palm's very happy here. It was just a bluff. However, I'll be having a quiet word with young Palm. I don't want my trainees watching what goes on in that arena of Cyro's.'

'What about Cyro?' I asked. 'He recognized Kwin and said he was going to have words with you about her and get you to stop training me.'

'Well, he certainly did his best,' Tyron said with a smile, 'but his best wasn't good enough. Let's say we parted on less than amicable terms. Consider it over – but I want you both to promise that you won't protest again. Next time somebody could get seriously hurt. Push Cyro into a corner and things might get very nasty.'

'So we're supposed to allow things to continue as they are and do nothing?' asked Kwin.

'He's got new plans,' I said. 'He intends to pit humans against lacs in his arena.'

'Does he now? Well, we'll certainly knock that scheme on the head,' Tyron growled. 'Let me deal with the situation in my own way. Many of us disagree with what Cyro does and it certainly is illegal. Give me time and we'll bring pressure to bear.'

'How much time?' Kwin demanded, her eyes flashing angrily.

'Until the end of the season,' he replied.

'That's too long! Lacs are dying down there.'

'This has been going on for decades. A few months more is too long? Let me try *my* way. Your way can't succeed.'

'Just until the end of the season – but if nothing changes, we'll protest again! In fact, we'll go further!' Kwin exclaimed. 'The lacs that fight down there are stored in a locked compound. I've never seen it, but I could make it my business to find it. Next time we won't just protest – we'll release those lacs!'

'That would be an extremely reckless and foolish thing to do. First of all, those lacs have owners – remember that. Releasing them would deprive those owners of their property. It would be theft. Somebody like Jefferson wouldn't hesitate to press charges. You could end up behind bars for a long time. Secondly, lacs released like that would band together in a mob. They'd be angry, afraid and out of control – their fighting instincts would take over. Innocent people could get hurt – maybe even killed. Anyone responsible for that could be charged with manslaughter by the Wheel Directorate. Your life would be over. They'd throw away the key. I'd be unable to help.'

Headed by Pyncheon, the Chief Marshal, the Directorate was the legal power in Gindeen that answered only to the

Protector. It had jurisdiction over the whole city, but its main focus was on the Wheel. It was an autocratic system, and once charged, people were invariably found guilty. Tyron wasn't exaggerating. To release lacs in that way was fraught with peril.

Kwin shrugged. 'Then you've got until the end of the season, Father dear,' she said with a smile. 'So bring a lot of pressure to bear in the right places.'

Tyron nodded and rose to his feet. 'Well, Leif, back to training. You've a lot of work to do before the start of the season.'

A TUMBLE

We all fall down.

Amabramsum: the Genthai Book of Wisdom

The months passed quickly. Deinon and I had worked hard and were now excited that the new Arena 13 season was underway. The mud in the streets had begun to harden and the late spring sun was warm. Now, early in the first week of the season, we reached the evening scheduled for Tallus's first contest.

I walked into the gallery with Deinon and Tyron, who had booked seats three rows up from the front. We'd have a really good view.

It was the first time I'd been into the gallery since the previous season, and once again it took my breath away. It was far superior to the other arenas, and not just because it held two thousand spectators. The tiers of seats had all been re-upholstered in expensive red leather and the smell pervaded the air. The torches had been newly gilded in gold and silver, including the huge candelabrum that was lowered from the high ceiling to illuminate the arena.

It showed that combat in Arena 13 was generating as much wealth as ever. This was a rich man's game.

As usual, the women were dressed in their finest silks, their lips painted black, while the men wore the coloured sashes that denoted their trades. Over the odour of new leather I could detect a variety of female perfumes on the air.

Only one smell was missing: the stench of blood that I'd smelled on first entering Arena 13 the previous year – probably because the season had only just begun. There would be time enough for that smell to be added to the mix.

I was looking forward to seeing how the new trainees would perform, including Tyron's. I wanted to weigh up the opposition. After all, hopefully I would be fighting against them soon. If it wasn't this season, then it would certainly be next. Tyron was afraid that if I did enter the Lists, Hob would come to the arena to claim my life. I didn't dare tell him of the challenge I'd issued to Hob down in the Commonality. Even to me it now seemed reckless and hot-headed – guaranteed to cause Hob to do exactly that.

Common sense told me that despite my need for revenge, I needed to make progress before I faced the djinni; I also needed a first-rate lac to fight with – one patterned to the highest level.

But although new young talent would enter the Lists this season, it was the contest between Tallus and Brandon that was most eagerly anticipated. It had drawn a big crowd; the gallery was full to bursting and there was excitement in the air. The gambling houses were doing a roaring trade, and as we walked down the steps towards the front, we passed close to an agent. He nodded to Tyron, who walked on past, and then stopped Deinon and me, thrusting a bunch of red tickets under our noses.

'Well worth a go,' the tout gabbled, spittle flying from his mouth as he spoke. 'Tallus could take a tumble.'

He talked so quickly that it was hard to follow his words. But slowly I began to appreciate the full horror of what was on offer. I'd watched a grudge match fought to the death, and noted the bets that it attracted. But this was a novice combatant, and the tout was offering odds on a range of results, from cuts to death.

'Bad cut gets you five times your stake,' he said. 'If he's maimed, it's worth twenty, but that depends on medical confirmation later. It has to be ratified. Death gets you a hundred. And he's green, my lucky lads, just a first-timer, still wet behind the ears. One in ten takes a tumble.'

We shook our heads and walked on. Neither of us was interested in gambling. It was a mug's game – as Deinon had demonstrated using simple mathematics. I'd never been interested in gambling on stick-fighting, preferring to take part than be a spectator.

'What does he mean by a "tumble"?' Deinon asked Tyron as we paused at the end of our row of seats. 'That's what the tout said is likely to happen to Tallus. Is that just a way of saying he'll lose?'

'It means literally what he said, boy – that he's very likely to fall – he'll probably trip over his own feet. Statistics show that one in ten novices do exactly that in their first contest. And if you fall and can't dance away out of trouble, the lacs come looking for you with their blades. You're very likely to get cut – occasionally very badly.'

I was proud of the fact that I'd won two contests in the Trainee Tournament. I had managed to overcome my nerves and avoid taking a tumble. However, Tallus's first contest was to be fought under the full rules: blades would be coated with kransin, so that even the slightest cut would be extremely painful. Then, after five minutes, combatants would have to fight in front of their lacs. It would be much more daunting than the tournament I'd fought in and likely to fill a novice with nerves. The danger that Tallus faced suddenly struck me with full force.

Those red tickets were mainly on sale for grudge matches, where one contestant was likely to die – though they were also available before *every* contest for those who wanted them. You named a combatant, and if he was injured, you won. Obviously, injuries were very rare or the gambling houses would have quickly become bankrupt, but it did happen. As I took my seat, I noticed that a large number of people were clutching the distinctive red tickets.

Tallus was a novice. Statistically it was slightly more likely that he would be injured. It was as simple as that. The gambling houses didn't offer favourable odds for such bets so that winnings were always relatively small. But there was such great interest in the chance of blood being spilled that lots of punters bet and when the novice didn't take a tumble the gambling houses raked in fat profits.

At that moment I noticed someone smiling up at us from the row below.

'Kwin's there!' I said, pointing her out to Tyron and giving her a wave.

'Have you seen who's sitting next to her?' he asked.

At that moment her companion turned and looked up at us. I noticed that her hair was cut very short, more like a man's than a woman's. This had to be Ada, the artificer Tallus had bought. She wasn't smiling, and I noticed something else right away.

The fashion was for women to paint their lips black, but the rebellious Kwin was different. Only her upper lip was black; her lower lip was a vivid blood-red. Ada had painted her own lips in exactly the same way.

Kwin stared at me, then abruptly looked away, her attention distracted by what was happening in the arena below. Had she stared at me just because I'd been staring at her? Or was it because she liked me?

My thoughts were interrupted by the sight of Tallus and his lac entering through the min door.

For a moment there was silence, and then suddenly, from high in the gallery, a male voice called out something that I didn't catch; it must have been some sort of joke because there was laughter from the people around us.

'What did he say?' I asked.

'That Tallus has been eating too many pies!' Deinon replied, laughing fit to burst.

I looked down into the arena, and one glance at Tallus showed me the reason for the jibe. I didn't feel like laughing. Instead I felt sorry for Tallus. The regulation shorts and leather jerkin were designed to offer flesh to the blades of the opposing lacs. Unfortunately there was a great deal of wobbly flesh on Tallus's arms and thighs. He was no fatter than many of the male spectators, but the difference was that he had dared to enter Arena 13.

You needed to be fit in order to fight here; you needed strong muscles, speed and stamina – things that Tallus lacked. He'd patterned lacs to fight in the other arenas of the Wheel, but had never set foot in one himself until this moment. If the contest wasn't over quickly, he would surely collapse with exhaustion.

I stared down at his lac. It looked very ordinary, its armour dull and dinted in places – no different to the battered lac we used in training. But with the addition of a few new wurdes and other changes in its patterns, Tyron had so improved our lac that it had helped me to win two contests in the Trainee Tournament. I had learned that you couldn't judge by appearances.

But how good was Tallus's lac? Could it save him? Had the female artificer patterned sentience into it? We were about to find out.

Brandon made his entrance through the mag gate. He was a squat, thick-set man, but light on his feet, with not even a hint of flesh surplus to requirements. His tri-glad of lacs wore polished armour that looked as if it had been bought new for the season. He was a successful campaigner and could afford it.

The candelabrum was lowered from the high ceiling, the doors rumbled shut and the trumpet shrilled. Soon the contest was underway, with Brandon drumming on the arena floor with his boots, using the sound-code Ulum to instruct his tri-glad.

Tallus looked clumsy, flat-footed and ungainly as he struggled to stay close to his armoured lac. At one point he stumbled and almost lost his balance. His own lac was being pressed hard by the three opposing lacs, and was forced back towards the arena wall.

And then disaster struck. As expected, Tallus did take a tumble. He tripped and fell full length on the arena floor – to a great roar of laughter from the crowd, followed by mocking applause.

It seemed that it was all over. All that remained now was to see how badly Tallus was injured. Brandon's lacs would now cut his flesh to achieve victory.

But the rapid reflexes of Tallus's own lac saved him from the razor-sharp death that arced downwards. It was no longer in retreat. Its blades moved faster than the eye could see, to stab right, left and right again, each blade unerringly finding the throat-sockets of its three opponents.

They went down in a clang and clash of tangled metal.

And then there was utter silence. Nobody was laughing now.

A mixture of cheers, boos and catcalls followed. Some spectators were happy at Tallus's victory; others aggrieved at having been deprived of their winnings. There was a full range of emotions: anger, astonishment and disappointment.

'Did you see the speed of that?'

'That was amazing! I've never seen a lac move so quickly!'

'That's not possible. He was as good as dead.'

To our left sat a wizened old man with a 13 tattooed upon his wrinkled forehead. He was one of the aficionados, the devotees of the Trigladius mode of combat that was fought in this arena. Some of them could give blow-by-blow accounts of contests fought years earlier.

'Never seen the like of that!' he exclaimed. 'It was beautiful, but it wasn't the Trig. That should be about a lac and a human working together in harmony. Any oaf could fight behind a lac like that.'

I watched a shower of crumpled red tickets being lobbed over the rail in disgust and disappointment – to fall around the victorious Tallus as he struggled clumsily to his feet. His lac moved forward to seal victory with the lightest of cuts to the unprotected arm.

It was clear that Ada had patterned a lac that was a force to be reckoned with. But Tallus had some way to go. Struggling to regain his breath, he even forgot to bow to his opponent.

'That was worth seeing,' growled Tyron. 'But is that lac sentient? Is it fully aware?'

The following morning he worked us hard, but at noon he had a surprise for us.

'You can both take the afternoon off from your usual routine,' he said. 'You'll be spending it in the company of my daughter. And you, Leif, had better take care not to ruin her marriage prospects. Bring her back with all her teeth.'

It was typical of Tyron's dry humour. He was never going to let me forget that I'd once fought Kwin with sticks and ended up hitting her in the mouth.

'Where are we going?' Deinon asked.

'To the dwelling of Tallus,' Tyron replied. 'You're going to meet Ada. So smile and be on your very best behaviour.'

SOMETHING HAS BEEN ALTERED

> Sycoda have multiple selves but a limited capacity to
> generate more.
>
> *The Manual of Nym*

As we emerged from the narrow streets into the large sunlit
open space that surrounded the Wheel, Kwin led us towards
the trades area, where a small army of carpenters, caterers,
chandlers and smiths worked, servicing the arenas.

A few wagons were backed up against the curve of the wall.
Inside was accommodation hired for the season by the patterners and combatants who didn't have permanent homes in
Gindeen. The wagons' shafts lay empty; as part of the deal you
also got your horses stabled or your oxen put out to grass.

The rear of each wagon was bolted to the wall. The owners
usually slept there, but rented a small private workshop and
training facilities and kitchen just inside the Wheel. This
gave them easy and cheap access to a secure area.

'So he's not from the city. Where does he come from?'
Deinon asked. 'Are his family farmers?'

'He's from the edge of the Genthai tribal lands. He used to
be a hunter before he got involved in patterning. He paid a

number of city artificers to teach him Nym, but he's mostly self-taught. And as for fighting behind a lac in Arena 13, as you saw last night, he's had no training at all.'

'He won't be pleased to see us, will he? He'll think we're here to spy for Tyron!' I said.

'That's why we're here now,' Kwin said with a wicked smile. 'If all has gone to plan, Ada should be alone.'

'Is she easy to talk to?' I asked. 'Your father said she had a strange accent.'

'It's incredible how fast she learns,' Kwin replied. 'At first she was hard to understand, but already her diction is almost perfect. She speaks in rather a grand manner; with anyone else you'd think they were showing off, but it's just her way. I like her. I think you'll like her too.'

There was a small door set into the wall beside the wagon, and Kwin rapped lightly on it three times. A moment later it opened inwards, and she entered, beckoning us to follow.

I stepped into a small windowless workshop. My eyes were immediately drawn to the far wall. Against it was a long bench bearing pieces of armour . . . and a lac some distance away, lying on its back, all but its head covered by a blanket. There was a torch in a wall-bracket above, and by that flickering yellow light I saw that its eyes were closed and its chest was rising and falling. It was exciting to think that this lac had astonished everyone in the gallery, and that I was in the presence of the woman who'd patterned it.

After glancing at the lac, I turned to Ada, who smiled at each of us and beckoned us towards a couch. On a table beside it stood a jug of water, a bottle of red wine, four glasses and two candles.

I saw that Ada was an attractive woman, with high cheekbones and a wide, full-lipped mouth, but where Kwin was fit and lean, she was curvaceous. This was false flesh, but it was impossible to detect any difference to our own flesh. But what struck me most, once more, was her very short hair.

Most women in the city wore their hair long. Ada's was shorter than a man's; it would draw lots of glances, many of them disapproving. City society was very conservative. Even the fact that Kwin sometimes painted her bottom lip red rather than black brought distaste to the faces of the more pretentious ladies of Gindeen.

'I am very pleased to meet you, Leif and Deinon. Kwin has told me a lot about you. Please be seated. Would you accept a glass of wine?' Ada asked. She had a very slight accent that didn't belong anywhere in Midgard.

Deinon and I shook our heads. 'Tyron doesn't like his trainees to drink alcohol,' Deinon told her. 'But thanks for the offer.'

'Will you accept water then?'

We nodded, and she poured some into two glasses and handed them to us.

'You keep looking at my hair!' she said with a laugh.

'Sorry,' I told her, feeling embarrassed. 'I didn't mean to stare.'

'When they released me from the casket, I didn't have a single hair on my body,' she said, 'but it is finally starting to grow back. I used to wear my hair very long – even longer than the women in Gindeen. I get a shock when I look in the mirror, but apart from that, this body is just as I remembered it. It's been recreated down to the tiniest detail.'

'When will Tallus be back?' Kwin asked her.

'It was not difficult to persuade him to take some exercise. He knows he needs to lose weight and get fit, so he took my advice. He has gone for a long walk. I think we have a couple of hours.'

'Good! So we're free to talk about anything we want!' Kwin exclaimed.

'Yes,' said Ada, turning towards me. 'Leif, Kwin tells me that you are hoping to fight in Arena 13 from the min position. She also told me about the death of Kern and Hob's threat.'

I was surprised to hear that Kwin had divulged so much. I thought we were gathering information, not telling this artificer our private business. But even Kwin didn't know that my father was Math and that Hob had killed my mother. Those were secrets that Tyron had kept even from his own daughter. As father and daughter, they were close, but there were some things that he kept to himself. Kwin thought that he was obsessed by money, always seeking to become richer. Little did she know the ultimate purpose of it all, which was to destroy Hob, then restore our knowledge of Nym and patterning skills to what they had been before the fall of mankind.

'Tyron thinks I should delay my appearance in the arena – perhaps for as long as a year,' I admitted.

'It will soon pass,' Ada said with a smile, 'although I know that the young have little patience. Kwin has nothing but good to say about you. She says you are strong and fast, and will make a first-rate combatant. She knows a lot about the Trig method of combat in Arena 13 and has been dancing behind Tallus's lac, helping me to understand what needs to be done to improve it.'

'Have you made it sentient?' I asked, trying not to sound too eager.

Ada shook her head. 'It is far more aware than previously, and can react much faster, but I cannot make it fully sentient because I do not have the tools.'

'What tools do you need?' Deinon asked, suddenly perking up.

'At the heart of each wurde there are *primitives*, the building blocks from which it is constructed. The wurdes within that lac,' she said, gesturing towards the bench, 'do not have the essential components. I suspect the same will be true of all lacs in Midgard. That is something that, in time, I will be able to overcome. I can build new primitives. But the second problem lies within the brain of the lac. Something has been altered to make it impossible to bring it to full awareness.'

'Then it can't be done,' Deinon said, disappointment on his face.

'I would need something that only your Trader could supply. Whether he can or will supply such an item – who knows? One day we must ask him.'

'The djinni Hob is a threat to all of us,' I told her. 'No doubt you've been told about him?' I still hadn't told anyone about Hob visiting me in the Commonality.

'I have indeed, Leif. We named such a creature a *djinn*, always using the plural form because it has many selves.'

'Do you have the knowledge to help us deal with him? After all, wasn't he created by imperial artificers like you?'

'He certainly was. From what I've been told, I think Hob is probably a type of djinni called a *sycoda*,' Ada explained. 'They were created and used by the military long ago, before the Empire was reduced to this pitiful state. Basically, Hob is a very advanced form of the lacs who fight in Arena 13, but he has not only multiple selves but also some limited capacity to generate more. Once I could have brought such a creature to its knees with a wurde,' she said, smiling politely. 'But . . .'

I could see that she was not being arrogant or boastful. The truth shone from her eyes. Her hesitation and silence at the end simply showed that this was no longer true.

'But you can't do it now?' I asked.

Ada nodded. 'Probably not, and I would not like to face Hob and try. He will have moved on, developing those abilities originally gifted to him by his patterners. In order to control him, I would first need to probe him using a wurde-tool. But first he would have to be my prisoner.'

'Tyron is the best artificer in the city,' I told her. 'If you were able, would you share your knowledge with him?'

'Of course, but sadly I'm not free to do so. Tallus owns me, and he is determined to protect his investment. He simply sees Tyron as a rival. Using my skills, he hopes to dominate Arena 13 and earn a lot of money. Please do not misunderstand me – he is not a bad man. He is kind and courteous and treats me with the utmost respect, but his faults are overweening pride and ambition.'

'Those are faults common to many men,' Kwin said, her mouth twisting in disdain.

Ada suddenly smiled at Deinon. 'Kwin has been saying good things about you too, Deinon. It seems that her father thinks you possess the best coding talent he has seen in a long time. How good are you? Let's put you to the test . . .'

She reached across and picked up the notepad and pen from

the table. Then she frowned and began to write. After a few moments she tore the sheet from the pad and handed it to Deinon.

'What function does this code perform in a lac?' she asked. 'This is similar to the test I gave to would-be novitiates. If they passed, I gave them a harder question. Eventually, if they continued to show promise, I began to train them.'

Deinon's face fell. I could tell that he had no idea what the code did. I glanced over his shoulder, and when I saw what Ada had written, I immediately knew why.

: ActionX – Peekloc#774321 * If > 29000 then Poke Contentsloc#774320 <into> loc#774321;

I thought that 'Peek', 'Poke' and 'If' were wurdes from *The Nym Dictionary*. But what did all the numbers mean? How could Deinon possibly work out what 'ActionX' did?

'I'm sorry. I don't know,' Deinon said, his face starting to redden.

'It's fine, Deinon. I don't expect you to come up with the answer right away,' Ada said with a reassuring smile. 'Go away and think about it. Don't ask Tyron. Work it out for yourself. When you have the answer, please send it back to me with Kwin.'

We left soon after that, and I delivered Kwin back to her father, complete with a full set of teeth, her marriage prospects undiminished. It took far longer for the three of us to make a report to Tyron than it had talking to Ada. But at last he was satisfied and pleased to hear that Ada had been so friendly and helpful.

'That's promising, very promising,' he said. 'Ada seems willing to help, but we need to win Tallus over. We might do it, given time. And what about that test she set you, Deinon? Think you can work it out?'

Deinon nodded, but he didn't look too confident.

That night, before we went to sleep, I raised the topic with him. 'How *will* you work it out, Deinon? What are those numbers?'

'They're locations in a lac's head, Leif,' he replied. 'What "ActionX" does is check a certain location: if it contains a number greater than 29000, then it replaces it with a number from another location. I need to use a wurde-tool like "Newt" and probe a lac to find out. I'll try it out on our training lac tomorrow. It shouldn't be too difficult. For a moment I thought she expected me to know the answer right away! Some patterners do, you know. They have most of the locations in their heads, and somebody like Tyron will have an incredible memory. He can probably remember every wurde in the *Slim Nym Dictionary*!'

'Rather you than me!' I said. 'Just the thought of sorting that out gives me a headache!'

Deinon shook his head. 'What you do is much harder, Leif. In Arena 13, a headache is the least of your worries!'

A HARD LESSON

Intense pain is the lot of the loser.
He must bear it lest all honour be lost.

The Manual of Trigladius Combat

Before the end of the week, Tyron had a surprise for me;
something that intruded into the routine of my training.

'I still don't want to risk you in the arena,' he told me, 'but
I think it's time we gave you a more rigorous workout.
Tomorrow morning Palm will bring his tri-glad to my house
and you can fight him here on the training floor. I don't
expect you to win, but I do want you to push him hard and
make a fight of it, boy.'

I knew that Palm's lacs were first-rate; it would be no dis-
grace at all to lose against him. But there was more than just
rivalry between us. I could already imagine the smirk on his
face when I lost.

I would push him hard all right. Tyron could be sure of
that.

Palm arrived early so that he could have breakfast with us
and we could begin our contests directly afterwards.

I sat next to Deinon, facing Palm across the table. Tyron and Kwin had already breakfasted and stood just inside the doorway talking. She had arrived from Tallus's quarters to talk about the day's business before setting off to work at the admin building.

Palm said little, but he kept glancing at my tattoos. My eyes were drawn towards Kwin and she caught me staring, but she gave me a warm smile that made my morning. Whatever happened afterwards, I'd have that to remember.

Once they'd gone I saw a change in Palm. His haughty expression reappeared and I could tell that he was about to try and score a few points.

'You must be disappointed not to have quarters in the Wheel,' he said with a smirk. 'I don't think I could have tolerated another year in this house. It's so claustrophobic. Of course, there are some things I do miss. Kwin looks more gorgeous than ever! Did you see that smile she just gave me? Looks like she's really missing me!'

Angrily I opened my mouth to reply, and no doubt I'd have said something stupid, but Palm didn't give me a chance: he carried on with hardly a pause.

'Tyron's already entered me in the Lists and I won my first two contests easily. He plans for me to fight at least five more times before the end of the season, against better and better opposition. Pretty good going for a second-year trainee, don't you think?'

'Let's hope you win all of them then,' Deinon said. 'They say the ritual cut is incredibly painful. When you watch it happening in the arena, it looks like nothing, but the combatants put on a brave face for the spectators. It hurts like hell!'

I saw dismay flicker on Palm's face. Someone so smug and over-confident probably hadn't even thought about that. Deinon glanced at me and winked. He'd hit a nerve all right.

Palm's tri-glad was everything that my lone lac wasn't. His three lacs wore shining armour without even the faintest scratch; the armour of mine was battered and dull, with patches of rust. His three co-ordinated perfectly, gliding effortlessly through a large repertoire of rapid moves; my lac seemed ponderous and slow.

We were both dressed in the regulation leather jerkins and shorts, but only in our clothes were we equals.

Palm was blond-haired, with clean-cut features and blue eyes. As he'd already boasted, he'd already won two contests and was starting to build up an enthusiastic female following in Arena 13.

I caught him staring again at the tattoos on the left side of my face. When our eyes met, he smirked. However, Deinon smiled and gave me a thumbs-up.

I noticed that Tyron had a timer – a shiny brass box about the size of a fist. There was a lever on top, which measured out five minutes – the first stage of a bout. After that you had to fight in front of your lac or lacs. This was a smaller version of the one that Pyncheon used to time bouts in Arena 13.

Were we going to fight following the full rules? The Trainee Tournament had special rules and I'd assumed we'd be using those.

Tyron suggested an initial warm-up. He sat next to Deinon at the table in the recess beyond the edge of the training floor, watching impassively as we fought.

I was eager to defeat my old rival and wanted to wipe that smirk off his face. However, I began cautiously, dancing close to the back of my lac. After a few moments my confidence began to grow. I used Ulum, the sound-code, to instruct my lac to begin an attack. We feinted to the left and then advanced towards the centre. I did everything correctly. There wasn't a thing I would have changed.

But Palm's lacs were simply too fast for mine. The central one reacted with lightning speed and slotted a blade into the throat-socket to call endoff. My lac went down and Palm grinned.

The contest had lasted less than a minute; I'd been defeated easily.

That wasn't surprising: the practice lac had been deliberately slowed down for training purposes. Tyron had modified it for combat in Arena 13 and it had been good enough for my two wins in the tournament. Now it was certainly faster than during our training bouts, but not quick enough to offer Palm more than token resistance.

I began to think that this practice was for Palm's benefit more than mine.

My morning had started well, with Kwin smiling at me; it had deteriorated with this quick defeat.

Now it got even worse.

'Now we'll try the real thing!' Tyron called out. 'This will involve full Arena 13 rules, including the five-minute rule. The loser will also offer his arm for the ritual cut.'

I stared at him in astonishment. Was there any need for that? I glanced at Deinon, who looked as if he couldn't believe it. He'd only just baited Palm with the prospect of being cut in a forthcoming contest. We both faced it now, but Palm's lacs were superior to mine. The greater danger was to me.

Tyron pressed the lever and a loud ticking began. The contest was underway and I was struggling to defend myself. This time, desperately drumming on the boards with my feet to communicate with my lac, I moved rapidly through the repertoire of my best moves, and we managed to offer a little more resistance.

But this only delayed the inevitable. A blade found my lac's throat-socket and it crashed down onto the floor.

Then Palm's central lac moved towards me, the blade in its right hand, ready to make the ritual cut. It was far bigger than me and looked truly threatening in its dark armour. The closer it got, the more afraid I grew. For a moment I felt paralysed, unable to do what was required, but I took a deep breath, steadied myself and offered my left arm.

Almost delicately, the creature made a cut on my left arm, just below the short sleeve of my leather jerkin. Initially there was just a sting and I felt relieved that it was all over. Then, suddenly, I felt a sharp, piercing pain that made me gasp. It was far worse than I'd expected.

The pain was so intense that I couldn't breathe. Every nerve in my body was on fire. My eyes began to water, and for a moment I was afraid that they might leak tears and I would be disgraced.

'It hurts a lot, doesn't it, boy?' Tyron asked.

I nodded, fighting to suppress the groan that was rising in my throat.

'That's because lac blades are coated with a substance called *kransin*,' he said, staring at me hard.

I knew that kransin did two things. Firstly it was a coagulant, which was important because sometimes a lac cut a little too deeply and the kransin stemmed the flow of blood. Secondly, it intensified the pain of the cut. To lose a contest in Arena 13 was to experience extreme pain. That's why the spectators were silent when that cut was made. It hadn't been used in the Trainee Tournament, but it was certainly a feature of proper Arena 13 contests. Being successful meant being able to control oneself and face danger and pain with courage. The spectators wanted to watch how the losing combatant conducted himself.

I'd often watched combatants suffer that ritual cut. None had so much as flinched, so I had never associated it with real pain. But now I realized that, as Deinon had indicated, this was because they wanted to show bravery in the arena. And now I knew what it felt like to lose.

'Right – get into position again and prepare to fight. The same rules will apply!' Tyron ordered.

I couldn't believe it! My lac had no chance against the triglad of Palm. I was bound to lose. Then I would be cut again.

Tyron pressed the lever and the timer began to tick.

I couldn't have tried harder. I stretched my knowledge of Trig combat to its very limits, drumming on the boards in increasing desperation to signal to my lac the steps that I wished it to take. And this time it took Palm longer to defeat me.

It took him all of three minutes.

Once more I suffered the ritual cut, this time to my right arm. Once more I fought to keep the pain from my face while Palm watched me and smiled in triumph.

'One more bout,' said Tyron, 'and we'll call it a day.'

My defeat led to a third cut. I already had one on each arm, so this was made to my left arm again, close to the first. It seemed to hurt even more than the other two; soon I was gasping with pain while Palm gloated. I felt a strong sense of grievance. It seemed so unfair. Arena 13 combatants only rarely fought more than one contest each night. Never would they suffer three cuts in so short a time period.

'What's wrong, boy?' Tyron demanded when Palm and his tri-glad had left. 'You look less than happy.'

'Is my lac as finely tuned as it was when I fought in the tournament?' I asked, bringing my simmering suspicion out into the open.

'It is patterned to *exactly* the same level,' answered Tyron. 'The difference is that you are up against a first-rate tri-glad, the best that money can buy. And let's give Palm his due. Although still a trainee, he used Ulum well and fought three excellent bouts. So you need to raise your game, boy. In five days you'll fight him again, and I expect you to do better! Hopefully the lac will improve as well.'

'So you're going to do some more work on it?' I asked, my hopes rising a little.

Tyron didn't reply but fixed his gaze upon Deinon. 'Did you manage to solve the code that Ada set you?' he asked.

Deinon smiled and nodded. '"ActionX" was simply Ada's new name for the pattern routine that calls endoff.'

He was proud that he had managed to work that out. It seemed that the systems inside a lac's head constantly checked the location that controlled its throat-socket. Once a blade entered it, the number increased to more than 29000; this automatically poked in another number, which turned off the lac so that it collapsed. Well, it was something like that, anyway.

'Well done, boy. So what was her response? Did she give you a reward?'

Deinon smiled ruefully. 'No, she gave me another code to work out. This one is much harder.'

'Well, I've got something for you to do too. I want you to try and improve this lac and give Leif a better chance of winning. Think you can do it?'

The colour had fled from Deinon's face. I knew he wouldn't want that job. He was conscientious and sensitive, and wouldn't want me to be cut again.

'I'll do my best,' he said, giving me a nervous glance.

'Good, I'm sure you will,' said Tyron. 'Then, to further advance your training, Leif, your next contest against Palm will be fought in Arena 13.'

I couldn't help smiling at that. 'Win or lose, it'll be great to be on the Lists!' I told him.

'No, Leif, you won't be on the Lists – we can't risk that. This won't be open to the public. I've hired the arena for an hour. These will be private bouts, with only Deinon and me to witness them. It's cost me enough, so make the most of the opportunity.'

Following Hob's threat, Tyron was reluctant to let me fight in the arena. He thought that Hob might come on a night when I was fighting. Strange things happened with the lottery that chose the combatant to face him in the arena. I could be selected, and that would be the end of me.

And down in the Commonality, I remembered, I'd actually challenged Hob to fight me in the arena. How could he resist that? I knew I wasn't ready to fight him yet. I wasn't good enough and I needed the best possible lac to work with.

'What if I lose to Palm?'

'Then you'll fight Palm again.'

'How long will this go on for?'

'It goes on until you win a contest, boy. I want you under pressure. You're like a plant in a hothouse. I'm forcing you to grow!'

So I practised even harder and extended my use of Ulum, improving the way I communicated with my lac. And Deinon went to work on the patterns inside the lac's head, putting in hours of extra work.

'Making any progress?' I asked him after his third evening working with the lac.

Deinon nodded, but he looked far from confident. 'I've managed to improve its speed slightly, but it still seems sluggish. I just don't know what the problem is. Given a few weeks, I could probably sort it, but there simply isn't enough time. I'm really sorry, Leif.'

'Don't worry, Deinon. Just do your best. I think it's unfair of Tyron to put you in that position. He could improve the lac if he put his mind to it. It all seems so unjust. He can talk as much as he wants about forcing me to grow, but the truth is, that lac just isn't good enough to withstand Palm's tri-glad. It's not your fault.'

But it wasn't all for nothing. I did get better, and Deinon did manage to improve the lac. And although the odds were against me, I was looking forward to fighting in Arena 13.

*

Palm was leaving the changing rooms as I entered and he gave a smirk as he passed me. I quickly pulled on my leather jerkin and shorts, tucked my blades into their sheaths and walked to the door.

Out in the corridor, a man emptying a rubbish bin nodded at me as I passed by. I saw that he was Genthai and had facial tattoos like mine. That meant he'd fought and defeated a werewight. So what was he doing working here? I wondered. I'd seen him around from time to time. He did menial jobs but always looked cheerful. As far as I knew, he was the only Genthai working in the Wheel. At one time, according to Tyron, there were a couple of Genthai combatants, but both had now retired.

He paused and glanced at the left side of my face. 'Good luck!' he called as he dragged the bin away.

I turned and smiled at him, then headed for Arena 13.

Moments later, as the candelabrum descended, I was facing the smug Palm across the floor of the arena. Although Tyron's practice floor had the same dimensions, this presented me with a different experience and would give me a better insight into fighting here. Arena 13 was much higher, and the gallery was visible from the combat floor. Even if the seats were mostly empty, it had a different atmosphere.

It was noon, but there were no windows in the gallery, and the thirteen-branched candelabrum burned brightly. I could still smell the new leather seats, but now there was also a taint of blood in the air. Two days ago there had been a grudge match, a fight to the death. The victor had granted clemency to his opponent, but he had already been cut to ribbons and he'd died from his wounds.

There was no trumpet to signal the start of our first bout. I looked up and saw the only two spectators in the gallery – Tyron and Deinon. They were both leaning over the rail, looking down at us. Tyron was holding the brass timing device.

'Ready?' he asked, his voice booming down from the gallery.

We both nodded. He pressed the lever, and I heard the ticking of the timer.

My heart was beating rapidly and I forced my breathing to slow, inhaling deep, steady breaths to calm myself. I tapped out my signal to my lac and we surged forward. I was determined to attack and keep a constant pressure on Palm. I had to force him onto the back foot.

To my delight, it began to work, and his fixed smile slowly faded. Now there were beads of sweat on his forehead. Again and again I pressed the attack home, forcing back his triglad, but when it came to finishing it off, my lac just wasn't fast enough; it could not find the other lac's throat-socket.

All at once it was over-extended, and a blade found its throat-socket to call endoff. It went down.

I'd lost the first bout and had to suffer the ritual cut again. The pain seemed worse than ever, and I doubled over and gritted my teeth, unable to straighten my body. The seconds ticked by and I felt humiliated.

Finally the pain receded, and I crouched behind my lac again.

I had to learn to bear the pain better than this! After all, I'd coped with the pain of the tattoos.

'That bout lasted two minutes and thirty seconds!' called Tyron. 'Try to do better, Leif!'

But things went from bad to worse. During the second bout my lac lost its balance, and that was that.

'Barely thirty seconds, Leif!' called Tyron as I was cut again. 'That's very disappointing. I paid for an hour. It seems that I've wasted my money.'

I couldn't believe what I was hearing. It didn't sound like the Tyron I knew.

I readied myself for a really big effort. I felt angry and humiliated, and the smirk on Palm's face made it worse. This time I was more cautious, trying not to over-extend my lac. I fought defensively and guided it into good positions. Things were going well. I knew that I'd lasted over four minutes.

But then Palm's tri-glad cornered me, trapping me against the arena wall. So I used what had been Kern's favourite defensive move. I bounced my back against the wall and moved sideways, attempting to escape.

I almost managed it, but my lac was forced back hard against me. Its elbow smashed into my left eye and my head shot back with some force against the wall. Everything went black.

In a Trig contest in Arena 13, that could have been very dangerous – perhaps deadly. When a contestant is down, the cuts lack the precision of the ritual end to each bout. Lacs are very fast and incredibly strong, so sometimes the cuts are so deep that the loser dies of shock and loss of blood; occasionally a limb or a head is severed.

Deinon told me later that Tyron intervened immediately. Quick words of Nym called down from the gallery halted all four lacs. Palm had won again, but he didn't get to gloat this time; no cut was delivered.

I was carried back to Tyron's house and up to bed. A

doctor was summoned, and it was three days before I was allowed to get up. They kept me sedated, and on the morning of the third day I opened my eyes to find that I wasn't in the room I shared with Deinon.

There was someone staring down at me. For a moment I thought it was Kwin, but as my eyes cleared, I saw that it was Tyron's other daughter, Teena. She was blonde-haired and had a fuller figure than Kwin. Teena was kind and had a very warm smile – though I hadn't seen it much since the death of her husband, Kern.

'Here, try to sit up,' she said, placing a pillow behind my shoulders, and handing me a large glass of water. I was thirsty and drank half of it without coming up for air.

'Don't gulp too much or it might make you sick. How do you feel?' she asked.

'I've a slight headache and my shoulder is sore,' I told her, 'but apart from that I feel all right.'

'No nausea?'

I shook my head.

'Then I'll bring you up some breakfast,' she said, smiling again, though I could see that grief was not far from the surface. How could she ever forget the sight of Kern being dragged out of the arena, giving a final anguished glance up into the gallery?

'The doctor said you should stay in bed for a bit longer. But no doubt you'll have visitors to relieve the tedium.'

My first was Deinon, who kept apologizing for the performance of the lac. He thought everything was his fault, so I spent most of the time putting his mind at rest.

'Look, you did your best. You're a good patterner. Who knows, you might be even better than Tyron one day. But Palm's lacs are just too good. Don't beat yourself up about this, please!'

'But it was so hard to watch you being cut like that, Leif. I really can't understand why Tyron allowed it. You always try your best. Doesn't he know that? There's no need to inflict pain on you. That talk of forcing you in a hothouse is stupid. I think I'll have a word with him—'

'No, Deinon, leave it to me. You'll only get into trouble. When the time comes, I'll tell him what I think.'

Deinon persisted, and arguing with him soon tired me out.

About an hour after he'd left I had another visitor. This time, to my delight, it was Kwin.

'My word, that's a shiner!' she exclaimed, looking at my black eye. 'How did it happen? Deinon said you were fighting a private contest in Arena 13.'

'Your father hired the arena to give me practice fighting there. I didn't last long, though. The lac pushed me back against the wall.'

'Well, it happens,' she said cheerfully. 'Who were you fighting?'

'Palm. That tri-glad of his is just too good for my lac.'

I watched the smile slip from her face. She was staring at my upper arms. 'What the hell is that?' she said, her eyes flashing with anger.

I shrugged and looked at the cuts. One was slightly infected and had been smeared with ointment; the others were red and livid.

'Each one tells you that I lost a contest to Palm,' I said, trying to keep my voice cheerful.

'Were the blades coated in kransin?' she asked.

I nodded.

'You were cut at the end of *training* bouts and with kransin-coated blades?' she said in astonishment. 'What stupidity is that?'

'Your father's just trying to toughen me up. He said the contests against Palm will go on until I finally manage to win.'

'Did he now!' hissed Kwin, almost spitting with fury. 'Well, we'll see about that!'

She stormed out of the room, and after a few moments I heard her shouting, and Tyron arguing back. Then a door slammed.

She didn't return to my room, but soon Tyron paid me a visit.

'You'll be on your feet tomorrow, boy, and back to light training. In that third bout you fought well until you were knocked out. Raise your game a bit more and you might win next time. You've a week to prepare before your next bout with Palm. I'll hire the arena again.'

Then he was gone, leaving me angry and close to despair. Despite what he'd said, I was a long way from beating Palm. My lac simply wasn't good enough.

AROUND HER LITTLE FINGER

Newt, an analytical wurde-tool used by an artificer
to explore a wurde-matrix, presents a novice
patterner with his greatest challenge.

The Manual of Nym

Soon I was back in training. Tyron still hadn't employed anyone else to take over Kern's duties, so he took personal charge
of we two trainees. But of course he had other older boys to
coach, and also qualified fighters and patterners working
for him who were based in the Wheel. He also had an office
in the admin building; Kwin worked there in the mornings,
but in the afternoons she went back to Tallus's house to
see Ada.

This meant that Tyron had to share out his time. We got
the mornings; in the afternoons he visited the Wheel. When
he was absent, our instructions were to try and improve our
knowledge of Nym; he usually left us a list of wurdes to look
up in the *Slim Nym Dictionary*.

On the third afternoon after I'd got back to work there was
a light rap on my study door. I opened it and found Kwin and
Deinon standing there.

Kwin smiled. 'Ada wants to talk to Deinon. She's going to give him some advice on how to improve your lac.'

'It's nice of her to offer to help,' I said. No doubt Kwin had begged her, I thought. But would Deinon be able to learn enough to make a difference?

When they left, I continued with my studies.

Deinon was away all afternoon and got back only just before Tyron returned. He was clutching a sheaf of papers.

'Ada's given me some wurdes for the lac,' he explained. 'We'll try them out tomorrow afternoon. Kwin's going to help.'

She came to my study at about three the following afternoon. 'We need to go down and help Deinon now,' she said. 'First we have to purge the creature. Ada warned us that it will be messy. Afterwards you'll need to hose down the lac and the floor.'

When we entered the cellar, my lac was on its feet. All its armour had been removed and it was completely naked. Deinon stood facing it, reading wurdes of Nym from a sheet of paper. He was speaking slowly and steadily, and frowning with concentration.

After a moment he turned and smiled at me. 'Get ready with the hosepipe, Leif!'

It was wrapped around a bracket on the wall, so I uncoiled it and turned on the tap. One twist at the end of the pipe and water would spurt out.

As he spoke to the lac again, it began to tremble and its eyes rolled up into its head. Now it was twitching and groaning, as if in pain. Suddenly a thin fluid began to ooze from the purple slit on the front of its neck. It was a bright yellow in colour, and flecked with denser globules of green, and the smell it gave off was very unpleasant.

Then the trickle became surge, and a slimy, stinking fluid ran down its chest and belly and began to drip onto the stone flags.

I readied the hose, but Deinon waved me back.

'That was just toxins that accumulate in the throat-slit,' he said. 'There's worse to come. Now I'll purge its body and get rid of the infections there.'

Reading from the sheet, he spoke only one wurde, but the effect was instantaneous. The lac's nose ran, vomit spouted from its mouth and it evacuated waste and poisons from every orifice. The stink was overwhelming, and I quickly hosed down the body of the groaning creature and the floor, trying not to be sick.

After everything had been sluiced down the drain, Deinon smiled at us and gestured towards the bench at the far end of the cellar. 'It's best if you wait over there while I finish,' he said. 'I'm going to try to over-write some of its patterns with new ones. But I've got a problem with reading out the wurdes. My pronunciation probably isn't that good, so I might have to repeat some sections. This could take some time.'

So Kwin and I sat down on the bench, watching from a distance while Deinon worked. 'What will happen if Tallus finds out that Ada has helped us?' I asked.

'That's nothing to worry about,' Kwin said, smiling mischievously. 'Ada can twist Tallus around her little finger. Last night I saw them sitting beside the hearth holding hands. They didn't know I was there.'

'So you were spying on them!' I accused her with a grin.

'Not at all!' exclaimed Kwin. 'I just happened to glimpse them through the kitchen door.'

'So is she playing him for a fool,' I asked, 'in order to get her own way?'

'She's definitely trying to get her own way – what woman doesn't try to shape a man to her needs?' laughed Kwin. 'But I can tell she really likes him. I suspect that last night they were generating more heat than the embers of the fire!'

Kwin's laughter was infectious and I joined in.

'Are you enjoying your time at Tallus's house?' I asked her.

'I certainly am. Ada sometimes says the strangest things, but she's very interesting. If you didn't know where she came from and what she'd been, you'd think she was putting on airs and graces. But in her other life she was really important – the most talented of all the patterners. I'm amazed how quickly she's adjusted to her life here. And, you know, it's good to get away from my father – he'd like to control everything about me, if he could. Of course, I do miss one thing . . .' Kwin smiled at me mysteriously.

Did she mean me? I wondered. But how could I ask? What if I was wrong? I felt my face begin to burn and saw her smile widen.

'When's Tallus going to fight again?' I blurted out to cover my confusion.

'It'll be next week, early on the Wednesday evening List. Why don't you come and watch? He trains hard and he really is getting better. Ada is pleased with him.'

Just then Deinon called us over. I saw that the lac was shivering slightly, but I'd never seen it look so alert.

'Leif, this is Thrym,' said Deinon, pointing towards it. 'Thrym, this is Leif! Defend Leif!' Then he read from a sheet again: '*Defeat opponents! Let no blade touch his flesh!*'

The lac began staring at me in a way that was very disconcerting. The expression in its eyes seemed different – almost curious.

'You've given it a name! Is it sentient?' I asked in astonishment.

'It isn't truly sentient in the way a human is. Ada can't do that yet. But Thrym has some awareness. And Ada gives all the lacs that she patterns names. I've just followed her instructions. According to her, it knows you so you're bonded together and it should fight all the better for that. Now there is another matter. No doubt in time Tyron will discover what's been done here, but for now Ada thinks it should remain secret. Palm should get a big surprise the next time you fight.'

'Palm's a conceited idiot. He deserves all he gets!' Kwin interjected. 'I can't believe my father allowed full Arena 13 rules in those practice bouts.'

'In order to keep our little secret, during any preparations witnessed by Tyron, Thrym will fight and behave exactly as he did previously,' Deinon explained. 'Only when you speak the wurdes "Awake, Thrym!" will his new, higher capabilities be activated. Understand? Then return him to his lower state with the command, "Sleep, Thrym!"'

I nodded. 'Thanks for doing that, Deinon. Kwin, please thank Ada for me. Now I'll be able to give Palm a real fight!'

'Yes, I think you will,' Kwin agreed, her eyes twinkling.

We weren't supposed to practise with a lac unless Tyron was present, but I couldn't resist putting it through its paces.

'Awake, Thrym!'

The lac looked at me in a way that was unnerving. The expression on its face was almost human.

Then we advanced across the floor and I drummed out a few commands, using Ulum. It responded well, and I was filled with a sudden surge of optimism. At last I had a real chance of beating Palm!

Of course, there was no way to evaluate its capabilities properly without facing an opponent, but I could see that the creature responded faster, and showed new agility and grace.

Suddenly I was looking forward to my next contest.

THE FLASH OF BLADES

Bravery is mandatory.

Arena 13 *Rules of Combat*

I went to watch Tallus's second appearance in Arena 13 in the company of Kwin and Ada.

Once again he won, but this time with much more style. Nobody laughed, and there were even a few cheers and a smattering of genuine applause at the end of the contest. He had lost weight and danced close to the back of his lac.

Combatants who fought from stables such as Tyron's had the corporate logo on the back of their leather jerkins. Others didn't bother with a symbol – though a few used their first name. Embossed onto the back of Tallus's jerkin was the word TAL.

Ada positively glowed with happiness.

But we weren't the only ones interested in the performance of his lac and the woman who had patterned it. The gallery was filled to capacity, the city still buzzing with speculation about the artificer Tallus had bought. Ada and Kwin left before me, and I turned and watched the spectators rubber-necking as they went up the steps.

After that, although there were three further contests scheduled, the gallery gradually emptied and I left early too. I needed a good night's sleep. Tomorrow I was to fight Palm again.

'Full Trig rules, as usual!' Tyron commanded from the gallery as the candelabrum slowly descended. Deinon sat next to him, smiling down at me. No doubt he was anticipating my victory.

My lac had improved, but would it be good enough to defeat Palm's formidable tri-glad? I wondered. It wasn't as if Ada had patterned the lac directly. I knew Deinon had done his best, but he was still a novice and might not have communicated all Ada's wurdes properly. His pronunciation was not perfect, and errors could have been introduced.

I looked at Palm. He was smirking from behind his expensive tri-glad; his lacs' armour shone in the torchlight. The air was warm and very still.

I stepped a little closer to Thrym's back. During the final preparations for the contest I hadn't been alone with the lac and hadn't had a chance to activate its new capabilities again.

'Are you ready to begin?' Tyron asked, holding his finger poised above the lever of his brass timer.

We both looked up and nodded. I took my chance and said, 'Awake, Thrym!' as quietly as possible so that Palm wouldn't hear. The acoustics were excellent, and there was also a danger that Tyron might overhear me.

But had I spoken loudly enough? Had the lac heard me?

It was too late to worry – Tyron had pressed the lever and the tick-tock of the timer began. Palm's tri-glad was already advancing, blades readied for action.

I'd decided to begin with a conventional retreating move: two steps to the left, two to the right, then a reverse diagonal to the right.

I thumped out the command with my boots, and we moved backwards together very smoothly. I signalled another command, a further retreat, still moving to the right, and then a sudden reversal that brought my back right up against the arena wall.

A memory flashed into my head of how I'd been crushed against it during the last contest. But this time there was no danger of that. I bounced along the wall, once again using Kern's favourite move, and emerged rapidly into the open space. That forced Palm and his tri-glad to turn and face me, but Thrym and I were too fast for them.

I'd drummed out my instruction with Ulum before bouncing along the wall. Thrym executed it immediately, attacking Palm's central lac.

It happened too fast to take it in. Thrym slotted a blade into his target lac as the others moved in quickly on either side. All I saw was a flash of blades, then there was a cacophony of clanging metal. In the immediate aftermath one thing was clear: Thrym was still standing – unlike all three of Palm's lacs. They lay in a tangled heap on the arena floor.

The astonishment on my face no doubt reflected Palm's. Thrym had been even faster than I'd expected, but I was also pleased with my own performance. By using the wall and suddenly breaking free before Palm had turned his tri-glad, I'd positioned Thrym perfectly for his attack on the central lac. That was one of the main contributions a human combatant could make – putting his lac in the right place to win.

But I could claim no credit for downing the other two lacs. They had attacked, and my lac had responded with terrifying speed.

Now I watched Palm as his astonishment quickly turned to terror. Thrym was advancing towards him to make the ritual cut. There were beads of sweat on Palm's forehead, and his arm was shaking as he held it out. He gasped as the incision was made, then groaned and gave a deep sob as the pain hit him.

I stared up at Tyron; his face was impassive.

'Next bout!' he commanded.

The next bout went the same way; the following one too.

When Palm received the third cut, he wept openly, tears dripping from his nose and chin. My feelings were mixed. I was embarrassed to see him cry, but at the same time I felt sorry for him. I knew from my own experience that he was in terrible pain – though when I'd been defeated, he'd smirked, so I was pleased he'd been brought down off his high horse.

Tyron shouted down the command 'Awake' to each of Palm's three lacs, and they clambered to their feet. They'd lost some of their sheen and were covered in dents.

I must confess, that pleased me too. Palm's rich father had bought him the best lacs that money could buy, and paid Tyron, the best artificer in the city, to pattern them. Now Palm's toys were no longer so shiny and new.

I was also grateful to Deinon, but it was Ada who had provided the code.

My lac had been patterned by someone even better than Tyron.

*

Once Palm had left, Tyron and Deinon came down into the arena. Tyron smiled, looking me directly in the eye.

'Well, that *was* something to behold!' he said, going over to look at my lac and whistling through his teeth. 'How long did it take Ada to bring about such a remarkable transformation?'

'She spelled out the wurdes out for me and I wrote them down. Then I spoke them to the lac,' Deinon admitted.

'Did she now! So I'll ask again – how long did it take?'

'Less than half an hour of writing,' Deinon answered, 'but it took me over an hour. Although Ada coached me, I don't think I was pronouncing all the wurdes correctly. Of course, I don't understand much of what they do. I wasn't much better than a parrot. But I know that the lac had first to be purged of accumulated poisons, then some of its patterns were modified.'

'Well, Deinon, don't put yourself down too much. You got there in the end and are to be commended. You probably learned more than you think. No doubt you still have those pieces of paper with Ada's wurdes?'

Deinon nodded.

'Well, you can bring them to me later. She did it out of friendship for my daughter, just as I'd expected,' Tyron continued. 'Once Kwin saw the cuts on your arms, I knew what would happen.'

'You planned this all along! You put me through all that just so she'd get Ada to help me!' I snapped angrily.

'Of course I did, boy. A few cuts did you no harm – they toughened you up for what you'll face in the arena. I did it for the best.'

I was still angry, but I said nothing more. I realized that we'd taken an important step towards defeating Hob. We had a lac patterned to a higher level than Tyron could achieve. He could learn from it.

'I heard you muttering at its shoulder. So tell me the wurdes to activate and de-activate the higher combat abilities of this lac.'

'It's just the usual "Awake" and "Sleep", but each time followed by its name, Thrym,' I told him.

'So she's given it a name!' Tyron exclaimed in astonishment.

Lacs were considered to be no better than animals, so I could understand his surprise. Giving lac a name somehow made it more human, even though it wasn't fully sentient.

'Now, let's see what this Thrym is made of!' Tyron continued. 'You can both stay. Watch and listen, if you've a mind to, but I fear you'll learn little, Leif. You'll struggle too, Deinon. This will take me far beyond what I know. Later, after I've interrogated the lac, I'll examine the written wurdes.'

Thus Tyron began to interrogate Thrym using the wurde-tool called *Newt*. Deinon watched and listened. After a while I left them to it. So engrossed were they that neither noticed me leave.

Tyron was persistent, a clever man who didn't give up easily. No doubt in time he would tease out a significant amount of new knowledge.

But events moved even more quickly than any of us could have guessed.

AN EVENING WITH TALLUS

A single deceit is like the first step of a child;
To maintain balance, others must follow.
The Genthai Book of Wisdom

The following morning Kwin called at Tyron's house on her way to work in the admin building. After talking to her father, she came across and joined us at the table.

'You're invited to a party tomorrow night,' she told us with a grin. 'Tallus wants to meet you.'

'Both of us?' asked Deinon.

'Yes, both of you. Want to come?'

I raised my eyebrows at Deinon, and he smiled and nodded. 'A party you say? Definitely! Who else will be there?'

'Well, not my father – he certainly isn't invited. But he's happy enough for us to go, as long as we keep our ears open and report back to him what's said while we're there. Tallus and Ada will be there, but we are the only guests. Ada just wants you to meet Tallus.'

'You say it's a party . . .' Deinon said. 'Is it some sort of celebration?'

'I think things are going well for him, and he and Ada are really happy together. That's all. He's always been a bit of a loner,' Kwin continued. 'He doesn't mix much with anybody – certainly not the other combatants. I think the party is Ada's idea, to be truthful. She thinks he should engage with other people more. He's starting to feel more comfortable in my presence, so now it's time to introduce him to my two best friends.'

'We're your best friends?' Deinon asked, raising his eyebrows.

'Of course you are!' Kwin grinned. 'You're the brains and Leif is the brawn! If only I could merge you together into one being, you'd be the perfect man!'

I smiled – I knew she was only joking; she liked to tease. But did she really think that I was just muscle without a brain? Did she think I was stupid? Well, I mused, it was foolish to feel hurt. But although my brain was certain that Kwin didn't mean anything by it, my heart was unsure.

'Why doesn't she invite Tyron?' I asked, attempting to put those dark thoughts away by changing the subject.

'There's no chance of that!' said Kwin. 'Tallus is very suspicious of my father – he's a rival. Don't go on about patterning, or he'll think you're trying to pump Ada for information.'

It was a warm evening, and as the sun set, the three of us walked across the city to Tallus's quarters at the Wheel. Deinon and I were in our best shirts and trousers, and Kwin wore a pale purple dress that fitted her body like a glove. It was hard not to stare. Once she caught me at it, but smiled rather than looking angry.

We were welcomed inside by Ada and Tallus. Kwin made the introductions. Tallus shook our hands and Ada gave us a brief hug.

The room had changed since last I'd seen it and no longer looked like a workshop. There was no sign of the lac – I guessed it was in the wagon – and the table was covered with a blue cloth. The chairs had been pushed back against the wall to create a space in the middle of the room, no doubt so that we had room to stand and chat while we ate. On the table there was a bottle of red wine, fruit juice and what looked like lemonade, along with sausage rolls, spicy dips and iced cakes, and we didn't need much encouragement to start eating.

Close up, Tallus looked taller than he did in the arena. Although stocky, he no longer appeared overweight. The regime of exercise that Ada put him through was finally paying off.

He had pale blue eyes and sandy hair, and I could see why Ada found him attractive. At first she did most of the talking. He was clearly shy and didn't make eye-contact or initiate any conversation beyond basic pleasantries.

Deinon and I kept to fruit juice, but after a second glass of red wine Tallus started to relax.

'For many years Tal's ambition has been to fight in Arena 13,' Ada said, pausing to take a sip of her wine. 'He started at the lower arenas, entering lacs he'd patterned himself. To fund that, he was a hunter. Isn't that right, Tal?'

'What did you hunt?' I asked.

'I was really more of a trapper than a hunter,' he said, meeting my gaze. 'I had a stockade down south. I trapped deer and wolves and a few bears. I sold the pelts in Mypocine, and most of the meat – any that I didn't keep for my own use – to the Genthai. You're part Genthai, aren't you, Leif? Ever visited their domain in the forest?'

I nodded and smiled. 'I went there for the first time last winter.'

'Well, they were good to me and paid me well. I had a small hut out in the forest, and they extended it for me and built a stockade around it. Strangely they wanted paying in currency. As most of the tribe never go anywhere near the city, I wondered why. But I got the feeling that it was best not to ask too many questions.'

I wondered if they'd used some of Tal's money to buy the gramagandar. Only the Trader could have supplied such weapons.

'Was it creepy all alone in the forest?' Kwin asked.

'It certainly was at times. Sometimes I found it difficult to sleep. I heard wolves howling out there amongst the trees. But I felt better once I had the protection of the stockade. I saw some strange things too . . .' Tallus didn't finish his sentence and suddenly seemed deep in thought.

It was Deinon who prompted him. 'What sort of things?'

'Well, you're going to think this is crazy, but one day I came across some decomposing bodies in the forest. They were pretty far gone – little more than skeletons. Most seemed to be the remains of wolves, but one was really odd. From the neck downwards it was without doubt human, but the head was all wrong. It was the skull of a wolf – I'm sure of it.'

'Do you think it was one creature?' Deinon asked. 'I mean, could it have been somebody's idea of a joke? You know – to replace the original human skull with a wolf one?'

'That's what I tried to tell myself,' Tallus said. 'But the remains were whole and the skull was still attached to the neck.'

'That sounds weird,' Kwin said. 'If I'd found something like that, I'd have packed up and run straight back to the city.'

'I did think about it,' said Tallus with a smile. 'But I needed all the money I could get. It's taken me years to get together enough to fight in the arena.'

'Well, enough talk of dead bodies and weird stuff,' Ada interrupted. 'This is supposed to be a party, isn't it? Come on, Tal, play us a tune!'

Tallus immediately went to the back of the room and returned carrying a small scuffed leather case. He sat down, put it on his knee and opened it to reveal its contents. I saw that it was a violin.

Not many violins were made any more. Playing them was almost a lost art. 'That looks really old,' I commented. 'I bet that set you back a few pelts.'

'It was my father's,' he said, his expression suddenly sad. 'He inherited it from his own father. He taught me to play it and left it to me when he died.'

Tallus put down the case, raised the violin to his shoulder and slowly drew the bow across the strings. Then he began to play.

It was a sad tune, and out of the corner of my eye I saw Ada grimace before putting her hand on his shoulder.

'This is a party, Tal. We need happy music. We need music to dance to!'

He smiled and began to play something much faster, a lively tune to set your feet tapping.

Suddenly Kwin grabbed Deinon and put her arms around him. 'You've got the brains, but have you got the rhythm?' she asked. 'Show me what you can do!'

'I can't dance!' he exclaimed, his face suddenly turning bright red.

'Then now's your chance to learn!' she said.

I was smiling at Deinon's embarrassment when Ada grabbed me. 'Don't tell me that *you* can't dance, Leif. Anyone who moves well with a lac can dance. That's what the Trig is – a kind of fluent, complex dance. This is much simpler!'

With that, she seized my left hand and put her arm around my waist and began to guide me backwards and forwards in time to the music. 'You can put your other arm around me, Leif. I won't break,' she scolded.

I did as I was told, and soon got the hang of it; within moments we were spinning round as well. As the male partner, I should have been guiding Ada – that was the way people usually danced. But by touch and gesture she was dictating our movements; I was like her lac. But I enjoyed it. After all, she knew what she was doing and I didn't.

With a laugh, she brought me to a halt and whispered in my ear, her breath warm. 'Now we'll swap partners,' she said. 'I know you're dying to dance with Kwin!'

The music paused while we changed partners.

'Tal! Play us that piece by Paganini,' Ada called out.

'Who's Paganini?' I asked.

'He was a violinist and composer – one of the ancients,' she replied. 'He was so brilliant and original that some believed he'd struck a deal with the devil. Tal's going to play my favourite piece.'

Now I had my right arm around Kwin and my heart started beating even faster. She felt warm and I could smell the scent of lavender. Tallus began to play again, the tempo faster than ever. The music was wild; it had a frantic, hypnotic quality, and I soon began to lose myself in the sound and the rhythm. All I was aware of was the music, the patterns our feet rapped upon the floor, the warmth and closeness of Kwin's body and the fact that we were moving almost as one.

At last the music ended and Ada began to fill four glasses with what I'd thought was lemonade. It turned out to be a sparkling white wine. While Ada poured, Kwin leaned against me, our arms still around each other's waists. Was I imagining it, or was she actually pulling me close?

But then we broke apart to take our glasses.

'A toast is needed, Tal!' Ada commanded.

Tallus smiled. He looked really happy, especially when Ada gave him a peck on the cheek and put her arm round him. He raised his glass and made the toast. 'To the joy of life!' he called out enthusiastically. 'To the joy of living! To the happiness of us all, and a long and successful future!'

We sipped the wine and it tasted delicious.

It was a great party.

All good things come to an end, and after we'd taken our leave of Tallus and Kwin, Ada walked Deinon and me out into the cinder space behind the Wheel. The air had cooled, and without a coat I began to shiver.

'Thanks for coming tonight,' Ada said, giving us both a hug. 'It was a great evening – just what Tal needed.'

'I enjoyed it. Thanks,' I replied.

'Me too,' added Deinon.

'Oh, and I wanted to thank you for working out those sequences of wurdes for Deinon,' I told her with a smile. 'It was great to beat Palm.'

Ada slowly shook her head, and out of the corner of my eye I watched Deinon's face redden for the second time that night.

'I think it's Deinon here you should thank,' Ada said with a frown. 'Tal made me promise not to work for anyone else, but because you were in trouble and it was Kwin who asked me, I made an exception. But Deinon wrote the code. All I did was answer a few questions when he got stuck. We had the usual dialogue between a student and a teacher – like lessons. Deinon is without doubt the best pupil I've ever had, and that's saying something; I taught some brilliant people back in my former life, but I've never had a student like this boy.' She put her arm round Deinon's shoulders.

Later, as we climbed the hill back to Tyron's house, I mulled over what I'd just been told. Why couldn't Deinon have been open with me? Kwin too had kept the truth from me. I felt excluded, yet at the same time they'd ended my terrible sequence of defeats.

'Thanks for patterning that lac, Deinon. I really owe you for that. But why didn't you tell me that it was your work? Why go to all that trouble of writing down and reading out your wurdes while pretending they were Ada's?'

'I'm to blame for that, and I'm sorry,' Deinon said. 'But you know what Kwin's like. She saw the cuts on your arms, had a row with Tyron – and quickly worked out that this was a scheme to get his hands on patterns created by Ada. Kwin was angry and didn't want to give him that, so she worked out an alternative. I would write the patterns, and Ada would only offer suggestions when I needed help.'

'So Tyron still doesn't know the truth?'

'Kwin told me to keep my mouth shut – that he need never know. And the longer I go without telling him, the harder it will be. I don't like deceiving people.'

How could I complain? I was keeping a secret too, I thought: Deinon and Kwin didn't know that Math was my father.

'You got really high praise there from Ada. Does Tyron know you're that good?'

'I think he's starting to realize,' Deinon said.

'You might be better than he is one day!'

Deinon smiled at that and shook his head, but I wondered if he was *already* better at patterning than Tyron. After all, Tyron had struggled to understand what Deinon had done; he'd been sure that it was Ada's work.

THE FATE OF TALLUS

Grudge match rules apply, but for one:
There is no clemency.

Arena 13 Rules of Combat
(Special Rules for when Hob Challenges)

Tyron was keen to see Tallus's lac in action again, knowing that it would be patterned to a much higher level than ours. Tallus's next contest was scheduled third on the Lists on the Wednesday evening, so Deinon and I accompanied Tyron to the arena, eager to see what Tallus and his lac could do.

The gallery was full of chattering, excited spectators. The women were there in force, filling almost a third of the two thousand seats. They were dressed in their silk finery, faces rouged and powdered, lips painted the fashionable black. I noticed a lot of young women and wondered how many of them were there to watch Palm, who was fighting first that night.

Tyron was putting him into the arena a lot – much more than was usual for fighters of his young age and limited experience.

We sat down in the front row. Ada and Kwin, just a dozen

seats away to our right, called out greetings, and we waved back. Once more they had both painted only their top lip black, the lower one the rich red of arterial blood.

In the aisles the gambling house touts were doing a roaring trade; as usual, quite a few red tickets were being sold. But soon the huge candelabrum with its thirteen torches began to descend, the first warning that things were about to get underway, and everyone settled down to watch.

With a rumble the two doors opened, the smaller min and the larger mag, and the two combatants and their armoured lacs emerged and quickly took up their positions. Palm was to fight a min combatant called Marcos, who had three years of experience in Arena 13 and was slowly working his way up the rankings.

I knew that Tyron wasn't too bothered whether Palm won or lost. He just wanted him to gain experience. I was jealous because Tyron wouldn't risk allowing me to fight.

There were a few shrieks, and the girls began calling out Palm's name. He smiled and waved up at them. His leather jerkin bore the silver wolf emblem that showed he fought from Tyron's stable. His fit, muscular body looked good in it, and he knew it.

There was no sign of the scratches and dents that Thrym had inflicted on the armour of his tri-glad. It looked as shiny and fresh as if it had come straight from the forge. No doubt Palm's wealthy father had paid to have it repaired.

However, there were two fresh scars on Palm's left arm and one on his right; the cuts inflicted by Thrym after each of our victories. But I had my own scars – and more of them – to remind me of the bouts I'd lost.

Out of sight, a deep bass drum began to beat with a slow, steady rhythm, and the tall figure of Pyncheon, the Chief Marshal, dressed in black and wearing a red sash, moved between the combatants. He was carrying his long silver ceremonial trumpet. He raised his hand and the drum ceased; silence fell over the noisy spectators.

'Let the proceedings begin!' he boomed in his pompous voice before strutting back towards the mag door. As he reached it, he raised the trumpet to his lips and blew a high shrill note, then disappeared from view. With a deep rumble, both doors closed and the contest got underway.

Palm was a cautious fighter and liked to play safe. After our private bouts, I knew his tactics quite well. He had a repertoire of about eleven moves, mostly defensive, and at times he became quite predictable. However, such knowledge wasn't enough to guarantee victory. His lacs were patterned to a very high level, their movements smooth and fast. If the lone lac defending a min combatant got anywhere near one, its throat-socket was vulnerable.

So it proved now. The contest lasted only four minutes. Marcos's lone lac got too close, and a blade called endoff, making it collapse on the floor.

The initial polite applause was drowned out by shrieks and whoops as Palm's fans showed their delight at his victory. Marcos received the ritual cut to his arm, and then the arena was cleared.

'A bit pedestrian, but Palm did well enough,' Tyron said, leaning towards Deinon and me. 'That performance might not please the aficionados, but the boy's young; once his confidence grows, they'll see what he is capable of.'

It was then that the torches in the arena suddenly flickered. The air turned icy cold, and suddenly we were all plunged into darkness. My heart lurched. Almost immediately the torches flared back into life, and screams filled the gallery, echoing back from the high ceiling – no longer cries of enthusiastic appreciation, but shrieks of terror.

Once again the torches flickered and died. When their flames returned, I saw that the aisles were full of terrified people seeking to escape.

Hob had arrived at the Wheel.

After five minutes the gallery was almost clear; only combatants and their kin and the aficionados remained. I found it difficult to understand why so many spectators fled the gallery when Hob appeared. After all, they were in no danger.

I'd asked Tyron, and he explained that some people had such an ingrained dread of Hob that they couldn't bear to be anywhere near him. Some believed that he chose victims to target in the future from amongst the spectators – though there was no evidence of this.

Tyron hadn't said a word. His face was grim and he was drumming his fingers on the arm of his seat, clearly agitated.

Down in the green room, Pyncheon would be presenting the lottery orb to the min combatants. Whoever drew the short straw would have to fight Hob. Fighting from the mag, Palm was in no danger, but I knew that Tyron had other min combatants scheduled to fight tonight. I remembered the terrible night when Hob had slain Kern.

Hob and his tri-glad, clad in ebony-black armour, entered

the arena first. I stared at him angrily, my throat constricted so that I found it difficult to breathe. He was clad in regulation jerkin and shorts, and wore his usual bronze helmet, with a wide black slit to look through. His arms were similar to a lac's – significantly longer than those of a human. His head was tilted upwards; he seemed to be staring into the gallery.

No wonder people believed that he selected victims here! Was he staring at me? I wondered.

As Hob's opponent entered from the min door, directly beneath us, I heard Tyron suck in his breath with relief. Looking down, I saw that the combatant didn't have the silver wolf logo on his back.

But I'd been staring at the jerkin without really seeing what was embossed there. Now I took it in and drew in my own breath sharply.

TAL.

I looked to my right and saw Ada's wide staring eyes, and Kwin talking to her animatedly.

Surely the lottery was fixed. Here was a man fighting with a lac crafted by a brilliant twice-born patterner about whom the whole city was buzzing. It was almost as if Hob had come to test himself against Ada's talent.

'Now we'll see just how good she is!' Tyron exclaimed, as if reading my thoughts.

'It's not fair! It's too early,' I replied angrily. 'Tallus hasn't had time to train properly.'

I'd only met the man once, but I'd immediately taken to him. Ada cared about him, and now his life was on the line. Apart from my father, every combatant who'd faced Hob in

Arena 13 had died there or been taken away, wounded, never to be seen again. Was this to be the fate of Tallus?

Pyncheon entered the arena only briefly, nodding to the combatants; then the doors rumbled shut, and lacs and combatants took up their positions. Tallus looked scared. He was very pale and there were beads of sweat on his forehead.

To my surprise, Tyron pulled a small sand-timer from his pocket and positioned it on the arm of his seat. He'd used it occasionally during training as an alternative to the brass device, but I'd never seen him use it to check the timing of a contest in the arena.

It consisted of two small glass orbs connected by a metal tube. The sand was funnelled down from the top into the bottom orb. Once the last grain had fallen, five minutes had passed. It was very accurate, far better than a clock-candle, and as good as the cumbersome mechanical wall-clock that Pyncheon would be using now to time the bout.

The contest began very suddenly: Tallus's lac attacked with great speed, driving Hob's tri-glad backwards. As they clashed, Tyron tapped the top of his timer to start the flow of sand. So fast was the attack that Tallus only just managed to keep up. He hadn't used Ulum, so the lac had surged forward of its own volition, its patterns sensing the opportunity to put Hob on the back foot. Ada had claimed that it wasn't sentient, but it did seem to have some initiative.

It was a very good start. Could Tallus actually defeat Hob? I wondered.

But Hob soon rallied, and his tri-glad fought its way to the centre of the arena. There was the constant rasp of metal on metal, and twice it sounded as if a blade had struck close to a throat-socket, though it was hard to be sure which lac had dealt the blow.

Up in the gallery there was absolute silence. The remaining spectators were enthralled, and sat holding their breath.

'Who's winning?' Deinon asked.

'It's very even, boy,' Tyron replied, glancing at his sand-timer. 'It's on a knife edge and could go either way. That lac is as good as anything Gunter ever patterned, and that's saying something.'

Gunter had patterned the lac that enabled my father to defeat Hob fifteen times. It wasn't for nothing that they'd called him Gunter the Great.

Then something astonishing happened. One of Hob's lacs went down. Almost too fast to see, a blade penetrated its throat-socket to call endoff. With a roar, the spectators rose to their feet. My heart lurched with excitement and hope, but I didn't jump to my feet, and neither did Deinon. That was because Tyron was still staring at the timer.

The upper glass bulb was already half empty.

19

THE MOTHER OF A DJINNI

A shatek is the mother of a djinni.
The midwife is a Nym artificer.

The Manual of Nym

The downed lac was lying close to the far wall, so it didn't obstruct the fighting, which raged close to the middle of the arena. The action was fast – very fast – and once again I heard the rasp of blades striking armour.

Tyron was staring at his timer as if that was more important than what was taking place in the arena.

He caught my eye. 'He has to finish it now!' he said. 'Once that first five-minute stage is over, he has no hope of winning.'

I understood exactly what he was saying. Tallus had improved his fitness, but it would still be nowhere near that of the average human combatant. Already his lungs and heart would be straining; his muscles protesting. Dancing behind a lac demanded supreme fitness.

And after five minutes the situation would get even worse: a gong would sound, and then Tallus would have to fight in front of his lac. That was why Tyron kept glancing at his sand-timer. During this stage of the bout, the long arms of his lac would have to reach over Tallus's shoulders to defend him; he'd need to dance very close to it. I doubted that he would have developed sufficient skills to do this properly. There hadn't been time. He would be vulnerable to the blades of Hob and his two remaining lacs.

Yes, he had to finish it now, I thought.

But the gong had already sounded.

Tyron cursed under his breath.

The combatants repositioned themselves. Gripping his blades so tightly that his knuckles were white, Tallus stepped in front of his lac.

Hob crouched before his two remaining lacs and flexed his knees. His eyes glittered behind the slit in his helmet. I noticed again how long his arms were. But for the bronze helmet he could have been a lac himself.

Right from the start it went badly for Tallus. Now his lack of skill was evident. He had two left feet, and they betrayed him again and again. What was worse, he was clearly impeding his own lac. He kept stumbling, preventing it from moving forward smoothly. It could no longer attack, and was hard pressed to deflect the blades that sought his flesh.

Suddenly Tallus tripped, this time completely off balance. He'd taken a tumble in his first contest, when the audience had laughed and jeered. This time the spectators remained silent or groaned softly. He fell back against his lac so that it was unable to wield its blade.

Hob came in fast, his two remaining lacs almost at his side. With its left hand, Tallus's lac thrust its blade into the throat-socket of its nearest attacker, calling endoff. But its right blade was blocked, and Hob stabbed forward, and suddenly the contest was over. Tallus's lac collapsed.

I didn't want to look, but I couldn't tear my eyes away.

Tallus was on all fours, desperately struggling to rise.

Before he could do so, Hob chopped down viciously, cutting clean through his neck.

Then he picked up Tallus's head by the hair and held it aloft, showing it to the spectators. As the blood trickled from the stump and ran down Hob's arm, there were groans and cries from the audience. I could smell the blood – and hear the screams of anguish from Ada. She was trying to throw herself over the rail into the arena; Kwin was holding her back.

Tyron pushed his way through to help: he seized Ada's other arm. She was struggling to free herself, and her face was twisted in torment.

Hob seemed to be looking directly up at her.

Then the marshals appeared; three of them managed to get Ada into the central aisle and escort her up to the doors at the rear. She had stopped screaming, but sobs racked her body and tears streamed down her face.

'Kwin! Go with her. Make sure that she's taken care of properly!' Tyron called.

Kwin nodded and climbed the stairs towards the doors.

Marshals were entering the gallery in force now, ushering the spectators towards the exit. When I glanced back into the arena, I saw that Hob was still holding the severed head, but he seemed to be staring down at Tallus's lac.

*

Three hours later a tearful Kwin brought news of Ada.

We came rushing downstairs when we heard her arrive. Teena had her arm around her and was trying to comfort her, but Kwin's face was red and tears were flowing from her swollen eyes. She kept trying to speak but couldn't get the words out.

Only when Tyron, drawn by the disturbance, came into the room did she calm down enough to speak.

'It was horrible . . . Ada kept screaming that it was her fault. She was hysterical. She fought like a fury, but then they sedated her and put her to bed.'

'Where was she taken?' Tyron demanded.

'To the small hospital within the Wheel.'

'Did Hob take Tallus's remains?' he asked.

Sobbing, Kwin shook her head.

'Well, at least that's something,' he said, without adding further comment.

I knew that he was thinking about Kern and what Hob had done with his head – and what the tassels had done to his body. At least Tallus had been spared that.

'They say that he took Tallus's lac though,' Kwin added.

Tyron nodded thoughtfully. No doubt Hob had taken it to learn what he could. That lac had downed two of his. If Tallus hadn't stumbled backwards and impeded it, Hob would surely have been defeated.

The following day, soon after dawn, Tyron took me with him to the office of Pyncheon, the Chief Marshal.

'I can't believe the lottery chose Tallus,' I observed as we strode through the deserted streets at Tyron's usual furious pace. After a visit from Hob there were few people about. The city would be quiet for days.

'It had to be somebody, boy,' Tyron said, 'but I don't trust the process one bit. Hob culls the rising stars of Arena 13; kills them early before they become a real threat.'

'So the lottery *is* rigged? Then Pyncheon must be involved. Is that why we're going to see him?'

'I'd be a fool to confront him over that,' growled Tyron. 'No doubt he's in Hob's pocket, but there's nothing I can do about it. No, we're going there to buy Ada.'

Was she still a slave? I wondered. That didn't seem fair.

'Isn't she free now that Tallus is dead?'

Tyron shook his head and then glanced down at me and frowned. 'Take that disapproving look off your face, boy!' he ordered. 'The woman's status doesn't change just because her first master's dead. There is a deed of ownership, which is very valuable in this case. She has almost two years still to serve, and can be bought by the highest bidder. If I don't buy her, then someone else will. That's a fact of life, so don't get on your moral high horse!'

We walked on in silence. The sky was clear and it would be another warm day. High above the great block of the slaughterhouse, the vultures were already circling.

The interview with Pyncheon did not go as Tyron had expected. He made his offer, and then slid a sealed envelope – as custom required – across the polished surface of the large desk.

The Chief Marshal simply pushed it back with a shake of his head. 'Tallus married the woman three days ago,' he said, placing a large piece of paper before Tyron. There was a smaller piece fastened to it.

Tyron picked it up and began to read.

'As you'll note,' continued Pyncheon, 'clipped to the marriage certificate is a cancelled deed of ownership. It's all perfectly valid – it was sworn in private before a commissioner for oaths. So the woman is free.'

Tyron's face fell, but there was nothing he could do about it. Ada was a widow, not a slave. No wonder she'd reacted so violently. She'd married Tallus just days before his death.

I was saddened by the news. To have been married for so short a time and then have your husband snatched away in so brutal a manner – it was tragic. But at the same time I was happy that Ada had her freedom.

Then a third piece of paper with a black border was handed to Tyron. It was the combined death and cremation certificate.

'The body was burned an hour ago,' Pyncheon said.

Tyron nodded but made no comment.

The interview was over.

The following day, at breakfast, Kwin arrived with a message from Ada. Her face was still full of grief. She didn't even glance at me but went directly to her father.

'Are you all right, girl?' Tyron said, coming to his feet.

'I was with Ada when she first woke up. It was bad, really bad. It brought back all the memories from last year when Teena lost Kern.'

Tyron hugged her, and she leaned against him, her shoulders shuddering. 'It's not right,' she sobbed. 'It's not fair. Somebody has to put a stop to this.'

He patted her back but didn't reply. She pulled away from him and straightened up, her eyes flashing with defiance. 'Ada wants to speak to you, Father. Could you go to the hospital this morning?'

'Of course I will. I'll go right away.'

Then Kwin looked directly at me. 'She would like Leif and Deinon to come with you.'

Tyron frowned. 'Did she say why?'

She shook her head. 'She doesn't say much. But she's angry, and I don't blame her. I think she has some sort of plan . . .'

'A plan? A plan for what?'

'A plan to deal with Hob. A plan to sort him out once and for all!'

Tyron shook his head, clearly exasperated. 'Did you *know* that they were married?' he demanded angrily.

'No. They were married in a private ceremony one morning. I work in your office then, don't I? So don't blame me!' she snapped back.

He patted his daughter's shoulder. 'I'm sorry for doubting you, girl. It's just that things are moving so fast I can't keep up.'

We left immediately. The hospital room was small; apart from the bed the only other furniture was a table beside it. On it were the documents we'd last seen in Pyncheon's office.

Ada was sitting upright with three pillows behind her back, her hands folded across her belly; she was wearing a simple white nightdress buttoned to the neck. There were dark shadows under her eyes and her lips, devoid of paint, were as pale as the rest of her face. Her black hair had grown and had been trimmed into the urchin style often chosen by mothers for their young sons.

We stood beside her bed. 'I'm sorry for your loss,' Tyron said.

Ada nodded and stared down at her folded hands in silence. Suddenly she looked up at him. 'I need to speak to the Trader,' she said. 'I need something from him.'

'He's due in eight days' time,' Tyron said. 'I'll fix up an appointment for you. We could travel together by barge, if you like.'

'No,' Ada said, shaking her head. 'We will travel together, but not by barge. If I visit him with the others, it will be common knowledge. What I want must be a secret – especially from Hob.'

'So you plan to act against Hob in some way?' Tyron asked. 'Yes.'

There was a silence while they stared at each other.

I wondered what she planned to do. I was also impatient to find out why she had wanted Deinon and me to visit her.

'If you want my help, woman, I need to know more than that,' Tyron said gruffly.

'I will do what I must – with or without your help,' she answered, her eyes flashing with defiance. 'But if I get what I need from the Trader – then I will tell you what you wish to know. You wish to learn more about Nym? Then I will be your teacher. Is that what you want?'

Tyron's eyes shone with eagerness and he nodded.

'Then it's settled. So can we meet the Trader in secret? Is there a way?'

Tyron scratched his head then gave a sigh. 'It might be possible. There is a way to summon him. He arrives after dark on the eve of the appointed date for his visit, laying up at anchor out of sight. There's a great bronze plate suspended by chains close to the tower by the Sea Gate. Beat that gong, and he will come ashore – though nobody has done so in living memory.'

Ada leaned across and picked up a document from the table, throwing it angrily onto the bed. I noted the black border. It was Tallus's death and cremation certificate.

'They burned Tal's body and scattered the ashes while I was still unconscious,' she cried, tears springing from her eyes. 'Couldn't they have waited for me? It was cruel.'

'I'm sorry for your grief and pain, but no cruelty was intended,' Tyron said in a kindly voice. 'Unfortunately, that's the custom. If someone dies at Hob's hands in Arena 13, the body is burned as soon as possible. He has been known to come back for the remains he doesn't take with him; he's capable of doing terrible things to his victims. He retrieves and preserves souls in order to torture them. The bodies are usually eaten by his followers. In this city we do not bury people lest the tassels eat the dead flesh. Speedy cremation is the norm. It's meant for the best.'

Ada did not speak for a while, and a heavy silence fell over the room.

'Did you want to speak to Leif and Deinon?' Tyron said, nodding across the bed towards us. 'You asked to see them.'

'Yes. I want them both to come with us to the Sea Gate and to witness what I do. Deinon has great potential as a coder and will benefit from the experience.'

Deinon's face lit up and he beamed at Ada.

'As for Leif,' she continued, 'in time I would have him fight with my lac in Arena 13. Would you do that, Leif?'

I gasped. It would be a dream come true. I would be fighting with a lac capable of defeating Hob. Revenge would finally be within my grasp.

However, I looked at my master. 'I'm being trained by Tyron,' I explained. 'Whether or not I fight behind your lac, I still belong to his stable. It would be his decision.'

Tyron looked at Ada rather than me. 'May I ask the reason for that choice? You've never seen him in action. Leif's just a novice,' he told her.

'Compared to him, those I've seen fighting in the arena are like slow old men. They belong to the past. He is young, fast and very hungry. He is the future. I've seen your daughter move, and she says Leif is her equal.'

'So with the help of something you hope to buy from the Trader, you intend to defeat Hob in the arena?'

'Correct.'

'I don't wish to be cruel, but your skills couldn't save Tallus. It was a close contest, but your lac wasn't good enough to win. Tallus had neither the experience nor the skill to fight to the fore of that lac. The contest should have been won in the first five minutes: you should have ensured that.'

'Your words *are* cruel, but I accept what you say,' Ada said. 'I underestimated Hob and didn't anticipate Tal having to fight him so soon. Poor Tal was an eager novice. He tripped and fell. I shouldn't have allowed him to fight so soon.'

'Why should I put my trainee at risk? He's a novice too.'

'My skills are adequate, but in this fallen world I'm denied what I need – as are all who pattern here. I believe the Trader will be able to provide what is missing. Even if you had it, your knowledge of Nym is not good enough to enable you to use it properly. Help me, and you will see how it is done.'

'The Trader may demand a high price for what you want. If necessary, I'll lend you the money,' Tyron offered.

'I may well take you up on that offer. Tal has left me a little money, but it may be insufficient.'

'Will we buy wurdes of Nym – the special primitives necessary to build sentience?' Tyron asked.

'That's no longer necessary – I've already developed my own primitives – but there is one further thing that I cannot create. It is a creature called a *shatek*.'

'What's that?' Tyron demanded, voicing the question on all our lips.

'A shatek is the mother of a djinni,' Ada replied, 'and I will be the midwife.'

'Then what about the father?'

'Thrym will be the father, but he will also be the son. He will be twice-born, as I am. He will be sentient. In partnership, he and Leif will slay Hob over and over again until his final self is dead. Before that djinni dies his final death, he will wish he had never been created.'

THE WARSHIP OF A WARRIOR

The Trader does not come bearing gifts.
Cross his palm with silver.
Even better, offer gold.
Amabramsum: the Genthai Book of Wisdom

Soon after dark on the eve of the Trader's midsummer visit to the Sea Gate, Tyron drove a wagon hauled by eight oxen towards the western edge of the city. Inside, strapped to a jig – a wooden frame with bindings at the ankles, wrists and throat, the usual procedure for transporting lacs – lay Thrym, in the deep sleep.

I was wide awake and sitting on the front seat between Tyron and Deinon. Ada and Kwin were immediately behind us.

It was an unusually warm, humid night, and I could hear faint rumbles of thunder in the distance.

I looked forward to our arrival at the Sea Gate with mounting excitement. What did a shatek look like? I wondered. Soon I was going to find out.

I'd assumed we would follow the course of the canal – the most direct route to our destination – but we veered away from it. When I mentioned this, Tyron just said, 'It's too dangerous. We might be seen.'

So we took a winding route through the edge of the forest that probably doubled the length of our journey. Soon it began to rain, the wind buffeting the wagon with increasing fury, thunder rumbling in the west. A summer storm was building.

At last the canal came into view once more. We had reached the Terminus on the cliff above the Sea Gate, and now began our descent through the woods on foot, having tethered the oxen and sealed the wagon against the driving rain.

As we approached the tower, a glimmer of yellow light spilled out from its highest window. Were we being spied upon?

'I thought the tower was deserted,' I said to Tyron.

'The Keeper watches over the Sea Gate. I don't think he'll approve of what we're about to do.'

Tyron led us across to the bronze gong suspended between two stone pillars. It was about six feet in diameter and over a foot thick. Leaning against one pillar was a long-shafted hammer, its heavy head covered with thick leather.

Tyron bent down and gripped the shaft. But Ada came to his side and shouted something into his ear, which was lost beneath a crack of thunder. Then, with a shrug and a grimace, he stepped back; now she seized the hammer.

For a moment it seemed that it would be too heavy for her, but I could see the anger and determination on her face. In a paroxysm of rage, she swung it up to shoulder height and spun her whole body round so that its head made sudden contact with the gong. She grasped it tightly, striking the gong again and again.

That summons boomed out across the choppy water, and before the seventh strike the door of the tower burst open and the Keeper of the Gate ran over to stay Ada's hand. But Tyron intervened, pulling him to one side.

On the thirteenth stroke, lightning forked above the harbour and the gong's boom was answered by a clap of thunder.

Ada laid down the hammer and stood there in the lashing rain. The Keeper pushed past Tyron, gesticulating and shouting at her, but she simply ignored him, knelt on the wet ground, buried her face in her hands and wept.

Kwin knelt by her side and put her arm round her shoulders.

Deinon looked scared, and my heart was pounding in my chest. Something momentous was happening here.

Then Tyron cried out, 'Look, Ada! The Trader's here!'

Lit by another fork of lightning, a dark ship was surging towards us between the narrow arms of the outer harbour, its black sails billowing in the gale. And upon its prow was a carved white wolf, so huge and life-like that it seemed to bound before the ship. Its tongue lolled from its mouth and its fangs were bared, its eyes blazing with fury as it leaped towards its unseen prey.

I had a sudden moment of insight. This was not the vessel of a Trader. It was the warship of a warrior.

The Keeper was pointing towards the tower, and we followed him through the narrow doorway and stood inside, shivering as water dripped from our clothes onto the stone flags. A single torch flickered on the far wall above a long oaken table; twelve chairs were positioned along the sides and a thirteenth at its head.

The man disappeared into another room and returned carrying towels, which he offered to us. Gratefully we wiped the rain from our faces. I saw that he was an old man with grey stubble on his chin and a gaunt face, but he had kind eyes. He pointed towards the table, gesturing that we should sit down.

We nodded and took a seat, but nobody spoke. When he left the room, I sat there in a daze, listening to the rain battering against the stones. The Keeper had left the door ajar, and it swept into the room, forming a large puddle, which glistened yellow in the torchlight.

He returned with a tray of steaming metal tankards, which he placed upon the table. 'Drink,' he commanded. 'It will drive out the chill.'

I lifted the tankard to my lips and sipped the liquid cautiously. It contained hot caudle – a sweet and spicy gruel which slid down my throat to warm my stomach. I sipped again and felt new strength spreading through my body.

Suddenly I heard heavy footsteps on the flags, and a giant of a man dressed in chain mail from head to foot stood framed in the doorway; he wore a silver mask, and luxuriant red hair spilled down almost to his shoulders.

The Keeper went across and bowed low, and I heard him whispering quietly. Then he returned to the table and pulled out the chair at its head. For the first time I noticed that this was larger than the others; on its back was carved the head of a snarling wolf.

Unbidden, we came to our feet and bowed to the stranger. Although he was dressed as a warrior, with silver chain mail and a long dagger sheathed at his belt, his hair and size told me that this was the same man we had met in the tent close to this very spot.

He bowed graciously in return and motioned for us to sit, before taking his own seat. I looked at the eye-slits in the mask, and saw the flicker of the eyes behind. There was no opening for his mouth.

The Keeper bowed to each of us and left the room. When he'd gone, the Trader spoke. The deep voice was somewhat muffled by the mask, but his words were clear.

'For what reason have I been summoned?' he demanded.

'I loved a man and now he is dead,' Ada said simply. 'And I cannot find peace until the thing that murdered him is also dead.'

'Name this murderer!'

'The creature is a djinni called Hob,' Ada continued. 'He slew my husband in the arena.'

'Then what do you wish from me?'

'A shatek,' she said, glancing towards Tyron. 'I will pay the required price.'

Tyron nodded. 'I'll be her guarantor. I am prepared to advance the money,' he said.

'Do you know what it is that you contemplate?' the Trader asked, turning towards Ada and resting his huge mailed fists on the table.

'Do you know who I am?' Ada countered, an edge of anger in her voice. 'Do you *know* me?'

The Trader nodded. 'I should, for I brought you to this

place and awoke you from the sleep that is akin to death, thus making you twice-born. Once, long ago, you were the High Adept of Nym, foremost amongst those in the Imperial Academy, and amongst your colleagues you had no equal. But now you are but a lone woman in a fallen land. The forces that oppose you are far more strange and terrible than you realize.'

'The shatek? Is one available?' Ada asked, becoming impatient.

'Yes, it's available. I can supply what you demand now. But my payment can wait.'

'I will pay you in full,' she insisted.

The Trader nodded. 'One year from this very night I will be at anchor in the harbour. If you still live, bring to me what is owed.'

Ada nodded and he rose to his feet. Throughout this interchange Kwin, Deinon and I had remained silent. Even Tyron had spoken only one sentence.

With Ada in the lead, we followed the Trader out into the darkness. The storm had abated, leaving behind a warm drizzle as insubstantial as mist. We waited on the quayside while the Trader boarded his ship and went down into the darkness of the hold.

It was some time before he emerged. When he did so, he was no longer alone. Behind him, four squat figures laboured to manoeuvre something up onto the deck; it was a cylinder of dull metal, big enough to accommodate a large human body.

They hefted it to waist height, supporting it on straps around their shoulders. When they clambered up onto the quay with their heavy load, I saw that they were not human;

their naked bodies were covered with a hide of dark hair that glistened in the fine drizzle. Although a head shorter than me, they were much broader and stockier.

Their heads were not human either: they had flat snouts and fangs that curved downwards over their bottom lips – though their eyes flashed with intelligence. They watched us with sideways glances even as they went about their business, and I sensed their threat. I saw Kwin's eyes widen in fear and heard Deinon gasp. I was glad that the Trader was standing between us and them, directing their movements with quick hand signals.

'What are those creatures?' Kwin asked Ada.

'They are called *rasire*,' she replied. 'They are a type of low-level singleton, brutal and debased, often used by djinn as beasts of burden to fetch and carry. But they are very strong, and are sometimes used in battle. However, they need strict discipline or they will turn on their master.'

As the creatures climbed the hill towards the wagon their bodies began to steam in the rain.

I heard the oxen snort in fear at their approach, but the four creatures had soon secured the cylinder aboard our wagon, moving back into the trees to begin their descent towards the Sea Gate.

We turned to take our leave of the Trader.

'Other than your title of *Trader*, do you have a name?' Ada asked him.

'I have many names,' he replied. 'But some call me Lupus.'

'Then I thank you, Lupus,' she said with a warm smile. 'Thanks for what you've supplied. You'll be paid in full. I always keep my word.'

He bowed, and as he did so, the red mane of hair fell forward over the silver mask. Then, without another word, he turned and followed his rasire.

'What now?' Tyron demanded.

'We take the shatek to Tal's stockade,' Ada replied. 'Then I will begin my work.'

'Where is this place?'

'It's in the forest on the edge of the Genthai lands to the south-east. He took me there once.'

'You say you only visited it once. Are you sure you'll be able to find the way?'

'The same skills I use when observing and developing patterns also enable me to recall routes. Don't you worry, I'll find it. I'll sit beside you and be your guide.'

We headed along a rutted track that ran roughly south. After a couple of hours we halted to get some rest. Tyron insisted that Ada and Kwin should sleep inside the wagon. It meant sharing with Thrym and the shatek. But Thrym was in the deep sleep and the shatek was still within its container. They'd certainly be more comfortable than us.

We were to use the wooden seats. It would have been more comfortable on the ground, but it had only just stopped raining and it was saturated.

Before we settled down on our blankets, Tyron beckoned to Deinon and me. He led us some distance away into the trees, well out of earshot of Ada and Kwin. Coming to a halt, he turned and faced us. His face was in darkness, but the tone of his voice told me that he was angry. It was directed at me.

'Don't build up your hopes of fighting behind that lac, Leif. I don't care how good it proves to be. You're still a novice.

I'm just playing along with Ada for now, until I find out what I need. Understand?'

'But what if it's so good that even a novice could dance behind it and win?' I protested, the words flying out of my mouth. 'And don't we *want* to defeat Hob in the arena? Don't we *want* to defeat him over and over again until we can attack him in his citadel? You said that Hob might come after me if I fought in Arena 13. Well, isn't that exactly what we want? I could be the lure that draws him to his destruction. Wasn't that your plan?'

'It was a plan that you were supposed to keep secret, but I suppose it doesn't matter if Deinon knows,' Tyron said, patting him on the shoulder. 'But remember, we're here to learn from Ada – you especially, Deinon. This is a golden chance and we've got to take it.'

Then, without another word, he headed back towards the wagon and we followed him.

I spent an uncomfortable night but I had plenty to think about. I was impressed by what I'd seen of Ada. She had stood up to the Trader, while we were nervous in his presence. Back when humans ruled the world, she really had been important. She was talented and she believed in herself. Hob had threatened me and, even worse, threatened anyone I might show affection for. He had to be dealt with, and quickly. This was our chance to do exactly that, and far sooner than I'd expected.

Despite what Tyron had said, I was looking forward to fighting with a lac patterned by Ada. I really wanted it to happen.

I was a lot nearer to getting my revenge.

THE SHATEK

Creation is a messy business.
Amabramsum: the Genthai Book of Wisdom

It was almost almost a week before we finally reached the
stockade. The rough track had long since given way to grass-
lands, and then to a dense forest of both conifers and deciduous
trees – beech, ash, oak, rowan and pohutukawa. I could see
mountains rising in the distance, partially obscured by the
mists of the Barrier.

Set within a large clearing, the huge wall of logs obstructed
our view of anything within. We came to a big padlocked
gate; Ada got out the key, and then Deinon and I helped
Tyron to push the heavy gate open.

We drove the wagon into the muddy compound. Around us
stood a number of crudely constructed, single-storey wooden
buildings. I noticed that one structure was set a little apart
from the rest. It had no windows and only a narrow door.
After unlocking this door, Ada entered, and I followed her
somewhat apprehensively into the darkness, Kwin at my
heels, with Deinon and Tyron bringing up the rear. Then
there was a scratching sound, and a sudden flare of yellow

light, and Ada was brandishing a torch which she'd taken from a metal bracket attached to the wall. Ahead of me, I saw wooden steps leading downwards.

'Take off your shoes,' Ada commanded. 'We don't want to drag any mud down there.'

Without argument, we began to unlace and tug off our boots. As I followed her down, the smell of damp earth filled my nostrils. The fifteenth step brought us to a large cellar.

'Not a bad practice floor,' Tyron said, looking around.

The whole room was panelled in wood – though these timbers were not rough, but polished and stained a rich mahogany, as was the floor. It lacked the high-quality finish of Tyron's training floor, but it was more than adequate: I realized that Tallus had been very serious about competing in Arena 13. He must have spent a great deal of time and effort constructing this.

I looked around, but saw no supporting pillars. Given the size of the cellar, this was surprising, and I glanced up nervously, wondering how the ceiling was held up, imagining all the earth above our heads.

'Did Tallus build this himself?' I asked Ada.

'Tal paid others to help him, but yes, he worked on it himself and it was built to his own design. To fight in Arena 13 was always his dream. He spent years scraping together the money he needed to get started. It's terrible to think that it ended in such a way. That was my fault. He should have practised for at least a year before entering the Lists. I should have insisted upon it. Then he would not have died in the arena. He would have defeated Hob.'

Sobbing quietly, Ada began to light the wall torches. I now

appreciated how clean this cellar was; no wonder we'd been ordered to leave our muddy shoes at the top of the steps.

But there was another reason for that, as I was soon to discover.

We all set to work immediately, unloading the shatek. However, removing the cylinder from the wagon proved difficult. It was too heavy even for our combined efforts; I shuddered when I remembered how the four creatures had carried it suspended from their shoulders.

Tyron took charge, and under his direction we piled logs up behind the wagon, constructing a crude ramp, and then carefully rolled the cylinder down onto the mud.

'Gently! Gently!' cried Ada. 'The creature inside is delicate!'

Next we moved the wagon away and unharnessed the oxen. Tyron selected the strongest four and yoked them into a team. Then, after we'd carefully rolled the cylinder into position on the very edge of the cellar steps, we tied ropes around it and, harnessing those four oxen to it, backed them slowly towards the building, easing the cylinder down the steps and into the cellar below.

'Now it's time to release the shatek,' Ada said.

One end of the cylinder was actually a lid which could be unscrewed. Tyron offered to help, but she shook her head firmly and set to work while we all steadied the cylinder. She struggled for a while, but eventually it began to turn and she looked up at us.

'Stand well back,' she said softly. 'We don't want to scare it.'

She allowed the lid to roll away and stood back.

Immediately, dark-brown liquid began to flow out of the

cylinder, becoming more viscous as it met the air and congealing to a jelly. I smelled a sudden pungent odour that caught at the back of my throat. I held my breath for a moment.

'The fumes are unpleasant but not dangerous and will quickly disperse,' Ada said with a smile as Kwin wrinkled her nose in disgust.

Then the shatek emerged.

It was about the size of a five-year-old child but with twice the number of limbs. It scuttled away from us across the floor to take up residence in the darkest area possible – a point equidistant between two wall torches. There it crouched, palpitating rapidly, its dark glistening body flattened against the boards of the cellar floor. It was clearly visible: apart from its face, which was turned away, I could make out every detail without getting too close.

It resembled an insect, but it had eight legs like a spider, and was covered in black fur. However, its body was segmented; its abdomen and thorax were oval in shape, its head large. I was curious to see its face.

'Not a pretty sight, is it?' Tyron laughed grimly.

'You said we shouldn't scare it!' I joked to Ada. 'I think we're the ones who ought to be scared! It's the most repulsive thing I've ever seen.'

'It's even uglier than a tassel!' Deinon quipped.

'We need to be cautious,' Ada told us. 'It's weak at present; the liquid in the cylinder both fed it and kept it docile so it should pose little threat. But after its first meal it will become fully alert and grow quickly; we'll need to show constant vigilance. At times it will be very dangerous; at other times it will do little more than sleep.'

I continued to study it: I saw that the three body segments were streaked with the gelatinous substance that had anaesthetized and sustained it in the cylinder. When it finally turned its head towards us, I heard Kwin gasp, and I felt a mixture of revulsion and fascination.

Its features resembled those of a woman: it had a wide, sensuous mouth with full lips, a feline nose and long lashes, behind which flickered expressive eyes. Attached to the body of a human woman, that face would have been considered exceptionally beautiful. I felt sure that, unlike the lacs of Midgard, this creature was sentient.

'As I told you,' said Ada, 'this shatek is the potential mother of either a djinni or a lac, or even some other hybrid. Using wurdes of Nym, the progeny can be shaped to an artificer's own design. But first it needs food – and lots of it. Let's not keep it waiting!'

After locking the cellar door, Ada led us out to a large shed that Tallus had used for storing meat. Salted carcasses of deer hung from the ceiling, and Tyron cut one down to provide the shatek's first meal.

After removing our shoes once more, we returned to the cellar. I drew back the bolts and opened the door cautiously. The shatek was still crouching against the far wall. I held the door open and Tyron lurched into the cellar, the carcass over his shoulder. He dropped it in the middle of the floor before joining us behind the door.

He'd barely got out before the shatek scuttled over towards its supper. It began to feed ravenously, its legs ripping and tearing, the head jerking convulsively as it devoured the raw meat.

'It'll make a mess of your training floor!' Tyron told Ada.

'It doesn't matter,' she said. 'I was just concerned about bringing soil in – shateks can be vulnerable to fungal infections. Apart from that it's hardy and strong. It'll eat all that carcass, bones included.'

'And what about the mess that'll come out the other end?' asked Tyron with a grimace.

'Ideally we'd have drainage and be able to hose its waste away,' Ada said, 'but that isn't possible here. We'll have to scrape it up and carry it out of the cellar.'

At that, Kwin wrinkled her nose again. Ada smiled at her. 'Don't worry – I think that's a job for our three men! This cellar is far from ideal, but we'll just have to make do. A shatek generally prefers warm blood; it should really be permitted to make its own kill. Eventually we'll have to sacrifice some of the oxen, but we'll kill them first.

'Cheer up,' she said, smiling at us each in turn. 'We are here to produce a lac such as Arena 13 has never seen – one with all the intelligence of a human but with enhanced speed, strength and reflexes. I know you aren't going to find this pleasant, but if we want to defeat Hob, this is the price we have to pay.'

THE BIRTHING PLATFORM

The beauty of the dream vanished,
And breathless horror and disgust filled my heart.
The Compendium of Ancient Tales and Ballads

That evening I helped Tyron make a fire in the open and we cooked a stew of meat and vegetables.

The sun was going down as the five of us sat gazing into the flames, eating hungrily. Despite the warmth of the day it was often chilly after dark in Midgard, even at the height of summer.

In the distance I heard the sudden cry of a wolf and glanced at the huge gate, reassured to see that it was locked. I remembered the werewights. Were they still around? After all, we were near the Genthai lands; they'd remain where they were until the end of the year, when that invisible Wolf Wheel turned again.

'Tal used to hunt both wolves and bears,' Ada remarked to Tyron. 'He sold their pelts – that's how he got started.'

'He was an unusual man,' Tyron said. 'He had this built and lived as a hunter before moving to the city and learning to pattern a lac. Not many men could have done that.'

'Yes, he was very special,' Ada said softly, and her face suddenly twisted in anguish.

'You say that Thrym will be the "father" of a sentient lac,' Tyron prompted, changing the subject.

Ada composed herself and nodded. 'The shatek has the eggs, but the seed has to come from another source. It's possible to use a human for this purpose – such an act is terrible to contemplate but can produce the most spectacular results. In the days of Empire, such practices were forbidden to civilians, but the military used them to produce ferocious and cruel djinn which could be unleashed against our enemies.

'My own creation here will be a form of djinni known as a *singleton*. It is more sophisticated than a common lac, but has only one self and cannot shift its shape. In order to create this I must use Thrym. I've patterned him to the highest level possible for a non-sentient lac, and those skills will be transmitted through the shatek to the offspring. But it is *not* a mating of lac and shatek in a conventional sense. Forget the biology of the natural world. Thrym will be devoured, and most of him absorbed by the shatek. But he will emerge again, twice-born and sentient!'

'How exactly will that help in the arena?' I asked Ada. 'And by "sentient", do you mean fully aware?'

'Yes,' she replied. 'Thrym will be just as conscious as you or me. Of course, he will still be directed by Nym commands, but will also show a high degree of initiative. He will be much more tactically aware than a non-sentient lac, and your partnership will be on a much higher level. He will also be much stronger and quicker. Of course, you'll still use

Ulum – that sound-code is vital in order to hide your tactics from your opponent.'

We spent the night sharing the two largest of the huts. Kwin and Ada took the one furthest from the gate whilst Tyron Deinon and I shared the other. The facilities were very basic and we slept in blankets on the floor. Tallus seemingly hadn't cared for home comforts.

But I was tired and I could have slept anywhere. Dawn came all too soon.

For the next two weeks, under Tyron's supervision, Deinon and I fed the shatek and removed what passed through its digestive tract. The creature grew rapidly, and by the end of that period it was almost twice the size of a human being. It had already devoured two whole oxen.

Ada also began to teach Tyron, gradually lifting his knowledge of Nym onto a higher plane. Deinon sat in on those lessons and made copious notes, talking them over with Tyron afterwards. In turn, Tyron continued my own lessons in Nym, but soon delegated them to Deinon.

This was because early in the second week, taking Kwin with him, he returned briefly to the city to check on his businesses and his stable of fighters and patterners.

Left alone with Ada, Deinon and I were able to ask her questions about the world from which she'd come.

'Your name is very unusual,' Deinon said. 'Was Ada common in your own time? It's unknown here.'

It was dark, and we were facing each other across the fire, chewing on some steaks from the ox we'd fed to the shatek. They were a bit on the tough side but I was hungry.

'No, it was not common even then, but my father re-named me Ada too. It was our custom for a child to be given a temporary name at birth, and then a true name chosen by the head of the family which was bestowed on his or her fourteenth birthday. I'd a rare talent for coding – we never used the word patterning. My father said that I had the art born with me – that I was Mozart-gifted! But he exaggerated and always thought his daughter special.'

'Mozart? What's that?' Deinon asked.

'Mozart was the name of a famous ancient, a musician. He was a gifted composer who excelled at a very early age. Mozart was born with the skills and knowledge that other lesser mortals would have taken many years to acquire. So, to a certain extent, it was with me. I became adept at Nym almost as soon as I learned to talk.'

'So why didn't your father call you Mozart?'

Ada smiled. 'That was the influence of my mother. My father might have been the head of the family, but she ruled it as only a woman can! She taught the History of Women in Science at the university, and it was she who really chose my name. I was called after Ada Augusta, Countess of Lovelace. She was the first coder. Imagine! That clever woman wrote the very first program, and for a computer that hadn't even been built!'

'What's a computer?' I asked. The world that Ada came from was very different, and there was so much that was mysterious and unknown to me.

'It was the forerunner of a lac, but was made out of dead, inert materials rather than flesh. A computer carried out complex calculations faster than humans and also stored vast amounts of data that could be searched and retrieved.'

'Were computers sentient?' Deinon asked.

'Not at first, but eventually they were made so; not long afterwards, what you call false flesh – that of lacs and djinn – was developed and the creatures born of it were also made sentient.'

'Were you born of a shatek?' Deinon asked suddenly. 'After all, your own flesh is "false flesh", isn't it?'

It seemed a very personal question, and I thought Ada might be offended. But I needn't have worried: she took it all in her stride.

'When the soul of a human is removed from Containment, a shatek is unnecessary because no mind needs shaping by the use of Nym coding. The body of false flesh is grown in a tank, and it is a replica of the original body. There is no essential difference between the flesh we are born with and that grown to accommodate a twice-born.'

I said nothing, even though I knew that wasn't quite true. I remembered Konnit showing me the gramagandar. That weapon could dissolve Ada's false flesh just as easily as it could that of a djinni. Humans, however, were not hurt at all by its deployment.

'You said the military created the djinn to fight on their behalf. But who were their enemies?' I asked.

'At first wars were fought between nations. Before the djinn rebellion, warring human states were highly militarized. Potential violence was diverted by the main leisure activity – arena combat where different types of djinni fought for the amusement of human spectators. Vast sums of money were bet on the outcomes of such contests. So what you have in Midgard – which is, by the standards of those times, an agrarian and relatively simple society – is the remnants of that way of life: the Wheel with lacs in combat. But your lacs are less than true djinn.

'However, by the time I was born, most of the world was unified under an imperial government – though we were already beginning to see what might become the next conflict. Pockets of djinn had rebelled and they were growing in strength.'

'Why did they call them djinn? It's a strange name,' I said. It was something I'd always wondered about.

'In legends and folktales, djinn are daemonic entities with magical powers. I am sure they never existed, but coders love to use acronyms, creating from the initial letters of a sequence of words a new short form. This could be applied to the words in which we converse and also the wurdes used by patterners. Thus *djinn* stands for *digital janus interface nano node.*'

'That's a mouthful,' I said, bursting into laughter. 'I prefer the shorter version!'

Ada laughed with me. 'There is much to be said for acronyms!'

'But what does it mean?'

She frowned. 'There's a lot contained in that five-word acronym,' she said. 'A nano refers to something very small, and Janus was an ancient god with two faces. This is very important because the essence of sentience is to have two aspects of the self mirror each other – two faces regarding each other and entering into dialogue. Do you ever talk to yourself?' she asked.

'Not when anyone else is around to listen,' I joked.

'We all talk to ourselves, whether we realize it or not. We call it "thinking". Have you ever puzzled over a question or tried to reach a decision, to find that the answer has suddenly popped into your head? The other half of your mind has supplied the answer, and that dialogue is the basis of consciousness. One day, when you've learned more, I'll explain it fully.'

But my mind was already flying in another direction. I hesitated to ask Ada what I really wanted to know. She might not want to talk about it. But my curiosity overcame my reluctance. After all, Deinon's question hadn't bothered her.

'What happened to you? Why were you placed in Containment?'

Somewhere in the distance a wolf howled, and then there was a scream of something in pain. We all turned our heads, but of course there was nothing to be seen. The high stockade wall lay between us and any threat – though I saw Ada shiver before turning back to answer me.

'The djinn were starting to mount terrorist attacks against the government. At first it seemed little more than a nuisance. Nobody at that time dreamed that they would grow in power to the extent that they could defeat the Empire and reduce us to this pitiful state. Their first major attack was on the Empress, but they failed to kill her. Then they identified a new target – the Imperial Academy, where artificers were trained. Nobody expected it at the time, but looking back now, it seems obvious.'

'Why obvious?' I asked.

'Because djinn are patterned using wurdes of Nym, and knowledge of such wurdes represents true power. Strike there, and the advantage that humans had enjoyed over djinn would be undermined. So that's what they did. I was killed by a terrorist bomb. The next thing I remember is being interrogated, floating in darkness, aware that I was no longer within my body. They told me that I was dead and offered me the usual choice – oblivion or stasis in Containment.'

'Why couldn't they simply place you in a body of false flesh such as the one you have now?'

'It was illegal. If everyone was permitted to adopt false flesh, the population would have increased unsustainably. It would have led to famine and the end of civilization.'

'So why bother to place *anyone* in stasis?'

'There was a faint hope that I would one day become one of what were known as the "twice-born". By special imperial decree, a few gifted souls were reborn in this way. I was the High Adept of the academy, and I hoped that I might become one of them. However, I almost chose oblivion: being "twice-born" in the future would mean leaving behind all my friends and family, who would be dead by then. But my fear of oblivion made me choose stasis.'

'It must have been terrible to wake up in our world knowing that everybody you knew was gone for ever.'

'Not at all: before being placed in stasis, the memory is selectively wiped. This ensured that if you were awakened to be twice-born, you did not carry with you a crippling burden of emotion and grief. I can't remember any individual that I was close to from my own time, so I cannot grieve. Though I found grief again soon enough. I grieve for Tal.'

'You can't even remember your parents?' Deinon said, his eyes widening in astonishment.

'Oh, I remember them very clearly, but they died years before

I did. The wiping is to remove losses that might be felt upon awakening far in the future. For all I know I might have had a husband and children. I simply cannot remember.'

There was a long silence, which I interrupted with another question. 'When djinn were first created, didn't anyone see the danger – that one day they might turn on their human creators?'

'Yes, many feared and opposed their development. They had their own name for djinn. They called them Franks, after Frankenstein's monster.'

'What sort of monster was that?' Deinon asked.

'It was a fictional creation from an ancient book written by a woman called Mary Shelley. In the story, a man called Frankenstein makes a creature from the body-parts of dead humans. Then he infuses it with life using the power of what we called electricity. But new developments do not always turn out for the best! Some humans would have prevented the creation of djinn. Looking back now, they were probably right. They were certainly correct to fear what might happen.'

When Tyron and Kwin finally returned, Ada announced that it was time to bring Thrym and the shatek together.

The lac had spent most of the time in the deep sleep.

'Awake, Thrym!' Ada ordered, after we had released it from the jig in the second wagon, and the naked lac followed her across the compound and down the cellar steps. Tyron, Deinon and I were at its heels, but Kwin had remained outside. The thought of what was about to happen turned her stomach.

At a command from Ada, Thrym went into the cellar. I

glimpsed the shatek quivering in the far corner, its long thin limbs glistening in the torchlight. Then we left, locking the door behind us.

The screams began almost immediately: although lacs of Midgard were not fully sentient, their bodies could still both feel and respond to pain.

'It's cruel, but there is no other way,' said Ada as we climbed the steps. 'The lac will be rewarded for its sacrifice. It will be reborn to sentience and will not remember any of the pain.'

Shuddering at the screams that followed me, I retreated to the far side of the stockade to find Kwin. Even there, the cries were carried faintly on the air.

Kwin stared at me, her face twisted in horror. 'The lacs that fight down in the Commonality scream too. Something that screams like that must feel pain,' she said.

I remembered the first time she'd taken me down into the Commonality. We'd watched an illegal fight between two lacs. One had died, cut to pieces by the blades around the arena. It had screamed just as Thrym was screaming now.

'They're more like us than most people realize!' said Kwin. 'Can't you see that, Leif? Surely you must!'

I nodded. She was right. Combat in the Wheel was an industry; it created jobs and made the gambling houses wealthy; it entertained the masses and added excitement to their lives. But nobody thought of the lacs. Nobody wanted to accept that they were in any way aware. If you believed that, how could you allow the fighting to continue?

'If my father does nothing about that illegal fights down there, then I will. I'll free those lacs! Just see if I don't.'

*

222

It was late in the evening when we returned to the cellar carrying torches with which to drive the shatek back if it proved necessary. We hoped that it would now be sated.

The scene inside was horrific and I started to tremble.

Most of the lac had been devoured, but there were strands of its skin across the ceiling, spun by a method too terrible to contemplate. But when we saw what had happened to the remainder of the skin, Deinon and I immediately vomited our suppers onto the floor.

It had been stretched in a taut triangle extending from the far corner of the cellar, where walls and ceiling met, to be anchored at two points halfway across the practice floor. Some fragments of bone and flesh were still attached to it and the floor was smeared with blood.

And there, at the centre of that cradle of skin, the shatek crouched, throbbing rhythmically like a beating heart; and at each convulsion of its body, the web of skin vibrated.

'Why has it done that?' I demanded angrily.

'That is its birthing platform,' Ada replied. 'Within the shatek's body is the egg that is already developing into what we need. Soon my work will start on a lac born of a shatek and a wurde which, in this fallen land, is the only sure way to gift it with the sentience, skill and speed to defeat Hob. I will begin to shape it.'

A GOOD PLAN

The best laid schemes o' mice an' men
Gang aft agley.

The Compendium of Ancient Tales and Ballads

The following morning Tyron slaughtered another ox to meet the demands of the shatek's voracious appetite. It was still growing at an alarming rate, and was now very fast and dangerous. We always visited it in threes, pushing the meat into the cellar with a long stick before closing the door.

On the seventh day after the death of Thrym, the shatek was waiting for us. As usual, Tyron carried the meat over his shoulder. I had the torch, and kept alert in case we found ourselves in danger. Deinon's task was to draw back the bolts and open the door slowly to check that the creature was safely in its web of skin.

This time it wasn't.

It was hiding behind the door.

A thin, sharp-clawed leg lunged through the narrow opening towards Deinon.

With a curse, he stepped back. I raced forward and stamped hard on the tip of the shatek's leg. The door was swinging wider now, and I could see its fierce, malevolent eyes regarding us. It looked ready to attack.

I thrust the torch into its face. With a hiss and a snarl, the shatek retreated, and Tyron quickly threw in the carcass.

Only after the creature had eaten its fill was it safe to go in. This was when Ada went to work on the new lac.

Occasionally Tyron, Deinon and I watched her.

She stood facing the birthing platform where the sated shatek crouched, speaking wurdes of Nym at great speed. Sometimes it would open one huge eye and regard her warily, but even when it slept, Ada explained, those wurdes continued to do their work, shaping within its womb the form that the offspring would take.

'I am weaving the warp and weft of my wurdes to create a labyrinth of high sentience,' Ada declared grandly, 'forming the singleton that will stand before Leif in the arena.'

Tyron made no comment, but he shot me a glance that told me exactly what he thought about that. For now, he was humouring Ada, while striving to learn all he could. He would never allow me to fight behind this sentient lac. He believed that I was still too young and needed further training. If we were to destroy Hob totally, as well as winning victories in the arena, we had to confront his final selves in his lair. For that Tyron believed we needed more sentient lacs. One would not suffice.

A month later the shatek pushed out a glistening, brown, tubular egg over six feet long, and attached it to the platform of skin with a gelatinous green compound from its mouth. As soon as this was done, the shatek died, and we faced the task of removing its body from the cellar before it began to rot.

The creature had grown to the size of a small ox, and we had to cut up the body before dragging the pieces up the steps and burying them outside the stockade.

One week later the egg split and, but for one significant difference, a perfect human emerged, crawling on hands and knees. At first glance it looked like a muscular man, with strong, well-developed limbs, the arms exceptionally long. But when Tyron and I helped it upright, we saw that the thickened neck and throat-slit marked it out as a lac created for combat.

It was kept in the deep sleep in the jig in Tyron's wagon, but woken for an hour each day to be fed, washed and exercised. But while the lac slept, Ada spent hours by its side, pouring a torrent of wurdes into its ears. From time to time Tyron and Deinon sat close by, trying to learn more about the process – though Deinon confided that much of what she said was beyond them.

'She speaks the wurdes so quickly that they merge into one and it's almost impossible to make any sense of them,' he explained.

'But you must be learning *something*?'

Deinon grinned. 'Oh yes, we are. I never thought I'd make so much progress with my patterning in so short a time. But that's only when she teaches me directly or Tyron passes on what he's learned. Even Tyron can't glean much from her when she's in full flow. He questions her at length afterwards.'

One evening Ada invited us to witness the final stage of her labours. She placed her hand on the forehead of the lac, which lay supine and relaxed upon the jig, clothed only in a loincloth, its arms and legs free.

'Thrym is self-aware,' she declared. 'He knows who he is and has a basic knowledge of our world. But in some ways he is like a child who must learn through experience.'

I noticed then that she referred to the lac as 'he' rather than 'it'; clearly she viewed it as more human than the previous Thrym.

'Awake!' she commanded, then, 'Selfcheck!'

The lac turned his gaze upon her, but did not give the usual reply.

'Listen,' she instructed. 'Listen well. The flesh of my warm hand is resting upon the skin of your forehead. Do you feel it?'

'*I feel it*,' the lac answered softly.

'Then you live,' she told him. 'You live to serve, to fight and to feel. You live to feel the life beating within you. To fight and win are your reasons for being. To feel and know life will be your rewards.'

'*Whom will I fight?*'

'You will fight others like yourself. You will fight them in ritual combat. And Leif will be with you. You will fight together. Then, in time, you will face a special enemy – one who is very powerful and dangerous. His name is Hob and he must die. That is your purpose. That is why I have made you what you are. You belong to Leif and you will do his bidding. Look at Leif now! He is your master!' Ada ordered, placing her other hand upon my shoulder.

At that, I heard Tyron suck in his breath in disapproval – but it was already done: the lac slowly turned his head towards me, his eyes glittering in the torchlight. And the expression in them radiated unmistakable intelligence.

I felt Kwin's eyes upon me, and when I glanced at her, she gave me a strange smile.

'Leif is your master!' Ada repeated, staring at the lac. 'And your name is Thrym!'

'So is it done?' asked Tyron.

'Yes, the process is finished. Now we need to get Leif and Thrym working together as efficiently as possible. We could clean up the training floor and do it here.'

'Yes, but my house would be better,' said Tyron. 'There we have all the facilities necessary. Not only that, people will be wondering at my absence from the city and some might get curious. I need to get back into my routine. You could be my guest and live in comfort. I'm at your service.'

Ada smiled and nodded. 'I'll take you up on that offer.'

Later, well after dark, I walked around the stockade walls with Kwin. I was carrying a torch to light our way. We often went for a stroll together after supper and talked over the day's events. I always enjoyed our chats.

'Why did you give me that mysterious smile before?' I asked.

'Mysterious? Is that what you thought it was?'

I smiled. 'Yes, it was mysterious because I couldn't guess what you were thinking.'

'I was thinking how happy you looked, and how angry my father was. Steam was almost hissing out of his ears! It looks like you are going to fight in Arena 13, Leif, and much earlier than my father thought.'

'He'll put a stop to it,' I said. 'He's already told me that he's just playing Ada along and has no intention of letting me fight so soon.'

'Don't be so sure!' Kwin said. 'I think you'll find that Ada is quite capable of getting her own way.'

Suddenly we heard the howl of a wolf. It sounded quite close to the stockade.

Kwin gasped and seized my free hand, moving closer. 'Could it get over that wall?' she asked.

I held the torch high above my head and looked up. 'No, a wolf couldn't scale that,' I said – though I suspected that the two-legged self of a werewight could. They fought the Gen-thai, but would they attack other humans? It was something I should have asked Konnit.

I guided Kwin back towards the two huts where we slept. She held my hand all the way. When it was time to part, she kissed me on the cheek. I tried not to make too much of it, but I was still reliving the experience when I finally drifted off to sleep.

The creation and early patterning of Thrym was over, and the following day we headed back towards the city much more slowly; the hunger of the shatek meant that only four oxen remained to pull the wagon.

Within the week we were back at Tyron's house in Gindeen, and almost immediately I began to practise with Thrym. Working with the new lac was a revelation. Soon we had developed an efficient version of Ulum, and Thrym proved to be a fast learner.

But the difference between this and other lacs was

unnerving. I had never felt comfortable when lacs stared at me. I'd always wondered what they were thinking. But Thrym was fully sentient; his utterances went far beyond the usual exchanges of Nym wurdes.

It was when I was alone with him on the training floor that he first engaged me in conversation. Deinon was putting in extra time patterning, while Tyron had just gone up to his study on business. Thrym was standing at ease while I sat cross-legged on the floor, trying to get my breath back after a vigorous workout.

'Who were you?' the lac asked.

I looked up at him in astonishment; I didn't know how to answer.

'Before you are, who were you?' Thrym persisted.

'I was nobody,' I said. 'I did not exist. I was just a twinkle in my father's eye.'

'A twinkle? What is that?'

'A twinkle is a glimmer, a spark of interest. My father loved my mother, and from his seed I was born, and from my mother's womb I emerged. Before that I was nothing.'

'Can you be sure of that?'

I shrugged. 'Nobody can be sure of anything in this world.'

'I am twice-born,' said the lac. *'I remember little of my first life. But there was pain. It seems distant now, but there was agony beyond bearing. I did not ask to be born.'*

It was disturbing to hear this. Ada had said that he would remember nothing of the horror of being eaten by the shatek. If he'd experienced and remembered that agony, it was surely wrong to have made him, in spite of our need to defeat Hob. Suddenly I felt guilty. Here he was talking to me just like a human, and yet he was a slave, easily silenced by a wurde and bound to do our bidding. He was still staring at me, so I replied.

'Neither did I,' I told him. 'No humans ask to be born. Do you wish that you hadn't been born?'

It is good to live. I like to fight. Fighting is good. I look forward to slaying our enemy.

'So do I. Hob killed my mother and brought about my father's death.'

We will pay him back for that, and for the death of Tal, said Thrym. *We will kill him many times until no selves remain as hosts to his dark soul. He will die many deaths. I will enjoy that. But you will not die, Leif. I will protect you. I will keep you safe.*

'I thank you for that, Thrym. But I want you to promise me something. If ever we face defeat by Hob but there is a chance of victory if I am sacrificed, then do it. I would willingly give up my own life to slay Hob.'

I would do that only if we could bring about the destruction of all Hob's selves through such a victory. The victory over one self would not be enough.

I nodded. 'So be it.'

Then Thrym fell silent. I wondered what strange thoughts were spinning through his head.

I was also wondering how long it would be before Tyron confronted Ada. She was working towards my speedy entry to the Arena 13 Lists, but as far as he was concerned, this season would be far too soon. However, he was happy learning from her, and there was a good atmosphere of industry and progress in the house. I knew that he wouldn't want to jeopardize that.

So Tyron waited almost two weeks before confronting her. He called a meeting. All five of us were present in his study that night.

He began by listing the reasons why it was premature for me to fight in Arena 13.

'We need to be ready for the time when Hob is finally weakened,' he finished. 'When he only has a few selves remaining, that will be a moment of great danger – not only for us but for the whole city. Who knows what weapons he might have in his lair? Weapons that, when threatened, he might unleash on us.

'I planned that not just *one* sentient lac but *many* should hunt him down in his lair. I have money to buy more shateks. We could begin the work in the winter when the Trader next calls. Then, *next* season, Leif could begin his battles against Hob in the arena and slowly deplete his selves while we prepare to strike at his heart. We could enter his lair and defeat him there.'

I looked at Tyron in astonishment. He had changed his mind and agreed that I could fight with Thrym in Arena 13. What he was proposing was reasonable. I would curb my impatience and spend this year readying myself for combat, practising until I was perfect.

Ada stared at Tyron for a long while before speaking. Then she smiled. 'It is a good plan, Tyron. But first hear me out because I have an even better one!'

BRING ME THE BODY OF HOB

The gorestad is the 'high mind'.
It is usually operative in all djinn with more than
one self.

The Manual of Nym

Tyron sighed, then went to his cabinet and brought a bottle of red wine to the table, along with two glasses. He drew out the cork, and poured a large glass for Ada and one for himself. Deinon and I didn't mind not being offered any, but I saw the corners of Kwin's mouth turn down in dismay. She would have liked one.

'Then let's hear your plan,' Tyron invited.

'Leif and Thrym only need to defeat Hob *once* in the arena. That will give me the opportunity to destroy all his selves,' Ada said, before pausing dramatically. She enjoyed making grand statements and watching the effect her words had on others.

Tyron raised an eyebrow and sipped his wine, waiting for her to continue.

'As I told you previously,' she said, 'I could once have halted a djinni such as Hob in his tracks with a wurde, then bound him to my will or eradicated his consciousness for all time.

I can no longer do that because Hob has had many long years to change and refine the patterns that inform him. He's a rogue djinni who has shaped his own being, which means that I don't know what I'm dealing with.

'But if one of Hob's selves were to be my prisoner, rendered safe while I worked upon him,' she continued, 'I could tease out the knowledge I need. His selves are governed by one mind called the *gorestad*, which is the *high mind* operative in djinn with more than one self. But within this group consciousness there is always some individual awareness particular to each self. Most importantly, the gorestad can be accessed through *any* of the selves; each is a portal. Thus by dealing with one of Hob's selves, I could obliterate *all the others*.'

I thought about this, and realized that werewights were probably types of djinni: each element had its own individual mind, but all four were also governed by that high mind Ada had spoken of. No wonder they were so difficult to defeat. Each creature could control its own body but the high mind could coordinate the attack.

The same was true of Hob. It would be extremely difficult to attack him in his lair. His many selves would work together and be formidable indeed.

'Hob has been defeated before in the arena, I understand?' Ada asked.

'Yes,' Tyron answered. 'Years ago it was done by Math, the greatest Trig fighter the arena has ever seen. Math defeated Hob many times.'

He didn't look at me, but it was strange to think that he was the only one who knew that Math was my father. I had never told Kwin or Deinon, and to Ada, Math was simply a legend of Arena 13 combat.

'What happened to the body of Hob after those defeats?' she asked.

'On each occasion the remains were collected by his servants, the tassels, and taken back to his lair.'

'How soon afterwards was that?'

'After his first defeat by Math, it was a couple of hours – no doubt because the tassels were taken by surprise. But subsequently they came in less than half an hour.'

'Twenty minutes would be enough,' said Ada.

'Enough for what?' demanded Tyron, a hint of impatience and annoyance in his voice. 'Didn't you hear me correctly? I said Hob's "remains". The only way to defeat Hob in the arena is to slay him, and the only sure way to slay him is to sever the arteries in his neck or cut off his head. Can you interrogate the dead?'

'I have no such skill with humans, but I can certainly interrogate dead djinn. But the head must not be cut off. Just sever the arteries. We can instruct Thrym to do that. I need the body in one piece. When Thrym and Leif win, I need you to bring me Hob's body.'

Tyron looked at her in astonishment. 'Surely that's not possible? Hob can animate the head of a dead human, but we don't even know how to do that to a lac. Perhaps the Trader can supply the technology? Is that what you're hoping for?'

Ada shook her head. 'We'll not need the Trader for this. There's a wurde buried deep within each djinni which can be called to make it possible, but time is limited – the interrogation must start within minutes of death. Could you get hold of the body for me?'

'Each time Math defeated Hob, the gallery was cleared of spectators and the arena secured by Pyncheon's marshals. Then the tassels collected the remains and the fallen lacs. We can assume that Pyncheon would do the same now,' Tyron said. 'I need to think . . . I would need help, but it's difficult to ask.'

'Why should that be so?' Ada asked. 'Wouldn't most people in the city be only too glad to overthrow Hob? Don't they want things to change for the better?'

'Yes, they do, but there are risks involved. If we fail to destroy him, Hob's reprisals will be terrible. The families of anyone involved will suffer his vengeance. But I'll ask Wode and two other artificers whom I trust – Brid and Ontarro. In turn, they'll ask the fighters in their stables to help, just as I'll ask mine. It'll have to be volunteers because the risk is great.'

'But do you see any difficulty in getting hold of the body?' Ada repeated.

'We'll need to plan very carefully. Pyncheon won't stand by and do nothing,' said Tyron. 'Still, what you propose is feasible – though I'd still prefer to delay it until next season. It would give us time to make our arrangements, and Leif could develop and increase his understanding with Thrym. There's another thing which worries me. Hob took the lac you patterned back to his citadel. No doubt he's been studying it there. So won't what he learns make his own lacs more formidable and dangerous?' Tyron asked.

Ada nodded. 'Yes, to a certain extent,' she replied, 'but I

have used a shatek and created a sentient lac. Without a lac, he cannot do that. Thrym is still more formidable than anything that Hob could develop by learning from my previous creation. We must not underestimate him. It is still three lacs against one. But we will win – that I promise you.'

I had been listening to their conversation with great interest, but I was torn. The wiser and more cautious part of me recognized that it was sensible to wait. But I was eager to fight, and desperate to avenge the death of my parents. And there was something else that made matters urgent. We needed to destroy Hob before he kept his promise to harm the person I cared for.

I thought that Tyron's argument would win the day, but then Ada proposed a sensible compromise.

'Then let's provisionally aim for this season, but only go ahead if we *both* agree that everything is ready,' she said with a smile to smooth his feathers.

Deinon, Kwin and I had taken no part in this discussion. Now I couldn't wait to play my part. And once all the talking and planning was over, I'd do exactly that. I'd be working with Thrym, developing our partnership. I'd be getting ready to face Hob. I was filled with excitement at the prospect, and adrenalin sent the blood coursing through my veins.

Now Tyron turned his gaze upon me and Deinon. 'I think we should increase the hours we put into training you, Leif. Perhaps Ada could work with you and Thrym in the mornings and I can take afternoon sessions. Deinon, you need to be there for both sessions too. Learn what you can, and don't be shy of making suggestions. And as for you, daughter,' he said, fixing his gaze upon Kwin, 'I'd like you to put in more hours at the office – take some of the burden of admin off my shoulders.'

Kwin's face fell at that. It was the last thing she wanted. She found her work at the admin building boring.

'May I make a suggestion?' Ada said.

'Of course,' Tyron replied.

'It would be useful to have Kwin working with Thrym as well. The lac won't tire, but Leif will. We don't want to over-extend him. A pulled muscle or a torn ligament would be disastrous. And we can learn by watching someone else work with Thrym. It would be useful if Kwin joined me first thing every morning – that would still give her time to work in your office.'

Tyron grudgingly agreed. So the pattern of the succeeding weeks was decided. At last we could get on with it. The waiting was over. Now the serious business of training would begin.

STAMP, THEN SPIT

Kali's waist is beautiful.
Her girdle is made of dead men's arms.
The Compendium of Ancient Tales and Ballads

Tyron also began to plan the snatching of Hob's dead body. As he'd explained, there were like-minded artificers in the city – artificers such as Wode, who were prepared to risk their lives – and he intended to enlist their help. That would be his priority.

Mine was to defeat Hob, and Ada's was to supervise my training, concentrating on increasing my understanding with Thrym. She drew up a timetable of four training sessions a day. The first involving me was to begin an hour after breakfast so that Kwin could make her contribution first.

When I reached the training floor that first morning, Kwin was already practising with Thrym while Deinon watched from the bench. He grinned and gave me a thumbs-up, but my gaze was drawn to Kwin.

She was dancing in front of the lac, matching him step for step, so close that her back was almost touching the metal armour on his chest. Both were wielding blades; hers held almost horizontally, Thrym's arched over her shoulders.

'Just look behind them!' Ada said.

The torchlight was casting their shadows back onto the wall; that composite shadow was three times their actual size. It looked like one creature with four arms.

'It's Kali!' Deinon shouted with a laugh.

'Who's Kali?' I asked.

'She's a goddess from one of the very oldest human religions,' Ada answered. 'As I've just explained to Deinon, she had four arms and fought daemons. Around her waist she wore a belt made of the arms of her slain enemies. She was terrible to behold. Just like Kwin and Thrym!'

Kwin's forehead was beaded with sweat and she was frowning in concentration as she moved before the lac. She was a picture of aggression and determination.

'She's good!' I exclaimed. 'It's a pity she'll never be able to fight in Arena 13.'

'That's something that needs to be changed,' Ada said quietly.

I looked at her in astonishment; there was no way that a female would ever be allowed to fight there. Ada was an outsider and didn't realize that it would never be tolerated in Gindeen.

'Kwin! Let's show Leif the stamp!' she called out.

Kwin grinned and danced towards me, Thrym close behind. Then, all at once, she scowled aggressively, her eyes glaring at me in feigned anger.

It was then that I noticed she was wearing the new red Trig boots I'd bought her – along with her usual war paint, the top lip black, the lower one a red that was almost the same as the red of her boots. The tattoo on her forehead seemed to glow.

They crouched as one, and stamped their feet hard on the wooden floorboards, left then right, left then right. *Thud! Boom! Thud! Boom!* That noise resounded across the room. It was strangely intimidating.

'As Hob enters the arena, I want you to do that,' Ada told me.

'Why?' I asked.

'Because it's never been done before and it will surprise him. Djinn are unnerved by anything different. They like order and stability, so we should offer disorder and change. It's a pity we can't paint your lips like Kwin's! That would shock him,' Ada said with a wicked grin.

Kwin's grin widened and Deinon laughed aloud.

'Forget the paint,' Ada went on, 'but there's something else I'd like you to do. Can you spit accurately?'

'Spit?' I asked in astonishment.

'Yes, spit – and it's important to be accurate. It's something you need to practise.'

'This is a joke, isn't it?'

Ada shook her head, her face solemn, though Kwin and Deinon were still grinning. For a moment I felt like an out-sider, the butt of some joke that I didn't fully comprehend. But I realized that all this had been discussed and planned in the hour before I'd arrived for training.

'When Hob enters the arena, first you stamp, and then you spit. Run up as close as possible and spit into the slit in his helmet. You need to get it into his eyes. He is not going to like it.'

'*Nobody* would like it!' I declared.

'But *his* dislike will be extreme,' Ada said. 'You see, there are certain djinn that form virulent poisons in their bodies. They can project that poison accurately over a great distance, killing or disabling an opponent. The logical part of Hob's mind will know that you are just a human and that your saliva can have no effect on him. But fear of such a weapon is deeply embedded in djinn consciousness. It will unnerve him.'

I nodded. Ada seemed to know all about the djinn. I was happy to follow her guidance. There was logic in what she said.

'I also want you to stamp your feet, but immediately in front of Thrym, as Kwin is now. That will unnerve him even further. He will remember Math defeating him and will not cherish that memory. The name of the game is intimidation. We carry the fight to Hob and teach him to be afraid. We're going to beat him, Leif! We're going to win! Start to believe that!'

'I do believe it,' I said with a laugh. 'We *will* win!'

Ada had astonishing confidence and self-belief. I suddenly felt so relaxed and at ease that I spoke without thinking.

'Did you know that Math was Genthai and that his true name was Lasar?' I suddenly blurted out. 'I'm half Genthai . . . Math was my father!'

Immediately I regretted my outburst. Tyron had told me to keep it a secret.

'You never told me that!' Kwin cried out in surprise; Deinon just stared at me.

'Well, we all have our secrets, don't we?' I countered. 'You never told me that it was really Deinon's patterns that enabled my lac to beat Palm's tri-glad. In any case, your father told me to keep it quiet – that way we'd get better odds from the gambling houses and win a lot of money.'

Kwin wrinkled her nose in disgust. 'Money, money, money! That's my father all right. He's always grubbing for money!'

'That's not fair, Kwin!' I said in defence of Tyron. 'Do you know *why* gathering money is so important to him?'

She shrugged. 'He wants to maintain his position as the best artificer in Gindeen with the best stable of fighters and lacs. He's a businessman first and foremost.'

'Not true!' I snapped. 'He paid out a fortune to bring back Kern's remains so that Hob couldn't torture his soul. And he didn't mind you borrowing money from him that night we fought the tassel.'

'But that's because of family. Any father would do it.'

'It's not *just* that,' I said quietly. 'That plan he told us about . . . he's had it for years. He's been striving to create a sentient lac for the purposes of defeating Hob. He wanted money for that – lots of money – to buy what he needed from the Trader. Earning money has merely been a means towards the destruction of Hob. Believe me, it's true.'

'As we're revealing secrets, I have something else to say about Tyron,' Deinon said. 'He's a generous man. My father's had a couple of bad years on the farm. The crop failed, and then his herd of cattle came down with a disease and had to be destroyed. When the payment for my second year's training was due, he couldn't find the money. I thought my time as a trainee was over. But guess what? Tyron waived the fee. This year he's training me for nothing.'

Kwin fell silent and looked down at her red boots.

'There was another reason why *your* father wanted me to keep quiet about *my* father,' I told her. 'If Hob knew that, he would be much more likely to visit the Wheel and seek me out. He wanted to try and keep me safe.'

'Things have changed, and that's *exactly* what we want now!' cried Ada. 'Let us tell the city who your father was, and word will get back to Hob. That will unsettle him further. For me the biggest danger is that Hob won't visit Arena 13 until next season. I just can't wait that long.'

Neither could I! So I still withheld the fact that Hob had visited me in the Commonality and already knew that I was the son of Math. If Tyron found out about that, he might be even more reluctant to allow me to fight this year. Despite our current preparations I didn't think he was totally convinced. He could call a halt at any time and delay my entrance into the Lists.

I began my first practice session with Thrym under Ada's guidance, fighting to the rear, as I would do in my bout with Hob.

It went well. I began to develop Ulum further, and Thrym was quick to learn and respond – far more adept at it than I was. Additionally, Ada showed how I might allow my lac to take the initiative and guide me – a thing unheard of in Arena 13.

There would be times when Thrym might see the opportunity to attack before I did. Then I would be in the same position as Kwin when our ankles were tied together fighting the tassel champion on the heights above Gindeen. I would need to respond rapidly and follow close at his heels, or be left unprotected and at the mercy of enemy lacs, forcing him to take risks as he fell back to protect me. So we developed elements of Ulum that Thrym would initiate; his warning to me.

Of these, the most important was the sudden, fully committed surprise attack.

A MIGHTY EMPIRE

Asscka are the highest classification of djinn.

These are true shape-shifters.

They can number up to 10,000 selves, and scores of
    shateks.

We must know our enemies.

Amabramsum: the Genthai Book of Wisdom

Tyron had mixed success in his mission to recruit allies.

Ontarro didn't feel he could offer help. Although sympathetic to what was to be attempted, he was afraid for his family. However, both Wode and Brid offered their full support and called for volunteers from their respective stables.

I had already met Wode. Tyron told me that he and members of his stable of combatants would provide back-up in case the first part of our plan failed. But it was Brid who would provide support in our attempt to seize Hob's body. He was a stranger to me, although I'd often watched his combatants win in the arena.

Brid visited us after dark, and we gathered in the study – which Ada now referred to as our war room. Tyron, Ada, Kwin, Deinon and I were there to meet him. Tyron had already told us a little about Brid: he'd fought from both the mag and the min positions and was adept at both. As an artificer, his stable was now, like Wode's, composed exclusively of mag combatants.

He was small and wiry, greying at the temples, his bushy eyebrows meeting above a hawkish nose. His face was almost without expression, but his eyes flicked from side to side like live things, independently sentient, and when he spoke, his words tumbled out one upon the other in their eagerness to be free of his thin lips.

'How's the training going?' he asked, addressing Ada as we took our seats. 'Are you confident that your lac can defeat what Hob brings?'

'Yes, we will win,' she said.

'But the boy's still a novice,' Brid protested. 'Wouldn't it be better to select someone with more experience – a combatant already high in the rankings? I know one we can trust—'

'Leif may be raw, but he is faster than anyone who presently fights in Arena 13,' Tyron interrupted. 'And he is the son of Mathias.'

Tyron knew that I had told Kwin, Deinon and Ada about my father. At first he had been angry, but Ada had persuaded him that the news should be filtered out into the city – though this had not yet been done.

Brid's jaw dropped open. 'You mean *the* Mathias? You mean *Math*?'

'The first time he fights and wins, watch him bow! Then you'll know.'

'Yes,' said Brid, staring at me hard. 'In spite of those tattoos, I can see the likeness in your face. I'll tell you something, Leif. I fought your father in the arena and I won. But that was in the early days – his first year. We fought exactly eleven times after that, and he defeated me each time. Still, I can say that I once defeated Math. It's my proudest boast! If you're half as talented as he was, Hob is as good as dead.'

'He'll be good enough to do the job,' Tyron said quietly. 'But how are we going to deal with the consequences of his victory?'

'We'll gather our forces in the Commonality.'

'What if Cyro finds out? He's likely to object,' Tyron pointed out.

'Cyro can be bought.'

'I don't trust him,' Kwin objected. 'He just serves his own interests.'

'Yes, and his chief interest is making money. Place enough gold in his fat hands and he'll turn a blind eye,' Brid insisted. 'Cyro won't cause any problems. Once the fight is underway, we should move our men into the green room. Nobody will think to go in there. It'll be empty. The other combatants will all have gone up to the gallery to watch. That's where we'll take Hob's body afterwards so that you can work on it,' Brid said, glancing at Ada.

'There is one more thing to concern us,' Ada said. 'That self of Hob will be dead, but as I begin my wurde-probes, it may become violent. It will need to be restrained.'

'We'll find a way,' Brid said, raising his eyebrows at that.

It was indeed strange to imagine a dead creature moving. But this was but one self of a djinni, and the gorestad, its high mind, which controlled all its selves, would still be directing it. As Ada had said, there would be reserves of energy in the corpse.

'Now we have to think about timing,' continued Brid. 'After Hob is defeated we must get into the arena quickly. When he arrives, everyone will be trying to get out of the Wheel. It will be chaos. You know how the candles and torches flicker and go out when Hob comes?' Brid asked, looking at Tyron.

Tyron nodded.

'Well, each time Hob was slain by Math, the same thing happened.'

'Aye, I remember it well,' answered Tyron.

'So when the lights dim, it will mean that the bout is over. That should be our signal to come out of the green room and into the arena.'

Tyron nodded. 'Do you think Pyncheon will try to make a fight of it?'

'He'll resist, but hopefully there won't be any bloodshed. I think we should use minimum force – just clubs and staves. We don't want to kill anyone. After Hob is destroyed, we want Arena 13 to go on as before. Let's hope there are no further consequences – I mean, from those beyond the Barrier.'

'From what I've learned so far, I think that's unlikely,' Ada said. 'Hob appears to be a rogue djinni – one that has cut himself off from others of his kind.'

'I hope you're right,' Brid said. 'We'd be foolish to attract their wrath.'

'But one day, might it not be possible to do something?' Tyron asked, looking at Ada. 'I mean, using the knowledge and skill that you have. Do you remember what I suggested? Couldn't we raise our own army of sentient lacs and fight back against those who hold us prisoners within the Barrier?'

'That might be possible in the future,' Ada replied, 'but

who knows what deadly strength lies beyond that Barrier? In this little domain called Midgard we've no way of knowing how insignificant and vulnerable we are. In ancient times, a race called the Romans ruled almost all the known world. They invaded a small island called Britain, intending to add it to their empire.

'But there was a rebellion led by a fierce queen called Boudicca. Though she defeated the Romans in battle, the struggle continued, and eventually she was slain. But imagine this. What if she *had* driven the Romans out of her little island and had then decided to build a fleet of boats and pursue them, thinking to sack Rome in revenge for what they had done?' Ada paused and smiled at each of us in turn.

'She would have found the task impossible,' Deinon said. 'She would be greatly underestimating the military might that she faced.'

'Yes, she would have found a mighty empire stretching thousands of miles, with great armies called legions that would have driven her small force back into the sea. I believe this is similar to the position we are in. We need to build our strength slowly and cautiously, in a way that does not attract attention.'

I was filled with curiosity about the land beyond the Barrier. 'What will the djinn there be like?' I asked. 'Are they roughly human in appearance, like Hob or the rasire we saw at the Sea Gate?'

'In truth I have no idea how they might have developed since the Empire fell,' Ada replied. 'I can only speak of what I remember – the djinn from my own time. The vast majority were not like humans. For example, there were some called catara, commonly known as sea-djinn. They had many subcategories, like crustacea, with hard shells and many legs and arms, which lived underwater, close to the shore. Imagine hundreds of such creatures emerging from the Sea Gate and moving down the canal to attack this city!

'There are more types of djinn than you can imagine; some were exotic indeed! There were hybrid djinn with ten selves called *decidons*, containing elements of both animal and vegetable, though from a distance you might just think they were unusual-looking trees. They communicated by wind-blown pollen. Their purpose was to be spies and sentinels, but they could be deadly, creating both poisons and antidotes. I dread to think how far the djinn might have evolved by now. But this is not natural evolution. The higher categories of djinn can *decide* the way they change from generation to generation.

'Like Hob,' Ada continued, 'many djinn are shape-shifters. They could enter Gindeen in human guise and spy out our weaknesses in order to devise the most effective method of attacking us.'

'They might walk amongst us even now!' suggested Kwin.

'Indeed they might,' Tyron said. 'No doubt the Protector's palace has one or two to keep an eye on us as well as him. There could be djinn that we don't know about inside that palace – spies from beyond the Barrier.'

I kept silent, but I remembered what Konnit had said – that they planned to remove the Protector and attack our enemies beyond the Barrier. The djinn might not react if Hob were removed, but it would be folly to attack the Protector. In view of what Ada had just said, it might call down upon us a terrible retribution.

HOLDING HANDS

Love never fails.
But where there are prophecies, they will cease.
The Compendium of Ancient Tales and Ballads

The week before I fought my first contest in the Lists, Tyron summoned Palm to the house for some final practice bouts.

Ada, Deinon, Kwin and Brid were present, the latter eager to see me and Thrym in action. Walking onto the training floor, Palm kept glancing at them nervously. He clearly didn't like this unexpected audience.

When Thrym and I faced his tri-glad, I noticed the layer of sweat on his brow. His face was even paler than his hair. Palm was terrified of being cut again.

'Full Trig rules but one!' commanded Tyron, putting him out of his misery. 'We'll dispense with the ritual cut for the loser.'

Palm rolled his eyes in relief, and Tyron pressed the lever on his timer. We attacked immediately, and pressed Palm and his tri-glad backwards. For a moment they rallied and held their ground. But then Thrym was amongst our opponents, his blades flashing in the torchlight, calling endoff on all three of his lac adversaries.

Everyone was grinning, except for the dismayed Palm, and Tyron, who kept a poker face.

Palm lost all three bouts; each defeat took less than a minute. He left the training floor with more scratches on the armour of his lacs and an even bigger dent to his pride.

Once Palm had left, there was backslapping all around. Brid was clearly impressed.

Only Tyron seemed somewhat subdued. 'That was hardly a workout,' he said. 'You need something more challenging. It's time for you to fight in Arena 13. This time the contest will be in public. You'll be on the Lists.'

'What if Hob arrives before Leif is ready?' Kwin asked, frowning with concern.

'It's a risk we'll have to take – Leif needs full combat practice, this time with a full gallery. He needs to adjust to the arena and feel comfortable.'

Ada gave Kwin a reassuring smile. 'Even if Hob does arrive, Thrym and Leif are ready. They'll win.'

The thought of fighting in Arena 13 excited me. It had been my dream, and now it was coming true. Soon I would get my chance to fight Hob. The moment of my revenge was approaching.

So it was that, two weeks later, I stepped into Arena 13 to face a man with white hair and a short beard, his bare arms crisscrossed with scars, some old and some new.

It was Epson, that veteran of Arena 13, the winner of the first contest I'd ever watched. Then he had fought behind a single lac and defeated a young man called Skule. Epson fought from both positions; tonight he had brought a tri-glad into the arena.

I was nervous. It was partly because it was my first contest in the Lists and a capacity crowd was watching from the gallery. But mostly it was because Tyron thought that Hob might come to the Wheel the very first time I fought. I kept glancing up at the torches in the huge thirteen-branched candelabrum, expecting them to flicker and go out to signal Hob's arrival. It could still happen, even though the evening's bouts were underway.

But I had to concentrate on what was happening now. I wanted to win, but I knew that Epson would be difficult to beat.

It took a while to gain the upper hand because Epson was very cautious and directed his lacs with great skill. But I danced effortlessly behind Thrym, and the lac responded quickly to each direction I gave him. We had agreed that tonight Thrym would not take the initiative and use Ulum to signal his intent to me. We would keep that surprise for when I fought Hob.

It proved to be exactly the workout I needed. I had to be put under pressure and taken beyond five minutes. The gong sounded the end of the first stage, and I had to fight to the fore of Thrym. This was the practice I needed more than anything. When I fought Hob, the bout would almost certainly extend into this more dangerous stage.

Now I was almost toe to toe with Epson. I was the target of his blades, just as much as my lac. He would cut me if he could.

I was reassured by the sight of Thrym's blades. His long reach meant that although I was in front of him, the tips of his blades were alongside my own.

Eventually he proved more than a match for the opposition. The first of Epson's lacs went down during the seventh minute of the bout, and endoff was quickly called on the other two.

I bowed to my defeated opponent, and he bowed back as the gallery above erupted in cheers and applause. Then Epson accepted the ritual cut without flinching.

We left the arena together, the appreciation from the gallery still loud. I even heard a couple of girls shout my name. Palm would be watching for sure, and he wouldn't like that!

Once we'd passed through the min door, Epson rested his arm across my shoulder. Away from the scrutiny of the gallery, his mouth twitched in pain from the cut. But then he gave me a smile.

'That will be my last contest, Leif,' he told me. 'It's becoming too much for my old bones, so I intend to set myself up as an artificer and train others. But it was an honour to be defeated by you. I never got to face your father in the arena – when he fought, I was still a novice with a lot to learn – but I think it's fitting that my final contest should be against his son. I wish you every success!'

'Thanks for those kind words,' I told him. 'I'd like to ask you something. I was told that my father worked for the Trader and even crossed the Barrier with him. Did you ever meet him then, in those later years? Did he ever tell you anything about that?'

Epson nodded. 'I saw him a couple of times at the Sea Gate. I remember thinking there was sadness in his eyes. He walked with a limp so that might have been its cause. He was friendly but didn't say much and I didn't feel able to question him about his experiences. You don't ask the Trader questions about crossing the Barrier and what is beyond it and I felt the same applied to your father. But it's a strange thing. Something that nobody knows the answer to. How is it possible to cross the Barrier and keep your sanity? The Trader and your father managed to do it.'

'He seemed happy enough when I was young,' I told Epson. 'But there were times when he became silent and would stare into space as if pondering something that he didn't want to talk about. When he did that my mother would sit close to him and put her arms around him. Then she'd whisper into his ears until he began to smile again.'

Epson laughed. 'That's what the love of a good woman can do, Leif!'

I went up to the gallery to watch the remaining contests. As I took my seat, Tyron patted me on the back. Turning to receive the congratulations of Ada, Deinon and Kwin, I noticed that people were staring at me.

I knew that it wasn't just because of my victory over Epson. Tyron had been slowly leaking the information that I was the son of Math. By now, everybody would know.

Later we walked back through the city streets. Kwin was talking to Ada, Deinon and her father. I was dawdling a few paces behind, playing over and over in my mind the steps that had brought us victory.

Suddenly Kwin dropped back to fall into step beside me. 'You were good tonight, Leif,' she said with a smile.

'Thanks,' I said. 'I was really nervous. Did it show?'

'Not at all,' she replied, shaking her head.

We'd nearly reached Tyron's house when she put her hand on my arm and brought me to a halt. 'It's a pity about the door,' she said softly.

'Which door?' I wondered what she meant. I was slow on the uptake, but suddenly I remembered. 'You mean the door between your room and ours.'

'What other door *would* I mean!' Kwin said with a laugh that caused her father to glance back at us suspiciously. 'I miss our late-night walks. Let's do it again. We can manage without the door. Meet me in the yard tomorrow night. Let's make it half an hour after supper.'

'I'll look forward to it – as long as there's no stick-fighting!' I joked.

Kwin was waiting for me in the yard, as we'd agreed. She wore a tight purple dress with small black leather buttons down the front. It had long sleeves that came down almost to the end of her thumbs. With a shock, I realized that it was the dress she'd worn when we'd first visited the Wheel together. She looked good in it. Without doubt she was the best-looking girl in the whole of Midgard.

Her hair wasn't pinned back. She wore it as she had that night – loose, the left side far shorter. Her scar gleamed in the light from the three-quarter moon. But I noticed that she hadn't painted her lips.

'Are we going to the Wheel?' I asked with a smile.

'Where else would we go?' Then, without another word, she set off through the city streets at a furious pace.

We entered the Wheel and headed straight down the long corridor I remembered from our previous visit. Kwin led the way past the first lounge – the one where women were not allowed – without even a glance towards it.

Soon we were in the second lounge where Kwin had bought and drunk two glasses of red wine; the lounge where I had proved so disappointing.

I remembered what she'd said: *I expected someone who'd be fun. I like boys who take risks. Boys who keep to the rules are boring!*

The bar was just as I remembered it – no windows, low lights, with a low roof like that of a cellar. But this time it was quiet and nobody was dancing. There were no drums, nobody jumping off tables, just a few couples sitting together, some holding hands.

'I'll get the drinks,' Kwin said, setting off towards the bar before I could object.

To my surprise, she came back carrying two glasses of iced water.

'You're not drinking wine tonight?' I asked.

'I need to keep fit. I'm in training!' she said with a grin.

'Training for what?'

'Arena 13, of course.' She took a sip from her glass.

I didn't reply. If I reminded her that females weren't allowed to fight there, she would only get angry. So I held my tongue and sipped my own water. It was cold and delicious.

'It will happen, you know,' she said, meeting my eyes. 'Next year I *will* be fighting there.'

I smiled at her. 'I really wish you could, Kwin. I know that's what you want most of all.'

'Most of all? You'd be surprised at what I want most of all. But Ada has had an idea to get me fighting in the Trig. We've worked out a plan. You see, when we destroy Hob, things will change. The old order will break down and the Wheel Directorate will be forced to listen to Ada. Then—' Kwin suddenly broke off and shook her head. 'I can see my words are falling on deaf ears.'

'No, Kwin, I am listening. What's your plan?'

'You'll just have to wait and see. Women are about to get a voice in this city.'

We lapsed into silence. I'd made Kwin angry, but it wasn't my fault. She was just banging her head against the wall. Surely she would never achieve her dream. It was so unfair, I thought. She was as good as I was. She could dance behind Thrym just as well.

I tried to change the subject. 'You're not wearing your lip-paint tonight,' I said. 'I've never seen you out after dark without it.'

'I didn't want to risk getting it on your collar,' she said. 'If my father saw it, he wouldn't like it. It's best to keep things just between us two.'

Then Kwin leaned forward, and very softly pressed her lips against mine.

We walked back through the streets holding hands. The feelings that I'd tried to keep deep inside me had been released. It felt unreal, like a dream. I was floating on air – but there was something I had to ask.

'What about Jon? Are you sure it's over?' I asked Kwin. I remembered how they'd walked close together when we protested in the Commonality.

'Why do you have to spoil things?' she said angrily.

'I'm not trying to spoil things. I'm just asking.'

'Look, if I was still with Jon, I wouldn't be holding your hand now. I told you at the end of last season that Jon and I were no longer seeing each other. We worked together to stage the protest, that's all. I'm with you now, Leif. That's if you want me.'

'I want you,' I replied.

When we entered the house through the side door, we got a shock. Tyron was standing there, staring at us with folded arms and hard, unfriendly eyes.

'Get to bed, Kwin,' he said. 'I'll talk to you in the morning.'

At first I thought she was about to refuse, but then she nodded and, without a backward glance, went up the stairs.

'I know my daughter's soft on you – that foolish gleam in her eye is unmistakable. But don't flatter yourself that it's your handsome face,' Tyron told me. 'It's because you fought her with sticks and beat her. It's because you treat her as an equal, not like any girl with a pretty face. But mark my words – you'll only ever be good friends!'

I felt my face heat up with anger. The words slipped out before I could bite them back. 'So why am I not good enough for your daughter? Is it because I'm half Genthai?'

Tyron glared at me, but answered quietly, an indication of his inner fury. 'It's nothing to do with you being of Genthai stock. I've not a racist bone in my body – you're making a big mistake to even think of such a thing. You're not husband material because you are almost certain to die young. You've got a death-wish as far as Hob is concerned. You'd happily die in the arena in order to get your revenge.'

'I've no death-wish,' I told him. 'Don't you think I can beat

Hob? Don't you believe that we're going to win? What was all this training and preparation for? Have we just been wasting our time?'

'Aye, I think you do have a fair chance of victory, fighting behind that lac, but I'm not sure about what happens next. A lot of things could go wrong. I've gone along with Ada's plan, but I'm starting to think that my way was better after all. I shouldn't have let that woman manipulate me. She's too clever by half. I'm not convinced that we will manage to destroy Hob completely; if we don't, you'll have to fight him again and again. You'll be following in your father's footsteps. Look, Leif, I have one widowed daughter who'll mourn for the rest of her life. She has a child to bring up without the help of a father. I don't want Kwin to suffer the same fate. Now do you understand?'

The anger left me and I lowered my head, unable to meet his eyes. He was just being a good father. Though it didn't change my relationship with Kwin.

'I understand how you feel,' I answered.

'Do you now?' said Tyron, shaking his head. 'Get to bed, boy. One day I hope you'll live to have daughters of your own. *Then* you'll know how I feel.'

I went upstairs, thinking over what he'd said. I remembered the threat Hob had made when he asked *Whom do you love?* I was probably putting Kwin in danger. Tyron didn't know about my second encounter with Hob. He had a right to be worried. Things were even worse than he thought.

Hob had to be destroyed as soon as possible.

A SPECIAL WAVE

Never for a moment did I think of defeat. I had
Gunter, I had Nym, and my feet were swifter
than thought.

The Testimony of Math

My next bout was against a young fighter called Korst who'd
just completed his three years' training and was tipped to do
well as a fully-fledged combatant in Arena 13. Tyron thought
he would give me a real test.

He gave me more than that: he gave me a scare.

Because of my partnership with Thrym, I suppose I'd
become overconfident. The contest had moved into the second
stage and we were both fighting in front of our lacs. I was
aware of Thrym's blades fending off the enemy as we pressed
the tri-glad hard. I was attacking Korst, when I slightly
over-extended myself. I lost my balance and found myself on
all fours. I looked up to see blades arcing downwards.

My blood ran cold. I remembered how Hob had sliced
downwards to sever the head from Tallus's body – surely this
would now be my fate.

But Thrym stood astride me and drove them back, giving

me time to clamber to my feet. After that I was more cautious. I won, but it took me almost twenty minutes. It was a proper workout.

Exactly one week later I was scheduled to fight again. Only light training was scheduled that day, so at noon I went for a run with Deinon, taking the route that Kern had usually followed; it made several circuits of the Wheel, and then back up the hill to Tyron's house.

I noticed a lot of guards about. They were in patrols of six, strutting around the Wheel, giving me hostile glances as we passed. I suspected it might have been worse, but we were running in our training vests with the wolf logo front and back, which marked us out as part of Tyron's stable.

Then, near the main gate, I saw someone I recognized. It was Jon.

He waved us over. 'Congratulations on your win the other night, Leif,' he said with a grin. 'You looked really good. I was seriously impressed.'

I smiled back at him. It was easy to feel friendly towards him now that he wasn't with Kwin.

'Why are there so many of the Protector's Guard around?' Deinon asked, wiping the sweat off his forehead with the hem of his vest.

'Don't tell me you haven't heard what's happened . . .'

We both shook out heads.

'You spend too much time holed up in Tyron's house – you'd be better off with the rest of the lads based in the Wheel. You've not heard about the weird stuff in the Medie?'

'The Medie?' asked Deinon, screwing up his face in puzzlement. 'What's that?'

'It's a small river that flows out of the Genthai lands,' I informed him.

'Yes, and it meets the sea not far north of the Sea Gate,' Jon continued. 'Bodies were seen floating along it and out into the sea – hundreds of them. They say the river was the colour of blood. Dozens washed up on the mudflats of the estuary. Most of them are wolves – or pieces of wolf. But here's the really weird thing. Some had human bodies but the heads of wolves. Their throats had been cut and their noses slit to reveal the bone!'

'You're making that up, right?' laughed Deinon. 'That's crazy.'

'It's the truth,' Jon insisted, and he wasn't smiling. 'The Protector's Guard have been there. They've collected the bodies and burned them in case they spread disease. Now they're on high alert. They've called up the reservists.'

'What? Do they think the killers are coming here?' asked Deinon incredulously.

'Nobody knows, but they aren't taking any chances.'

But *I* knew, and my blood ran cold. It was the Genthai. They'd hunted down the werewights, killed them and then thrown their bodies into the river. The time of waiting was over. Now they were truly on a war footing. But why had they slit the noses of the human-shaped selves of the werewights? Was it just some sort of savage revenge for years of being culled by those creatures? Or did it serve some other purpose?

Did the Protector and his Guard know that the Genthai

had done this? I wondered. Did they fear an attack was imminent? Was that why they were out in force?

As we ran back up the hill, Deinon suddenly put his arm on my shoulder to bring me to a halt. 'Remember what Tallus told us he'd found in the forest?'

I nodded. 'The skeleton of a human with a wolf's skull attached . . .'

'So it wasn't a clever hoax. That skeleton was for real! I wonder who slaughtered these others and threw them into the river?'

I said nothing. I'd promised Konnit to keep their secrets. As we made our way back to Tyron's house, my head was spinning with the news. I was probably the only person in the city who knew what those bodies meant. And now the Genthai sought not just to remove the Protector. They wanted to attack the djinn beyond the Barrier.

My bout was scheduled for late in the evening, so I had joined Kwin, Tyron, Deinon and Ada in the gallery, waiting for the first contest to begin.

Suddenly every torch and candle flickered and went out and the air grew icy. Screams filled the darkness.

A second later the light returned – to reveal the usual panic of people fleeing up the aisles.

This was what I had been waiting for: Hob had arrived at the Wheel to issue a challenge.

'Relax and let them get clear,' Tyron said as the light momentarily failed again.

Kwin reached across to squeeze my hand, and I saw Tyron glance down, though he said nothing.

Brid, Wode and their men would already be in position down in the Commonality, ready to ascend into the Wheel. This precaution had been taken each time I was scheduled to fight.

I glanced up at the exits. The last of the fleeing spectators were disappearing from view. About a hundred remained in the gallery: aficionados, combatants who weren't due to fight tonight, along with their families. And, of course, there were the touts, no doubt eager to sell their red tickets.

As I got to my feet, Tyron patted me on the back. 'Our thoughts are with you, boy. Just keep a cool head and you'll win all right.'

Then Ada leaned across and gave me a hug. 'Stamp, then spit!' she said with a brief smile. Then her face hardened. 'Then kill him for Tal and Kern. Kill him for your father and mother – for all the poor souls he's murdered and tortured. You can do it, Leif. I've cost one poor man his life. I haven't made that mistake a second time. Thrym will do the job, and you are the best partner he could have!'

I wanted to give Kwin a hug too, but didn't like to in front of her father. Her eyes were brimming with tears, so I left quickly, choking with emotion.

Down in the green room, I waited with the other eighteen Arena 13 min contestants due to fight that night. The air was filled with tension. Nobody spoke. My mouth was dry.

I'd raised the question of what to do if I wasn't selected. Surely I should simply demand the right of combat with Hob, I'd said. Nobody would stand in my way. They knew that I was Math's son and would understand that I needed to avenge his death. Besides, surely nobody else would want to fight Hob.

Tyron hadn't thought it worth discussing, feeling sure that I'd be the one chosen.

Pyncheon lifted the lottery orb from the table and offered it to us.

We selected our straws, one by one, then compared them.

Mine was the shortest.

I was excited and tense at the prospect of the fight ahead, and I strode into the arena brandishing the two Trig knives, holding them high above my head. Then, quite deliberately, following Ada's advice, I stepped forward and took up a position in front of Thrym.

I heard the collective gasp from the gallery above. I glanced up, hardly able to believe my eyes. Almost all the seats were taken. Had people returned because I was fighting Hob? Because I was the son of Math, fighting with a lac patterned by Ada?

Whatever the reason, there was now a far larger audience than when Hob had fought Kern or Tallus.

Thrym and I crouched, as one, and stamped our feet – left, then right, left, then right – pounding out a challenge on the wooden boards of the combat floor.

Thud! Boom! Thud! Boom!

The faces looked down from the gallery in astonishment. We repeated the performance, booming our challenge out across the arena again and again.

This wasn't just bravado. The moment Hob entered Arena 13, this is what he would see and hear. It was designed to send him a message: that I was not afraid; that I believed I could win. And in taking up a position in front of, rather than behind, my lac, I was reminding him of the last time he'd been defeated in the arena.

We thundered out our challenge for the third time just as Hob and his tri-glad entered through the double mag doors. He was dressed in short-sleeved leather jerkin and shorts – the regulation costume for a human combatant – but wore the bronze helmet with the slit for his eyes. Behind him, his lacs, in their black armour, radiated malice.

I felt a surge of anger; for the deaths of my father and mother; for the deaths of poor Kern, Tallus and all the other souls that Hob had snuffed out.

I immediately did what I had been practising daily. I ran towards him in a fury and spat accurately past the tri-glad that closed around him at my approach. To my satisfaction, my spittle went straight through the slit of his helmet.

Hob's lacs moved towards me, brandishing their blades, but Thrym used his left forearm to send the leader crashing back against its companions in disarray.

The gallery was in uproar. Pyncheon and his marshals quickly entered the arena to intervene, ignoring Hob and his lacs and gesturing angrily that I should retreat to the far corner.

I danced backwards and took up the normal position, behind my lac. Satisfied, the marshals withdrew, and moments later the doors closed.

Now we were alone.

I attacked immediately, following Ada's advice to take the initiative and carry the fight to the enemy. So swift and perfect was our first attack that victory was almost ours. We were amongst Hob's tri-glad before it had even moved.

Thrym darted forward to aim for the throat-slit of the central lac. His right blade missed by only an inch, rasping against the armour. It was a very satisfying sound.

All combatants knew that sound. It made the tri-glad retreat slightly, allowing Thrym to press home his advantage. Hob moved back towards the scarred wood of the arena wall, and we went after him.

As Thrym's blades swept down and the tri-glad fell back, Hob stumbled ... and it was only that chance stumble that saved him. My lac had been close, so very close, to cutting his throat.

That stumble, that evidence of mortality and fallibility, was a sure promise of victory. The djinni could be beaten.

I could hear the howls and groans of the spectators, the rasping of my own breath and the rapid pounding of my heart, feel the blood surging through my body. It seemed to me as if we'd only been fighting for a minute, but suddenly the gong sounded.

The five-minute rule applied, so we took up new positions in front of the lacs. Now I was face to face with Hob. I was close to his blades, but I didn't fear him. Give me half a chance and I'd kill him. My back was close to Thrym's chest, and his blades were next to my own. We began to fight and move as one. Again and again I used Ulum to signal moves, and each time we executed them flawlessly.

A bigger pattern began to emerge. We would feint, then attack from a different direction. But the quickness and variety of our real and sham moves kept Hob's tri-glad on the defensive. We dominated through the sheer multitude and complexity of our attack patterns; patterns that rumbled like distant thunder without betraying the nature of the deadly bolt we might hurl forth at any moment.

There were just the two of us, but Hob was now also facing the myriad daggers of Ada's mind; daggers whose points shifted like the flicker of lightning, always seeking out weakness. And each attack, when it finally came, was swift and direct. Reaching out over my shoulders, Thrym's blades extended beyond the tri-glad, threatening Hob's throat.

Occasionally, when we were forced to retreat, Thrym was very unorthodox in his movements. He swung left and right, using his feet and hands like hammers, bludgeoning heads and bodies.

But then Hob launched a series of rapid attacks, forcing us back into full defensive mode. The struggle was now evenly balanced and my hopes of a swift victory began to fade. My confidence ebbed too. How long would this go on?

I wondered if this was how Kern had felt, suddenly realizing that he could not win.

Thrym might not tire, but I certainly would. No matter how fit I was, I knew that eventually my reactions would slow.

And as that poisonous thought slid into my mind, a great weariness seemed to settle over my body so that my limbs felt heavy. All at once I saw in my mind's eye the distraught face of my father as we came upon my mother lying dead, drained of blood. I heard again his cry of anguish and saw him beating his face with his fists.

Suddenly I felt fierce heat upon my bare forearm – hot wax dripping from the torches above the arena: a routine hazard and a nuisance only to those who lacked the single-minded concentration necessary for success.

Focus! I told myself. *Give it everything you've got.*

There was a sound in my ears like a click, and then a great silence came down and I thought no more of defeat. I was filled with new energy. Within that silence, Thrym and I fought as one; fought to the limits of what could be done. I used Ulum without conscious thought. My feet knew what message to send, and Thrym instantly obeyed. We attacked again and again, driving Hob and his tri-glad back.

My face was just inches from Hob's helmet when, through the slit, I saw his eyes; they locked upon mine. I felt a wave of weakness and my legs buckled; once more he was holding me in thrall, and I was helpless.

I felt a sense of outrage. When he hunted his prey outside the arena, the djinni used these powers to subdue his victims. But in Arena 13 I'd assumed he always kept to the rules.

As I staggered under the power of that terrible gaze, the djinni aimed his blades at my face.

Reaching over my shoulder, Thrym blocked the right one, but the other sliced into the side of my head. I felt a hot searing pain, and then wetness running down my neck.

The spectators gave a deep groan, and I knew that something bad had happened.

Thrym and I retreated, my blood dripping onto the floor of the arena. But then I saw that my wound was even worse than I'd thought. An ugly blood-splattered thing lay on the boards by my feet. With shock and horror, I realized that it was my right ear.

I staggered backwards, the arena spinning about me, nausea coming in waves, thoughts of defeat filling my mind.

We retreated further, and for a moment there was a pause. Now I could feel the searing pain of the kransin in the wound, and fought to hold onto the contents of my stomach. I was grateful that I had already experienced that pain when practising against Palm. I was used to it. One cut was nothing. But my ear . . . it had been severed from my head!

I forced myself to remain calm. I knew that at any second Hob would hurl his lacs forward to overwhelm us. However, now we renewed our own attack. Again and again we surged against his tri-glad, like waves against a great granite cliff. Attack and retreat, attack and retreat; wave after wave after wave, seemingly without end.

Then, suddenly, my blade was slicing through Hob's leather jerkin, into his chest, and I was gratified to see his blood. There was a great cheer from above, and the spectators began to drum on the floor with their boots; it sounded like some kind of manic Ulum, urging me to even greater efforts.

The wound I'd inflicted was not life-threatening; I needed to cut Hob deeper than that. But still his tri-glad would not yield.

Once again, as the long struggle approached the hour mark, my weariness increased. The lacs would not tire. Perhaps Hob too could continue indefinitely. But I recognized the frailty of my flesh and bone. And I was still losing blood. I was beginning to slow down again. My reflexes seemed less sharp, my steps less sure; even my concentration was going. My breath was hot in my throat and my body ached with exhaustion.

I summoned my will for one final attempt. It had to be now. I had to make a supreme final effort while my strength still remained. But before I could use Ulum to signal my intent, Thrym's feet were thundering out a message on the boards; drumming out instructions that drew a roar of excitement from the crowd.

My lac had taken the initiative. This was what we'd held in reserve. He had signalled an all-out attack. It was all or nothing!

We went in hard and fast, and I avoided Hob's eyes lest he cheat once more. As one, Thrym and I surged across the arena like a wave towards a distant shore where our enemies waited like a rock that has forever stood firm against the elements. But there is a special wave that strikes a cliff at the exact moment when its time has come.

Together, we were that wave, and the tri-glad of Hob broke and crumbled before us. For the second time Hob was brought to his knees and, using his left hand, Thrym buried his blade deep within the throat-socket of an enemy lac.

And in that moment victory was within our grasp. We attacked once more. Over my shoulders, to right and left, Thrym's blades struck, and the two remaining lacs hit the boards simultaneously; at last Hob faced us alone. He waited silently, his blades slightly raised.

It was over. Didn't he know that he had lost? Was he going to try and defend himself?

In a fury, I rushed forward and struck his blades aside. They both fell to the boards. I almost killed him then. There was a red mist before my eyes.

But reason prevailed. We wanted him dead, but I knew that his head must not be severed from his body. The cut had to be exactly right. We needed to destroy Hob totally – not just this one self.

My whole body was shaking, but I stood aside and let Thrym past. He advanced with his blades raised, ready to strike. As the spectators stamped their feet and cheered, exultation filled me. This was the moment of victory for which we had worked so hard.

This was the first step of my revenge, which would soon be total.

Thrym's cut was precise. Hob fell backwards, blood spraying from his throat. He crashed onto the boards and lay on his back, twitching and shuddering for a few moments. Then he was still.

He was dead, but his body was still in one piece.

Now it was Ada's turn.

CURSED ARE THE TWICE-BORN

Twice-born, twice the pain.
Thrice-born is to be cursed again.
Amabramsum: the Genthai Book of Wisdom

Hob's blood was now pooling thickly around his body; it was a far brighter shade of red than human blood; far brighter than that of any creature. Even as it soaked into the wooden boards of the arena, it remained that bright crimson.

Both mag and min doors rumbled back to allow Pyncheon and four of his assistants into the arena. They came to a sudden halt, their eyes wide with shock as they stared down at Hob's blood, which was still spreading out around the body.

An ashen-faced Pyncheon mumbled a command, and two marshals nervously approached the thick red pool, each carrying a bucket of sawdust. They kept their distance and began to throw down handfuls to soak up the blood.

Pyncheon looked bewildered. He clearly hadn't thought I would win, and had not yet composed himself. But I knew that he wasn't the Chief Marshal for nothing; any moment now he could seal the arena. I glanced up and saw that the gallery was already being cleared.

Suddenly I heard the sound of running feet, and a group of men brandishing clubs entered by the mag door. Brid was in the lead, and he ran straight towards Hob's body. Two of his men carried a stretcher, which they set down on the boards, each seizing a boot and dragging Hob's body onto it.

Pynchon took an uncertain step forward, his mouth opening and closing as the men lifted their load and began to head back towards the mag door. He stared at them in outrage, and made to cut them off. In response, Brid lifted his club to intervene, but it proved unnecessary.

The Chief Marshal stepped into the large pool of Hob's blood and slipped. He went down head first, arms flailing.

One of Brid's companions handed me a folded piece of cloth, gesturing to my wound. I took it and held it against the stump of my ear to staunch the blood. It was throbbing, and I was beginning to feel light-headed.

'Follow!' I commanded Thrym, and then we set off after Brid. I noticed that some of his men remained in the arena, clubs at the ready, to prevent Pyncheon and his marshals from following us.

Hob's body was carried into the green room and laid out on the large wooden table. Ada and Tyron were already waiting there, and as I entered with Thrym, I was beckoned forward to their side. Only two other men and Brid remained with us; the rest waited outside to guard the door.

But how long would it be before the tassels arrived? I wondered. Perhaps we wouldn't get the twenty minutes that Ada had said she required in order to destroy Hob. And they would arrive with spears and blades rather than clubs. There would be a great many of them. How many men did Wode have in reserve?

Hob's helmet was tugged away to reveal the big hairless head and predatory nose, the eyes sightless in death. Ada had stipulated that the body must be restrained and I expected to find chains there to bind the djinni to the table.

But Brid had a different plan. He lifted a hammer in his right hand; with his left he placed a long nail with a broad head against the flesh of Hob's upper arm. Three times he struck the nail, driving it through the flesh and cloth beneath, and deep into the wood. The second nail was driven through the other arm; the third and fourth through the legs.

Throughout this procedure, Hob's flesh didn't even twitch. The djinni seemed totally inert, and I wondered how Ada hoped to get any response. But she started immediately, uttering a torrent of wurdes.

We stood there in silence, watching her work. I'd witnessed Tyron adjusting the patterning of a lac, but Ada worked in a very different way, as she had with the shatek and then Thrym. Wurdes of Nym flew from her lips so that one was impossible to distinguish from another. Occasionally she paused briefly, as if in thought.

The blood was still flowing from the gash in Hob's neck, which gaped like a red mouth; it flowed across the table to drip onto the brown carpet and splatter over our shoes.

Within moments Ada's wurdes brought a visible effect. Hob's dead body gave a shudder. Then he rolled his eyes.

That torrent of wurdes continued, and the djinni's body began to jerk and convulse. It seemed to be trying to escape from the table, but the nails held it in place. Finally the body lay still. Hob's dead eyes stared up at the ceiling and a terrible groan burst from his lips, erupting from deep within his belly.

Ada paused and looked down at him. Then she took a deep breath.

'Is it done?' demanded Tyron.

'The first stage is completed,' she replied. 'I've subdued this self and bound it to my will, but the next step is much more difficult. I must reach beyond it, through the portal, and extinguish the gorestad, the high mind that controls all his selves. That gate is guarded by layers of code and encryption. I must penetrate it quickly or all will be lost.'

Ada began again, flinging wurde after wurde against the djinni, and the dead body began to twitch and groan once more.

All at once I heard a commotion outside, and suddenly the door was flung open. Brid's men were backing into the room, dropping their clubs to the floor.

Were the tassels here already? I wondered. Why were we surrendering without a fight?

But then I saw that men in the distinctive blue uniforms of the Protector's Guard were pushing their way in. There were sheathed blades at their hips, but their projectile weapons were pointing at us. Those spinning metal discs could blind, break bones, tear flesh and sometimes kill.

We all turned to face the threat. For a moment everything was still and silent, and then Ada carried on chanting, still working to destroy the djinni.

'Tell her to stop or we fire!' a voice barked out. An officer was pointing his weapon at Ada, his finger already squeezing the trigger.

Suddenly Thrym moved between me and the guard. '*Stay back!*' he rasped.

He was still defending me. I had not yet ordered him to stand down. I was suddenly filled with hope. He was fast, dangerous and fully armoured. Even his throat-slit was not vulnerable: a disc projectile was too large to penetrate the metal socket, and the guards lacked the skill and speed to use their blades and call endoff.

It was Tyron who shattered my hopes. 'Put Thrym to sleep, boy!' he shouted.

Everything within me rebelled at this. How could we surrender now, when we were so close to victory? I heard Ada, still hurling wurdes of Nym at Hob. 'No!' I cried.

'Please, Leif! Do as I say or there'll be a massacre here.'

I was still minded to refuse, but then I saw the desperation on Tyron's face, and something within me, something deeper than my conscious will, decided for me. It was as if I were a lac and he had called a wurde to compel me to obey.

'Sleep, Thrym!' I said softly, and the lac bowed his head and became still.

'Why?' I asked, turning towards Tyron in disappointment. 'We could have won!'

'There are too many of them,' he snapped, and then turned and pulled Ada away from the body of Hob. She struggled against him for a moment, but soon more guards burst into the room; I was seized and forced down onto my knees. I glanced round and saw the others being dealt with in the same way. Only the inert Thrym, head bowed, sightless eyes staring down, remained standing.

'Eyes down! Eyes down!' a guard shouted behind me, and I was cuffed hard on the back of the head.

I stared at the brown carpet, shaking with anger, still holding the cloth firmly against my throbbing ear.

How close had Ada been to destroying Hob? I should not have obeyed Tyron. We might still have won. I felt sick with disappointment and pain.

I heard others being taken out of the room. And then it was my turn. My arms were seized and I dropped the cloth I'd been holding. I was dragged through a series of doors and out into the open area before the Wheel.

Immediately I saw that Tyron had been right. There were far too many guards for us to fight. Squads were lined up outside; rank upon rank of them – three or four hundred armed men. How had they turned out so fast? Who had warned them?

I felt cold inside. It had to be Cyro. Brid should never have asked his permission to hide in the Commonality.

A line of wagons waited nearby, four horses harnessed to each. I was pushed up into the back of one and forced onto a seat. Four armed guards accompanied me, and we set off. Where was I being taken? The guards' barracks on the outskirts of Gindeen? I couldn't see out of the curtained windows. I wondered what would happen to me when I got there. Was it a crime to attempt to destroy a monster such as Hob?

The Protector! What a joke that was. He and his men should have put an end to Hob and *protected* the city.

We came to a halt and I was dragged from the wagon. Despite the dark, I could just make out a large grassy area.

Directly ahead was a large building. I suddenly recognized its stone walls, its portico with marble pillars. Tyron had told me that it was the only stone building in the city. It was the Protector's palace.

I was marched across the lawn towards the stone steps that led up to the entrance. More guards stood there, waiting for me. Then I was pushed up the steps, the men bunching about me so closely that they trod on my heels. I couldn't see Tyron or any of the others. Was I the only one being brought here? All around I saw only hard, hostile faces.

Inside, we crossed a large throne room, the soldiers' feet echoing as they marched over the marble flags. Then I was thrust through a door at the far end, down wooden steps that suddenly gave way to stone, and we entered another chamber.

Along the walls stood guards armed with both long blades and projectile weapons. Their eyes were hard, their fingers hovering over their triggers as if ready to fire.

Tyron, Wode and Brid were already seated at a long table covered with a purple cloth. But where was Ada? I wondered. The men were staring towards the figure at its head, who was seated in a chair larger and more ornate than the others. He was a solid and imposing man in his early fifties. Although his beard was white, his broad face was unlined and there was not an ounce of fat on his body. His expression was regal, and a faint smile softened the stern lips. He exuded the gravitas and wisdom of one fitted to rule over men.

I immediately knew that he was the Protector. He radiated authority and presence – it *had* to be him. He seemed almost too good to be true. Had he been trained for the role?

I was pushed down into the seat next to Tyron. Brid and Wode glanced across the table at me, their eyes flicking to my ruined ear; but Tyron was looking at the Protector.

'Do you *know* what you almost did?' The man's voice was very deep and it resonated around the room. I felt it through the soles of my boots.

There was a moment's silence and I was filled with anger. I was going to reply, but then Tyron spoke.

'We've just defeated Hob in the arena,' he said. 'We were within moments of destroying all his selves. If you hadn't interfered, we'd have rid this land of a monster and a tyrant who's preyed upon innocents for centuries.'

The Protector shook his head. 'You were within moments of calling down death upon all the people of this land. Here, within the confines of the Barrier,' he said, 'we, the remnants of a defeated and broken humanity, have lived in safety for more than half a millennium. This is a place reserved for us; a place where we are protected; a haven where we are tolerated and allowed to live out our little lives. But you came close to ending that. You almost broke the Covenant and ended the cycle of life here.'

'What covenant?' demanded Tyron.

'I speak of the Covenant between djinn and mankind. The djinn judged mankind and found us wanting. So they ended our pitiful empire and reaped billions of souls. However, a few humans were set down here within the Barrier and given a chance to live. At first they planned to sterilize us and end our race. But they were magnanimous in victory, and permitted us to breed. Still we live – though only on sufferance.'

'But how, in trying to end Hob's tyranny, have we broken

that Covenant?' asked Wode, his voice quavering. He suddenly looked older, his brow etched with lines, dark circles under his eyes.

'The answer should have occurred to you by now. I am human and have been put here to rule you. But I rule alongside another. That other is Hob. We are a dual authority. We are the eyes and ears of the djinn beyond the Barrier. Do you understand? I am your Protector, but Hob is potentially your Destroyer!'

'Hob is a rogue djinni. How can he have any authority?' Tyron asked angrily. 'How can he be fit to rule alongside you? What kind of ruler kills innocent women and terrorizes a city?'

The Protector smiled at him as if at a naïve child. 'Long ago, Hob rebelled against higher djinn authority, but rather than being executed for his crime, was imprisoned with us as a punishment. He was also given the task of sharing the rule of Midgard. The djinn are not like us; they have elevated themselves to the level of gods while we are merely human. You cannot judge them by our standards. A child might pull off an insect's wings in order to amuse itself. So it is with Hob. Who are we to say what he can or cannot do? Some of us must be sacrificed so that the majority may live.'

'That's madness!' Wode said.

'Yes. It is the madness of the gods,' said the Protector, his voice hardly more than a whisper.

Tyron shrugged. I couldn't see his eyes because he was still facing the Protector.

'What of us? What do you intend now?' he asked in a voice of resignation.

The Protector held his hands out, palms upwards, and answered. 'Providing you cooperate, I intend to return you to the routine of your lives. Trigladius combat will continue to be fought in Arena 13. To ensure our very survival, things must return to normal as soon as possible. The djinn must see that things are under control within the Barrier. Additionally you will apologize to the Chief Marshal for interfering in his duties. If there is to be a punishment for your transgression, it will not come from me; Hob will inflict it at a time of his choosing.'

'What of the others?'

'Those who acted under your orders are also free to return. They also must make a formal apology.'

'Is that also true of Ada?' Tyron asked.

'There is an ancient proverb – "Cursed are the twice-born". In this case it is very apt. You will not see that foolish, arrogant woman again, and the lac she created will be dismembered and ground into dust. It will be as if they never existed. Only in that way can the balance be restored. Is it agreed?'

Tears came to my eyes at the thought of Ada in the clutches of the Protector's Guard. Would they kill her? Her second life had been so very short.

Tyron stared at the Protector for a long time before giving a reply. For a moment I thought he would refuse. When it came, it was just a curt nod.

Then we were released into our misery.

I LOVE KWIN

It is easier to die than to live for ever,
So we must prepare for the worst.
Amabramdata: the Genthai Book of Prophecy

Back at Tyron's house, Kwin, Teena and Deinon were waiting to greet us. There were tears of joy at our safe return.

'I thought we'd never see you again!' Teena sobbed as Tyron embraced both his daughters.

A doctor was called and he attended to my ear, doing the best he could. He cleaned it, then smeared it with an antiseptic cream that also acted as a coagulant. In time, I knew, the pain would go, but I was disfigured. Again I thought of Kwin; it was one further thing that might make me less attractive to her.

After the doctor had gone, we sat down together at the large table in the dining room and Tyron gave an account of what had happened. He began with our arrest and ended with what the Protector had told us.

'Who would have thought that Hob ruled alongside him!' Deinon exclaimed. 'It's madness.'

Tyron nodded in agreement. 'Aye, and it explains a lot.

I thought the Protector weak for not dealing with Hob for his crimes. Never for a moment did I imagine that they ruled together. Hob rebelled against the other djinn and should have been executed. Instead they exiled him here, inflicting him on us!'

Kwin began to sob, and her tears dripped down onto the table. There was silence as Tyron waited for her to compose herself.

'Poor Ada!' she said at last. 'Poor, poor Ada! She didn't deserve that.'

My own throat tightened with grief for her.

'Aye, poor Ada,' echoed Tyron. 'She was born again into a new life and gave us hope for a while. Little did she know what a truly foul place Midgard is.'

'How can you bring yourself to apologize to Pyncheon?' Kwin asked. 'I'd rather spit in his face.'

'What choice is there? Leif will have to apologize too, along with all who were taken to the palace. So calm yourself, girl. This is no time to be hot-headed.'

The hour was late, but after Teena had gone to bed Tyron gestured upwards. 'I want a word with you two upstairs,' he said, nodding to Kwin and me. 'I've a family problem to sort out. But you get yourself to bed, Deinon. It's been a difficult day, so you can lie in tomorrow.'

My heart sank at this. No doubt he was going to warn me off Kwin. He didn't want us to be together.

Tyron led the way up to his study. Soon Kwin and I were seated in the leather chairs facing him. He had a large glass of red wine on the table before him; Kwin and I had water.

It was to me that he addressed his first words. 'Cast your mind back, boy. Do you remember what Hob said to you that night in his citadel after you drew your blades on him?' he demanded, staring at me hard.

I remembered it word for word, but my mouth was twisted in anger, and before I could reply, Tyron had spoken for me.

'Then let me remind you. He said "Whom do you love?" and you replied "Nobody". Then he said that one day you *would* learn to love, and then, piece by piece, he would cut away those you loved until only you remained. Not until *then* would he kill you. Not until then would he take your soul. Do you remember that? So now I ask you again, boy, the same question that Hob asked – whom do you love?' He sipped his red wine, awaiting my reply.

I knew where this was leading. I had no choice but to follow the route he'd chosen. So I replied carefully, 'I care for you. You've become almost a father to me. I care for your family – Teena, Kwin and your grandchild. I care for Deinon – he's become my friend.'

'I'll say it one more time – whom do you love?'

I saw that there was no way I could deny him the truth. 'I love Kwin,' I said softly.

Out of the corner of my eye I saw her staring at me. We'd held hands and kissed – that was all. She'd think me a fool to make such a declaration. Was she staring at the ugly scar where my ear used to be? I felt the heat flow into my face.

Then I saw Tyron's face turn white.

'Yes!' he roared, banging his fists down hard so that his glass overturned, spilling the red wine.

I watched it flow across the table and drip onto the floor.

It looked like a river of blood. I realized that there was nothing I could say to make him feel better. But then, suddenly, a hand was holding mine. I turned towards Kwin. She was smiling at me.

'And I love Leif!' she declared to her father.

Tyron nodded and sighed. He stared at me again, ignoring his daughter. 'Hob will be aware of your feelings for Kwin. He has spies and knows almost everything that goes on in this city. He will know that you fought together against the tassels. You will have been seen holding hands. So it's just a question of how he goes about things. He could defeat you in the arena, then keep your head as he kept poor Kern's. Then he could snatch Kwin and kill her in front of you, thus fulfilling his threat. Or he could snatch her tonight. He could kill and torture us all tonight. Oh, how I wish we'd been cautious and followed my plan rather than Ada's!'

I remembered my conversation with Hob in the Commonality. Could Tyron be right? Was Kwin in immediate danger because of my feelings for her?

'Is there no hope?' I asked.

'I wish it was different, but for Ada, nothing can be done. Though while *we* breathe there's still hope, boy. Still hope for us. The Protector said that he and Hob were a dual authority. He released us. He might be a moderating influence on Hob: he wants things to return to normal. So I think it's unlikely that we'll be murdered in our beds tonight. But you'll be the first target. Hob will visit the Wheel within the month . . . I learned a lot from Ada,' Tyron went on. 'I have no shatek, so I can't create sentience, but I can pattern a lac to a very high level – maybe even up to the standard of Gunter.'

'Ada did that, but it still wasn't good enough to save Tallus,' Kwin said, her voice full of fear and bitterness.

'Leif is ten times the fighter Tallus ever was,' Tyron said, leaning forward to pat her shoulder in reassurance. 'I don't want to speak ill of the dead, but it's the simple truth. As I said, I learned a lot. And though Ada knew patterning, we know combat in Arena 13. I have a wealth of experience in here!' Tyron said, tapping his forehead. 'Your father, Math, fought behind a lac without sentience, and he won again and again. We can do the same. We can buy time until the Trader visits again before the start of the next season. Maybe we can get him to sell us another shatek . . .'

'If we're found out, the Protector won't give us a second chance,' said Kwin, squeezing my hand again. 'And what if we win and somehow find a way to destroy Hob? Won't that just bring down the fury of the djinn on us?'

'No, Kwin, you're mistaking my intention. We aren't going to try to destroy Hob. But we can deal with him. Somehow we have to survive. We can't change what Hob does outside the arena, but within Arena 13 he mostly keeps to the rules—'

'He didn't keep to the rules when I fought him!' I shouted angrily. 'He stared into my eyes and my knees grew weak. That's how he managed to chop off my ear! And what about my father – he made him fight a whole bout in front of his lac! He cheats there as well!'

Tyron stared down at the pool of red wine on his desk. 'Well, we'll have to find a way to deal with that. But if we can match him in the arena, if we can defeat him a few times, we might be able to negotiate for our lives. Hob can never get enough gold. He always bets large sums on himself, so if he loses, his supply of gold will diminish while ours will grow. Don't look at me like that, girl! What else can we do?'

Tyron looked like a defeated man. I was disappointed. Was that the best that he could come up with? Our optimism of just a few weeks earlier had all but gone. There was no victory over Hob to be won here. We could only bargain for our lives. One part of me wanted to flee south and join the Genthai – though their plans were also doomed. And how could I leave Kwin now?

If we followed Tyron's advice, all we could do was try to survive. There had to be a way to carry the fight to Hob.

One way or another, I was determined to find it.

As Kwin and I left Tyron's study, I glanced back at him. He was holding his head in his hands, staring down at his desk and looking utterly sad and weary.

I forced myself to smile at Kwin, trying to look cheerful, but she looked grave.

She squeezed my hand. 'Come to my room now,' she said. 'I have a present for you.'

On the small table before the mirror was a basin of water, a pair of scissors and a razor. Kwin pulled up a stool and positioned it in front of the table. 'Sit down and look into the mirror,' she whispered.

I gazed at myself, my eyes drawn to the remnants of my ravaged right ear. 'It's ugly,' I said. It was still throbbing with pain.

'It's an honourable wound,' Kwin said. 'A badge of courage. Think of it in the same way that I regard my scar. I fought a lac face to face and defeated it. I wear the scar proudly. I cut my hair short in order to show it off. Think how much more you have to be proud of! You defeated Hob in the arena. You should draw attention to it!'

I thought about it, but only for a moment. Why not! 'Do what you think looks best,' I told her.

So Kwin went to work on my hair. First she used the scissors and then the razor. When she'd finished, the right half of my head was shaved.

'It's a pity I don't have the Genthai tattoos on the whole of my face,' I said. 'Having a shaven head draws attention to the ear, but that right side of my face looks empty.'

Kwin smiled and pointed to the 13 on her own forehead.

'I should do that?'

'Why not? It will show what you are – half Genthai warrior and half Arena 13 combatant.'

'Then maybe I will!' I smiled.

She looked at me in the mirror. 'You were magnificent in the arena tonight. Covered in your own blood, you fought him toe to toe. I'd have sacrificed *both* my ears to have done that. Your father would have been very proud of you.'

At those words my throat tightened. I was thinking of my father and mother, and how their lives together had ended. But at last I said, 'Thanks for the present.'

'That wasn't the present,' she replied. 'That begins now . . .'

Kwin leaned down. Then she kissed me.

I kissed her back. At first it was gentle. Our lips barely touched. Then it was a deeper kiss; soft and warm.

Finally it became fierce, and with that heat, the room faded away and nothing else mattered.

*

The following morning, straight after breakfast, I went to the practice floor. Ada had been taking my morning training, and now her absence hit me hard.

Tyron was alone, speaking wurdes of Nym to a lac. When I entered, he stopped patterning, glanced at my shaven head and frowned. He seemed about to say something, but instead he let out a sigh. Then he smiled.

'I have one piece of good news,' he said. 'Thrym escaped the clutches of the Protector's thugs, damaging several of them in the process.'

'How did he do that?' I asked. 'I put him into the deep sleep.'

'Ada built a fail-safe into him. If the danger to him was extreme, he could override that command. He escaped before he was taken out of the Wheel. It's believed that he went down into the Commonality and ripped off one of the gates to the deep sealed areas. If that's the case, even the Protector's Guard aren't going to follow him down there: they'll simply replace the gate and weld it shut.'

So perhaps Thrym was now down among the feral, dangerous lacs who had apparently turned to cannibalism. How would a sentient lac fare down there? I felt sorry for him, but at least he'd escaped his intended fate. I was pleased that he'd survived.

Tyron went over to the table. Next to the brass timer was something large covered with a green cloth. And next to that lay a book. On the spine it said: *The Testimony of Math*.

Tyron handed it to me. 'This is your father's account of his experiences in Arena 13. It begins with his training and ends just after his final contest with Hob, when he knows that his injuries will prevent him from ever fighting again. I'm not giving you this, Leif, I'm just lending it to you. So read it, learn from it and take good care of it. Understand?'

I nodded. 'Thanks. I will.'

I was looking forward to reading my father's account and felt sure that it would be useful to me.

Tyron then turned and picked up the cloth. When he faced me again, he was holding a large metal object that gleamed in the torchlight. He held it out to me. 'This was Math's,' he said quietly. 'Your father gave it to me as a memento when he left Gindeen. You can wear it when you next face Hob. It will protect your head.'

It was a silver helmet in the shape of a wolf's head; the helmet that my father had worn in combat against Hob.

'If he chooses to wear a helmet, then so can you.' Tyron pointed to the horizontal slit. 'And this might make it harder for him to use his eyes to weaken you. Well, Leif, you'd best forget all that for now. We're a long way from being ready to face Hob; we have a lot to do. Kwin's gone off to work, and I've set Deinon some advanced patterning exercises, so this morning we two can concentrate on working with your new lac. I'm afraid it's back to basics.'

We were going to miss Ada, I thought. The fight would go on, but things would be much more difficult now.

Suddenly I realized that Deinon should have been present. I didn't think Tyron was aware of just how brilliant he was. Deinon was going to have to admit that he'd written the patterns for the lac that had helped me to defeat Palm.

I'd mention it to Tyron – just as soon as I'd spoken to Deinon.

INTERNMENT

A singleton is a djinni with only one self.

This is the lowest form.

But it is superior to the barbarian human in speed,

strength and reflexes.

The Manual of Nym

'Well, this is your new lac, Leif,' Tyron said. 'What do you think?'

It was clad in shiny new armour, but I knew that the patterns that informed it would be far inferior to those of Thrym. I would have to start from the beginning, using Ulum, developing the sound-code that I would use to communicate with it in Arena 13.

'It certainly looks good,' I replied, trying to put some enthusiasm into my voice.

'Well, it's not bad on the inside either. I think you might be pleasantly surprised.'

Just then there was a knock on the door. Tyron frowned; there was a strict rule that practice sessions were not to be disturbed, but he walked across to open it.

Over his shoulder, I saw that it was one of his servants, looking worried. He seemed to be passing on some bad news.

Tyron dismissed the man and beckoned me to the door. 'It seems we've got a problem. The Protector's Guard are here with an arrest warrant. They want to take you into custody.'

'But they released us,' I protested. 'I thought we were to be allowed to carry on with our lives. Why me?'

'Let's hope it's a mistake and the Protector hasn't changed his mind,' Tyron said. 'Let's go and find out. Unless they question you directly, let me do the talking.'

Four blue-jacketed guards and an officer were standing in the large reception room where Tyron received his business contacts and other visitors.

'What is the meaning of this?' Tyron demanded as he walked into the room ahead of me.

'Here is the arrest warrant, sir,' said the officer, handing Tyron a scroll of paper and nodding politely at him, though he stared at me with hostile eyes.

Tyron broke the wax seal, unfurled it and scanned the warrant quickly. 'It gives no mention of any crime. What is Leif actually accused of?'

'It is signed by the Protector under the emergency powers that he assumed at midnight. All Genthai or those of Genthai extraction living within the city are to be interned.'

'This is news to me. Why are they being dealt with in this way?'

'I cannot comment other than to say that the Genthai have proved to be hostile to the rule of law.'

'But how can this possibly apply to my trainee?' protested

Tyron. 'Leif is a law-abiding, hard-working young man who contributes to the economy of this city. He is an important member of my stable of combatants. Surely an exception could be made?'

'I am only carrying out orders,' said the officer, taking back the scroll.

Tyron turned towards me with an expression of resignation. 'Go with them, Leif. I'll try to get to the bottom of this and have you released as soon as possible.'

With that, I was marched out into the street. The sky was overcast and it was raining heavily. There was no wagon waiting outside this time. The officer strode at my side, with two of his men in front and two behind.

The streets were mostly deserted, but the Protector's Guard were out in force, standing at all the major crossroads, armed with their deadly projectile weapons. My own escort had only clubs at their belts; the officer carried a sword, his right hand resting lightly on the hilt.

Judging by the direction we were taking, we were making for the Protector's palace. I wondered if I was going to be questioned. And what had the Genthai done to justify the internment of innocent city dwellers? What did 'hostile to the rule of law' mean? Had they attacked the guard?

Then, in the distance, I saw smoke, and after a while the flicker of flames. Soon I had no doubts about their source.

The wooden barracks of the Protector's Guard was burning.

We reached the grounds of the Protector's palace. In the dark the previous night I'd not seen how truly spectacular they were, with ornamental trees and brilliant green grass, cut very short; the upkeep must have cost a fortune.

This time I was taken round the side of the palace towards the buildings at its rear, all enclosed by a high stone wall. Squelching across a saturated lawn, we approached a large wooden gate, which stood open. We had to move aside as a column of guards, riding three abreast, cantered out onto the broad cinder path. As they headed off towards the distant smoke, I was led into a large flagged courtyard, densely packed with rank after rank of armed guards.

The majority stood facing us, their faces grim, blue uniforms dark with rain. These were preparing to follow the horsemen to the barracks; others waited behind the walls, ready to defend the palace.

Directly ahead, set into a second stone wall, stood another wide double gate, this one metal. It was closed, and I glanced up and saw a dozen guards standing atop the wall, all carrying projectile weapons.

The officer beside me looked up at them and gestured towards the gate. Seconds later there was a grinding noise, and one side was dragged inwards, creating a narrow gap just wide enough for us to pass through in single file.

The gate itself was about a foot thick, but the wall was well over six feet deep. It was a formidable defence.

We crossed a smaller inner courtyard towards a three-storey building. The windows of the top floor were barred. Was this used as a prison? I wondered. If Ada was still alive, she might be somewhere inside.

We went through an open doorway and I was marched down a long corridor, then up two flights of stone steps before we halted in front of a door. The officer produced a key and unlocked it, pulling it open. Without further ceremony, I was pushed inside and the door was locked behind me.

I glanced around my cell. It was very large – about twice as long as Arena 13 and perhaps slightly wider – with a wooden floor and a single narrow barred window, the only source of light.

I wasn't alone. There were a dozen other prisoners sitting on the floor with their backs against the walls, all of them Genthai. There were only two sounds – a man groaning and the heavy rain thundering on the metal roof.

The man had obviously been badly beaten. His head was covered in blood and his face was swollen, his nose broken. The others stared at me silently. Most of them showed signs of ill-treatment: bruises, cuts and torn clothes.

I wondered if I'd been spared that because I was Tyron's trainee. Looking around, I recognized only one of these Genthai: the attendant I sometimes exchanged nods with – the one with the facial tattoos. He performed menial work in the Wheel; he swept the floors, emptied the bins, cleaned the spittoons and the latrines.

He beckoned me over, so I went and sat down next to him.

'You did well beating Hob,' he said. 'I'd have loved to see that. And what was attempted afterwards was very nearly successful. We could have been rid of that monster for ever.'

'You know about that?' I asked, surprised that the news had got out so quickly.

'There's little that escapes my attention, Leif. I clean up everybody's muck, but I'm invisible to most and perfectly placed to see what's going on. My name is Dentar,' he said, offering me his hand.

'I won, but afterwards everyone involved was imprisoned,' I said bitterly. 'I was released with a warning. I didn't expect to be arrested again. I hope what we did hasn't led to this . . .' I gestured towards the other prisoners.

'No, this is because of something else – you needn't feel guilty. You saw the barracks burning?'

I nodded.

'Then you'll know what's happened. This is the beginning of the end for the Protector.'

Dentar's words filled me with unease. If the Genthai won – what then? It might bring disaster to the whole of Midgard. With the Protector and his guard gone, what would follow?

After a while I began to realize that the worst thing about being a prisoner was boredom. Nobody talked; most of the men slept.

It was late afternoon when I heard shouting in the distance – though whether from inside or outside the building I couldn't tell. I kept thinking over what had happened. If the Genthai were now attacking the Protector's Guard, I didn't give much for Tyron's chances of getting me released.

Suddenly there were voices outside the door. We all turned as it opened and more prisoners were thrust in to join us. Then the door was closed with a bang.

These were also Genthai – although they looked different from those already in the room. They wore chain mail, which was splattered with blood, and they were soaking wet. They had clearly been fighting. They were warriors.

They swept the room with their eyes, finally fixing their stern gaze on Dentar and me.

'I believe that you and the big man are already acquainted,' Dentar said, nodding towards them.

One of them was big all right – he stood head and shoulders above the rest. I suddenly realized that it was Garrett.

He was almost as I remembered from the forest, though now his long hair was bunched up on top of his head and ended in a pigtail. As the Genthai warriors approached, Dentar and I got to our feet.

Garrett grinned at me. 'Good to see you here, Leif. You couldn't be in a better place. Now you'll be able to play your part in what needs to be done!'

Before I could ask what he meant, he turned to Dentar. 'Nice to see you too, Dent. Your last report on guard movements was really useful – the best one yet.'

'How's the battle going?' Dentar asked.

I expected bad news. After all, these men had been captured. But I was soon proved wrong.

'Couldn't be better!' Garrett said with a grin. 'They took the bait and rushed reinforcements to defend the barracks. But that was a diversion. This is our real target. We want the Protector alive. We've a few questions to put to him.'

His gaze settled on me again. 'But these buildings will be difficult to take, Leif. This isn't just wood we can burn or smash our way into. It could cost lives. We allowed ourselves to be captured, knowing there was a good chance that we'd be brought to the holding cells. Come here and look at this,' he said, walking over to the narrow barred window. I followed him.

'The outer gate is wood and will pose no problem, but the inner one could spell disaster. We need to break out and open that metal gate to let our lads in,' he said, gesturing downwards.

The window gave a view of the inner courtyard and the high wall. There weren't many guards immediately below, but there were still a dozen armed men on the wall. The heavy double gate was fastened with a long metal bar that ran through a row of brackets. This would have to be lifted clear to open the gate fully.

I realized that those guards would have a clear shot at anyone crossing the courtyard from the building to the gate. It seemed hopeless.

Any attempt to open the gate would be suicidal.

THE BATTLE FOR THE GATE

Our first victory will be bloody,
But bloodier still will be the aftermath.
Amabramdata: the Genthai Book of Prophecy

'Why not attack the front of the palace? Wouldn't that be easier?' I asked.

Garrett shook his head. 'Those projectile weapons are the biggest threat to us. We'd have to cross the lawn; we'd be easy to cut down. They won't expect us to attack the inner gate. It's the most formidable part of their defences. It'll take them by surprise!'

He turned away from the window, reached up into his hair and pulled out two thin paper tubes, one red, the other green.

'This should do the trick!' he said. 'It wouldn't help us with that gate, but this little lock should be no trouble.' He nodded towards the cell door.

I was about to ask him what the coloured tubes were when he turned to face the other prisoners. The rain had finally eased to a light pattering on the roof and he hardly needed to raise his voice.

'Some of you, I know, are in no fit state to help. But if any wish to join us, it'll be appreciated. We're going to get out of here and fight our way to the gate to let our brothers in. Stand up if you're with us! This is a day you'll tell your grandchildren about – one you'll remember with pride! There'll be no more Protector ruling Midgard after today. This whole land will belong to the Genthai.'

Garrett's words filled me with foreboding. What about people such as Tyron who lived and worked in the city? What about the farmers? How would they fit into the new order?

About seven of the Genthai came to their feet, including Dentar. One of them looked frail and too old to fight, another was bloody and battered and seemed unsteady on his feet, but their eyes were filled with determination.

'Whether you feel able to help or not, sit as far away from the door as possible!' Garrett instructed. 'Turn your backs to it. Do it now!'

Apart from me and Garrett, everybody repositioned themselves as he'd indicated, including the two warriors who'd accompanied him.

He grinned at me. 'You too, Leif. But not for a couple of moments. I'm waiting for the fun to begin. It shouldn't be long now.'

We both stared out of the window. After a couple of minutes I realized that the attack was underway. Some of the guards on the wall were gesticulating to each other and pointing downwards. Then I heard shouting and the clash of metal. The guards aimed their weapons and fired down into the outer courtyard. If the Genthai had managed to get through the first gate, they would be easy targets.

But these soldiers weren't having it all their own way: I

watched as one of them toppled from the wall with an arrow through his throat.

'Right, Leif! Against the wall like the others!' Garrett shouted.

I went to sit next to Dentar, but before turning round I glanced back to see what Garrett was doing. He tore two pieces from each of the coloured tubes and twisted them together. Then he squashed them against the lock before running towards us.

'Cover your ears!' he shouted.

The two mail-clad warriors cupped their hands over their ears. I copied them – and not a moment too soon.

I heard a dull boom, then felt a fierce blast of heat on my back. I turned to see that the door was hanging off its hinges, surrounded by a cloud of smoke. An acrid smell of burning filled my nostrils.

'Right! Follow me!' Garrett cried.

Moving very fast for a man his size, he leaped to his feet and ran towards the opening. I followed him, the two warriors slightly ahead of me and Dentar at my heels. Outside, a guard lay face down on the floor in a pool of blood. Hardly pausing, Garrett snatched the sword from the dead man's belt and raced along the corridor to the top of the stairs. Now he was armed, but what about the rest of us? I wondered. How many of the Protector's Guard lay between us and the gate we must open?

Garrett had only taken one step when a blue-jacketed figure appeared at the foot of the stairs. He aimed his projectile weapon, and with a high-pitched, whirring sound the deadly disc spun towards us.

It hit the first of the Genthai warriors, embedding itself in his forehead. He made no noise; simply fell forward and rolled down the stairs. Before the guard could reload his weapon, Garrett was down the steps, his sword slicing into the man's neck.

He screamed and fell to the floor, dead. Garrett picked up the projectile weapon and the belt of discs, and handed them to the second warrior. Then he leaped over the body and ran down the corridor. I followed at his heels, unarmed, but determined to help.

We turned left, and halfway down the next corridor saw another guard with his back to a door. He drew his sword, but Garrett soon cut him down, then gestured that we should get down and cover our ears.

Why weren't we continuing along the corridor? I wondered. Wasn't our priority to get down into the yard and open the gate?

I watched Garrett twist two more pieces of coloured tube together; this time I knew what to expect. The explosion was smaller but it did the trick. Moments later we found ourselves inside the room, and my questions were answered.

It was an armoury.

Of the eleven who'd left the cell, nine remained. One had been slain by the disc; maybe the other had been too weak to keep up.

We ran down the final flight of steps, and Garrett led us towards the door to the courtyard. He seemed to know the layout of the building. No doubt he'd had spies like Dentar giving him information.

Outside, I saw that the guards on the wall had gone, picked off by Genthai archers. But there were six or seven standing between us and the gate. They weren't armed with projectile weapons, so we charged straight at them, splashing through the puddles, swords raised.

From beyond the gate I heard shouts and screams and the din of battle, but the roaring challenge from Garrett's throat was louder still. In seconds we were upon the enemy. They stood their ground, and one swung his sword towards my head.

I suddenly wished I'd spent my time in the forest training with a sword rather than chopping down trees. My weapon felt heavy and unwieldy, but I used its weight as Garrett had taught me, and somehow I managed to block the blow without checking my pace. He was soon felled by someone at my side, and then we were at the gate.

There was no need for anyone to issue orders. We all knew what to do. Putting down our weapons, we spread out in a line and began to heave the heavy metal bar clear of its brackets. As we took its full weight, I stumbled, my knees almost giving way.

'Ten paces backwards!' shouted Garrett.

The bar was incredibly heavy, but we managed to stagger back the ten paces.

'Now, on the count of three, drop it – but mind your toes! One, two – *three*!'

We let the bar fall. It made a tremendous clang as it hit the flags. The subsequent silence was soon filled with shouts. I glanced back and saw scores of guards coming through the door behind us. These must be reinforcements from the palace.

I itched to pick up my sword, but we knew what had to be done. We began to drag the gate open, the bottom scraping on the stones. At any second I expected to feel a blade slicing into my back.

But the gate was opening faster now, as those on the other side pushed. Suddenly, through the widening gap, I saw more Genthai, and in the lead a man on horseback. He wore heavy armour and whirled two huge swords about his head, but I recognized the heavy, drooping moustache and facial tattoos. It was Konnit.

We stepped aside and he rode past us and galloped straight towards the advancing guard.

He smashed into them, laying about him with his swords, fighting like one possessed. And behind him were more Genthai warriors on foot, many with swords and shields. I picked up my own sword and made to follow them. I wanted to play my part, but I felt a heavy hand on my shoulder, drawing me back.

'No, Leif, you've already put your life on the line,' Garrett told me. 'We've both done enough for today. The battle is as good as won. But this is just the beginning. There will be more dangerous encounters in the future. Save yourself for that!'

More and more Genthai were pouring through the open gate. The guard had already been defeated; Konnit had dismounted and was leading his men into the building.

Garrett was right. The battle was almost over. I wondered if they'd take the Protector alive and what secrets he would divulge. Did he know what it was like beyond the Barrier?

Suddenly I remembered Ada. 'There's a woman called Ada

in one of the cells – that's if she's still alive,' I said. 'She patterned the lac that helped me to defeat Hob last night. She's an expert on the djinn too. I need to make sure she's safe!'

I made to walk towards the door, but Garrett tightened his grip on my shoulder.

'We know all about Ada – don't you worry, Leif. We know how important she is. If she's still alive, she'll be kept safe, as will all the other prisoners we find. They'll have to be questioned and assessed. There are probably a few robbers and murderers in the cells back there. There's no point in setting *them* free to cause mischief, is there?'

I nodded. That was reasonable enough. Not all the prisoners would be enemies of the Protector. Gindeen had criminals too.

I just hoped that Ada was still alive.

EVERYTHING WILL CHANGE

When a man rules the Genthai,
A woman shall rule Gindeen.

Amabramdata: the Genthai Book of Prophecy

We waited by the inner gate. After a while the Genthai started bringing bedraggled lines of prisoners through. Some were wounded but had already been tended to. They were taken into the building, no doubt to be held in the cells on the top floor.

I would have liked to return to Tyron's house to let everybody know that I was free, but it didn't seem right to leave while there was still fighting at the barracks.

After about an hour, a big cheer went up in the outer courtyard, and Garrett went to investigate. When he came back, he was grinning from ear to ear.

'It's over – we've won!' he said, slapping me and Dentar on the back. 'A message has just arrived from the barracks. What's left of the Protector's Guard have surrendered.'

'What about the Protector?' I asked. 'Have they got him? And Ada – any news of her?'

Garrett shrugged. 'Let's go and find out. We'll go round

the outside. It'll be easier than picking our way between the buildings.'

He led the way out across the soggy grass. Dentar and I followed him round the wall until the front of the Protector's palace was directly ahead. Genthai warriors stood in groups on the front lawn or sat on the marble steps that led up to the portico.

'Wait here,' Garrett said. 'I'll go and find out what's happening.'

Dentar and I watched as Genthai arrived at the palace, many on horseback.

'So you supplied Garrett with information on the guards' movements?' I asked Dentar.

'I certainly did, Leif,' he replied. 'I hope my contribution helped.'

'Wasn't it risky being seen near the barracks and the palace?'

'I didn't actually need to go anywhere near them. My job meant that I had keys to almost every area in the Wheel. I used to go right to the top of the dome. It's surprising what you can see from up there!'

I remembered the view well. Kwin had taken me up there when I'd first arrived in the city. You could see the whole of Gindeen spread out below, and beyond it the palace and the barracks.

I wondered what Kwin was doing now. Would she be worried about me?

'Look! That's a sight for sore eyes. Grub's on its way!' Dentar exclaimed.

There was the muffled thunder of hooves. Fresh groups of

Genthai horsemen were galloping onto the lawn, churning up the grass, dragging carcasses behind them. I realized that they must have raided local farms. That would lead to trouble – but what chance did the farmers have against the Genthai army?

It was starting to get dark, but soon there were over a dozen fires burning on the lawn. How they'd managed to get them started in such wet conditions I didn't know, but it wasn't long before meat was cooking on huge spits. The smell made my mouth water. It seemed like a long time since breakfast.

A couple of hours later, after joining the queue for food, I was sitting on the steps again, tucking into a plate of beef, waiting for Garrett to come back. I'd almost finished when he emerged between the pillars and came to sit next to me.

'Good news, Leif. Ada's well. There's not a scratch on her. She was talking to Konnit when I left. What she knows about the djinn will be invaluable. We've got the Protector too. Tomorrow we'll start to interrogate him ... And talking of tomorrow, Konnit wants to see you at noon. There's to be a meeting to decide a few preliminary things and he wants us both to be present.'

I was surprised by that. Obviously Garrett was important; by opening the gate he had played a vital role in the victory. But what did Konnit want with me? I wondered. I'd only been there by chance.

'I'd like to go back to Tyron's house tonight,' I replied. 'They'll all be worried. I'll return tomorrow in plenty of time for the meeting.'

Garrett shook his head. 'I'm sorry, Leif, but it's too risky at the moment. We've already had a couple of skirmishes with the city folk. Now they've barricaded each of the major roads into Gindeen with piles of logs. And don't forget that the Protector's Guard are recruited from city dwellers. Many have died and they have family still living in Gindeen. They won't take too kindly to seeing you with those tattoos on your face. Some will see us as the enemy. Better wait until things have calmed down a little and we've managed to negotiate with them.'

I tried in vain to sleep on the hard marble floor just inside the entrance to the palace. In the morning the sky was clear, and I went outside to let the sun warm me. Later I queued for breakfast – cold beef; I was hungry and went back for a second helping.

I spent the remainder of the morning chatting to Dentar. He told me about his early experiences in the city. He too had worked in the slaughterhouse, then on a farm, before finally getting his cleaning job in the Wheel.

Then I remembered how Garrett had destroyed the lock to get us out of the cell. 'What were those coloured tubes Garrett used to blow the door off its hinges?' I asked.

'They're called plastics.'

'Plastics? What does that mean?' I asked.

'They're explosives that can be squashed into different shapes – even squeezed into a lock. The two tubes are stable until mixed together. After that you have about thirty seconds to get clear.'

'We've nothing like that in the city. Where did you get it from?'

'The Trader. He visits us in the forest and supplies what we need.'

I remembered Konnit showing me the gramagandar weapons that he kept down in a cellar. They could destroy false flesh – they'd be devastating when employed against djinn. Had the Trader supplied those weapons too? I wondered.

'He supplies the city with the lacs that fight in the Wheel,' I told Dentar. 'I wonder who he really is. How can he sail through the Barrier?'

Dentar shrugged. 'Nobody knows, but some of our people believe that he is the wolf-god whom we call Thangandar. They say that's why he wears a mask – to hide his face because he has the body of a man but the head of a wolf. Whatever the truth of the matter, he's certainly been a good friend to our people.'

At that moment Garrett came to collect me; we headed into the palace, but were stopped twice and made to state our business, even though everyone knew Garrett. Security was tight.

The meeting was held in the throne room. The throne stood empty, but seated at a round table were nine people, some of whom I recognized.

Konnit was there, and on his right was a woman with grey hair and a broad, kindly face with intelligent eyes; she was probably in her sixties. On his left sat Ada. As we approached, she gave me a friendly smile. She looked tired, but didn't seem to have been harmed.

'Garrett and Leif, sit there!' Konnit commanded, gesturing to two seats across the table. Garrett bowed before sitting down, so I did the same.

'Welcome, Leif,' Konnit said. 'The lady here on my right is the Obutayer of our people. When the war is over and victory is ours, I will relinquish power and she will rule once more. But for now she is only here to witness what is decided.'

I glanced at her, but she didn't acknowledge me in any way.

'I have an important role for you, Leif,' Konnit continued. 'You may refuse – I would not attempt to force it upon you because it is not without danger. But first listen to what I have to say.'

He stared at me hard and I nodded. 'Yes, lord,' I answered. What did he want me to do? I was puzzled.

'You have Genthai blood, but are also of the city. Although some will view you as the enemy . . . after your victory over Hob, many will hold you in esteem. I'd like to appoint you as our envoy. This afternoon I want you to carry our preliminary proposals to those who now rule the city. Is that acceptable, Leif?'

'Yes, lord, I'd be happy to do that.'

'Secondly, if we can reach agreement on our proposals, I would like you to be the Mediator between the city and our people. Here – read this and tell me what you think,' Konnit said, pushing a piece of paper across the table towards me. 'I would welcome your comments.'

I drew it close so that I could read it.

Proposals for the Future Governance of Midgard

1 Leif, son of Matthias, has been appointed as the Genthai Envoy. Subject to your agreement, we nominate him to become the future Mediator between Genthai and city dwellers.

2 The Genthai will withdraw to their forest domain but keep small forces close to the city of Gindeen and the township of Mypocine. They will also patrol the main thoroughfares to and from the city and keep order.

3 Within the forest, the Genthai will rule themselves. The city will also be self-governing.

4 A joint Ruling Council should be formed, with equal numbers of Genthai and city dwellers.

5 That Council will be based in the palace and will be responsible for directing joint military operations.

6 The city will raise an armed force of three thousand men to join with the Genthai in defence of Midgard.

7 The city and the Genthai will cooperate in an operation to destroy the djinn known as Hob.

8 The arenas within the Wheel should continue to operate as normal, and a tax on the gambling houses should fund the upkeep of the palace, the city army and the operation to destroy Hob.

9 Females should be permitted to fight in Arena 13. Female artificers should be licensed to train stables of combatants.

I almost gasped aloud when I saw the ninth item. Surely the Wheel Directorate wouldn't agree to that. When I looked up, Ada was staring at me, a faint smile on her face. That must have been her idea.

'Well, Leif,' Konnit said. 'Let's hear your thoughts.'

'Lord, I can't predict the reaction to all this, but I think numbers eight and nine might be considered interference in the affairs of the city,' I said.

'The eighth point is just sensible advice. The ninth point is there at Ada's insistence,' Konnit replied. 'It is the price of her full cooperation. But everything is negotiable up to a point. All I want you to do is begin the process. Put the proposals to them and return to us with their reactions.'

'Could I make a further suggestion, lord?'

Konnit nodded.

'We raided farms yesterday and seized cattle. We dined well, but it will have caused resentment. It would be good if we could offer to pay for what we've taken. That would make the negotiations easier.'

Konnit paused before replying and gave a slight frown. Ada put her hand on his arm, and he leaned down while she whispered into his ear. When he looked up, the frown had gone.

'You are wise beyond your years, Leif. Yes, we will do that. It will become the second item on the list. Anything else?'

I was still eager for vengeance against Hob. I was impatient. I couldn't bear to wait for the city and the Genthai to draw up a plan to destroy him.

'I was there when you pounded on the gate of Hob's citadel and dared him to come forth and fight,' I said to Konnit. 'Why do we need the cooperation of the city? Can't we raid his citadel tonight and slay all Hob's selves? I defeated him once in Arena 13. Now I would like to fight him in his lair. Let me be a part of his destruction.'

'We must proceed with caution,' Konnit replied. 'There are ancient devices that can burn like a sun and reduce a whole city to ashes in seconds. He may have such weapons at his disposal. As far as we know, the djinn never used their like against humans. But a dual authority ruled Midgard, so we are told. The Protector was its benign face; Hob is a rogue djinni, capable of anything. We must not act against him until we are certain of a speedy and safe victory.'

Suddenly Ada spoke aloud for the first time. 'Without doubt you *will* play a part in his destruction, Leif. Be patient. The day will surely come when he pays for his crimes.'

Just over an hour later I was walking down the hill towards the city with Garrett at my side. A tall Genthai warrior strode ahead of us carrying a white flag on a spear which he held high to show that we came in peace. Dressed in chainmail, he wore a hood and a bronze mask with eye slits.

For a moment I wondered if this was the Trader. After all he'd been a good friend to the Genthai and had supplied them with the weapon called the gramagandar. But because of the hood I couldn't see if he had that distinctive red hair.

I knew that this flag of truce was unnecessary. Contact had already been made, and the Wheel Directorate were now convening in the admin building, ready to listen to the Genthai proposals. Tyron and his servants were going to meet me at the barricade and escort me there.

I wondered if he'd bring Kwin with him. As I thought of her, my heart lurched. We'd been apart little more than a day, but already I missed her.

A memory flashed into my mind: she was dancing in front of Thrym, their blades gleaming in the torchlight, their combined shadows reflected on the wall of Tyron's training floor. They'd looked like one creature with four arms. Deinon had said that it had the appearance of Kali, a goddess who'd fought daemons.

How formidable she had looked, dancing with Thrym! She was at least as fast as I was. Was that why Ada had asked for that ninth item to be added to the Genthai proposal? Did she intend Kwin to fight with one of her lacs in Arena 13?

I shivered. I didn't like the idea of her being in danger. How would I feel watching her fight?

An even more worrying thought occurred to me. It might be weeks or even months before an attempt was made to destroy Hob. In the meantime, would he still visit Arena 13 and challenge the min combatants? What if the lottery chose Kwin to fight him? How would I cope with that?

I could see the high barricade of logs ahead of me. Tyron was standing in a narrow gap to its left. I was disappointed to see no sign of Kwin. A couple of servants stood beside him, along with half a dozen men wearing red sashes – marshals from the Wheel. No doubt they were policing the city now; they wore short swords rather than clubs at their belts.

There'd already been a lot of changes, I reflected; I knew there'd be a lot more.

Tyron was frowning and seemed deep in thought. He would frown a lot more when he read that ninth proposal.

He'd know immediately what was likely to happen if it was adopted.

Kwin's dream of fighting in Arena 13 would be fulfilled.

About halfway down the slope Garrett nodded to me and stepped to one side. 'I'll wait here, Leif. Remember that this is just a preliminary negotiation. Keep it short and be back before noon.'

As I reached the barricade Tyron came forward to greet me. I saw him glance at the warrior with the flag and frown but he stepped beyond him and clapped me on the shoulder.

'Good to see you, Leif. I was worried when I realized you were caught up in the fighting. And now you're the Genthai envoy. Events are moving fast. We need to keep clear heads and do nothing rash. You're in no danger but the Directorate are anything but pleased by what's happening.'

'Things have changed in a big way,' I said. 'We all need to work together. So the Directorate will have to adjust to the new situation.'

Tyron raised his eyebrows and stared at me hard when I said that but then he patted me on the shoulder again. 'Well let's go and get it over with!' he exclaimed turning to lead the way through the gap in the barricade.

I walked after him but to my surprise the warrior with the flag came too. Tyron strode on my left and he was on my right.

Tyron's two servants followed behind with the marshals making up the rear. We walked at a fast pace through the streets which were deserted, heading for the admin building where the meeting was to take place.

My stomach was churning with nerves but I was determined to give a good account of myself and do the best I could to begin what I hoped would be successful negotiations.

Right from the start, things began to go wrong.

There were over a dozen marshals guarding the main door to the admin building and they would only allow us to enter if we didn't carry weapons inside. Tyron's servants were armed and at a nod from him waited outside. But the tall warrior pushed through the marshals still carrying his spear.

No effort was made to take it from him; maybe that was because it was also a flag of truce. Flanked by marshals the three of us entered.

The meeting took place in Pyncheon's office. We faced a long table. On this side of it there was only one seat. I assumed that it was for me. No marshals followed us into the room but two were standing with their backs to the wall either side of the seated Pyncheon and, to my surprise, they were armed with the projectile weapons once used by the Protector's Guard.

'Sit down!' Pyncheon, the Chief Marshal, commanded imperiously. He was dressed in his formal attire – black with the diagonal red sash denoting his office. It was the first time I had been so close to him and I saw that his eyes were set very close together and his nose was thin. It gave him a predatory appearance.

My hackles rose at his peremptory manner but I sat down. There was no point in getting angry. That wouldn't help matters at all. I was aware that Tyron was standing close to my left shoulder and the tall armoured warrior was on my right.

Then I realized that there were six seated people facing me across the table when there should only have been five.

The Directorate was headed by Pyncheon; the four other members were the heads of the four main gambling houses.

The new addition was Cyro.

Anger surged within me. What right had he to be here? He was the man who had probably betrayed us by alerting the Protector about our attempt to destroy Hob.

Words came out of my mouth before I realised that I'd spoken.

'That man is not a member of the Wheel Directorate and his presence at this meeting is not acceptable,' I heard myself say.

Tyron made a noise halfway between a gasp and a groan and Pyncheon's face almost turned the colour of his sash.

'*We* will decide the composition of the Wheel Directorate!' he snapped. 'Cyro is now an additional member.'

I came to my feet and addressed my words to Cyro. 'I defeated Hob fair and square in Arena 13. We could have rid this land of him for ever. But you betrayed us to the Protector. You don't serve this city, your masters are the Protector and Hob!'

Cyro came to his feet and sneered at me. 'The Protector was always a puppet,' he said. 'My true master was always Hob and I still serve him now. That is why I have claimed my place as a member of the Wheel Directorate. I represent his interests.'

Suddenly, the tall warrior spoke, his voice loud but muffled by the mask. 'You, Cyro, are guilty of a crime beyond forgiveness. You forced the lacs under your control to fight illegally under conditions in which they were maimed and slain in a manner akin to torture. You had a duty of care but abused your office. For that the sentence is death!'

With great force, the tall warrior hurled his spear straight at Cyro. It went through his chest pinning him to the wall behind. He was probably dead before he saw the danger. It all happened incredibly quickly.

The two marshals tried to raise their weapons and fire

but they didn't have time. As if by magic two blades appeared in the warrior's hands. Then they were buried in the throats of the marshals.

The warrior tore the mask from his face, threw it onto the table and pulled his hood back onto his shoulders.

When he spoke again his voice was clearly recognizable. 'As for Hob, Leif and I will meet him in combat in Arena 13 at any time of his choosing. Let him come and challenge us if he dare! And now let the negotiations begin.'

I looked up into the face of Thrym, nodded and smiled. Then I sat down and pushed the Genthai terms across the table towards Pyncheon.

When the Chief Marshal picked up the document, his hands were shaking and his face was the colour of fresh mountain snow. With the sound of blood dripping onto the floor behind him he began to read.

Now Kwin would be in no danger. When Hob came to Arena 13 he would have to fight us. Thrym and I would defeat and slay him again and again. Victory after victory would be ours. Then, when the time was right we would enter his lair and destroy him.

THE MIDGARD GLOSSARY

This glossary has been compiled from the following primary sources:

> *The Manual of Nym*
> *The Testimony of Math*
> *The Manual of Trigladius Combat*
> *Amabramsum: the Genthai Book of Wisdom*
> *Amabramdata: the Genthai Book of Prophecy*
> *The Compendium of Ancient Tales and Ballads*

ADA AUGUSTA

The High Adept of the Imperial Academy, who was slain by djinn terrorists at the beginning of the First Insurrection. Her soul was placed in Containment. She was named after Ada Augusta, Countess of Lovelace, who wrote the very first computer algorithm.

ADJUDICATOR

A type of djinn responsible for overseeing all forms of djinn combat, from those in the arena to battles of open warfare. They rarely show themselves to the participants until the combat is over, when their gungara absorb the blood of the weakest. By that means do they profit from their labours, and their shateks are the most proficient and prolific of all, generating shapes with ease.

Although performing a similar function, the Chief Marshal, he who oversees combat within Arena 13, is not a true Adjudicator. He is just a barbarian human.

AFICIONADOS

These are the devotees of the Trigladius; spectators whose knowledge of the proceedings − of the positions adopted by lacs and their tactical manoeuvres − is often greater than that of some combatants. Some specialize in the history of the Trigladius and can remember classic encounters of long ago by recalling, step by step, the patterns that led to victory.

AGNWAN

The Agnwan, known by barbarians as a horse, is a cowardly beast unsuitable for use in warfare. It undoubtedly has a certain grace, but it is outside the wurde and belongs to an age when the fecundity of nature was haphazard and chance spawned strange forms of life, each lone small mind encapsulated within a single host of flesh.

AMABRAMDATA

This is *The Genthai Book of Prophecy*. Although this holy book is written by a multitude of Genthai authors, it is believed that it represents the voice of their god, Thangandar.

AMABRAMSUM

This is the name of *The Genthai Book of Wisdom*. It contains observations on djinn, Midgard and the world before the fall of the ur-humans. This is the collective wisdom of Genthai scribes. It is not a holy book.

ARENA 13

This is another name for the Trigladius Arena. Once it was compulsory for human combatants in this arena to have the number 13 tattooed upon their foreheads. Once this rule was rescinded, it was still fashionable for many years, but the custom is now dying out.

ARTIFICERS

These are adepts skilled in patterning the wurdes of Nym. The first artificers were ur-human, and they developed their power to its height in the Secondary Epoch of Empire. Asscka, the most advanced form of djinn, are now the greatest artificers, having total control of Nym and the ability to shape themselves. The poorest artificers are barbarian humans, who pattern lacs who lack sentience. They build into them the steps of the dance that informs Trigladius combat in Arena 13.

ASGARD

In Norse mythology, this signifies the Place Where the Gods Dwell. Some inhabitants of Midgard use this name to signify the place beyond the Barrier, which is the rest of the earth occupied by the djinn.

ASSCKA

Asscka are the highest classification of djinni. These are true shape-shifters and, unless limited by the wurde, can number up to 10,000 selves and scores of shateks. During the Tertiary Epoch of Empire, djinn grew in power and ur-human artificer control of them diminished.

BARGE MASTERS

The barge masters are responsible for overseeing the transit of goods from the Sea Gate down the canal to Gindeen. There are seven of them, working a shift rota.

BARRIER

The Great Barrier is the zone of mist, darkness and fear that encircles Midgard, preventing entry or exit. Those who approach too closely either never come back or return insane. The Trader passes through the Barrier unharmed, but he makes the journey by sea.

BARSK

A barsk is the higher partner of a binary warrior djinn. Four-armed, with keen sight and great ferocity, his mount, and partner, is the orl, a two-legged creature with hands capable of wielding weapons. Barsk and orl were created each for the other; the first has a higher mind and greater access to the gorestad, which they share unequally. The barsk is dominant yet still dependent upon that which carries it. Such binary djinn are born of a shatek but lack the power to be born again. By this limitation were they shaped as warriors, for those who can die only once fight most fiercely to hold onto life.

BINARY DJINN

Binary djinn are the next rank above singletons. Theirs is a symbiotic relationship, but this partnership of two is not always equal as in the case of barsk and orl.

CATARA

Catara are sea-djinn which take two basic forms. The first are crustacea, with hard shells and many legs, which live close to the shore; the second are cephalopods with eight arms and two tentacles, which inhabit deep water. Both were developed by ur-humans for purposes of warfare.

CHIEF MARSHAL

This official is the highest authority within the Wheel with many assistant marshals to enforce his decisions. The main focus of his attention is Arena 13 where he supervises combat. Although his function in that arena may seem largely ceremonial, in the case of any dispute his decision is absolute and there can be no appeal.

COMMONALITY

This is the name given to the underground zone beneath the Wheel where lacs are stored by owners who cannot afford to lease private quarters.

COMPENDIUM OF ANCIENT TALES AND BALLADS, THE

This is a compilation of writings by humans before the fall and the subsequent construction of the Barrier. They take the form of lyrics, poems and prose fragments. Most are without a named author.

CONTAINMENT
This is the digital store within which a soul is preserved with the possibility of being born again into a body of false flesh. An alternative name for this condition is 'Stasis'.

COVENANT
The Covenant is the agreement made between the djinn and mankind following the defeat of the latter. Humans were set down within the confines of the Barrier and given a chance to live there providing that they accepted the rule of the Protector. The Genthai were to submit to ritual culling by the werewights; non-Genthai were to accept culling by Hob. As time passed the Covenant was forgotten about by city dwellers. Some believe that no such agreement was ever made.

CYRO
He is the official responsible for the Commonality, the large underground zone below the Wheel. With the help of a small army of assistants, he supervises the storage of lacs, the kitchens, the training areas and the combat zones. Cyro rules his domain with absolute authority and nobody interferes in his activities some of which are illegal.

DECIDONS
Decidons are hybrid djinn with ten selves, containing elements of both animal and vegetable but resembling trees. Largely static, they communicate by wind-blown pollen. Ur-humans developed them as sentinels and also for purposes of espionage. They have offensive capabilities and generate both poisons and antidotes.

DJINNI

A djinni is the wurde made flesh. The different types of djinn are more numerous than the visible stars. They range from low singletons, who may hardly be higher than base simulacra, to high djinn known as asscka, who may now generate selves almost beyond counting. Almost all djinn are subordinate in some way – some major, some minor – to the patterns of the ur-humans who first gave their progenitors shape. But of all these, most deadly is the djinn who is no longer subservient in any way to the wurdes that shaped him. Originally they were created by the military to serve the Human Empire. Djinn is an acronym which stands for *digital janus interface nano node*.

ENDOFF

This is the close-down function called when a blade is inserted into the throat-slit of a lac, which becomes temporarily inoperative. For the min combatant, it signals the end of the contest. All that remains is the ritual cut to the arm of the defeated human combatant.

EXTENSIBILITY

This is a characteristic of Nym which allows a patterner to add new wurdes and features or modify existing ones. The language can be increased by those who have the skill to do so.

FALSE FLESH

False flesh is the derogatory term first used by ur-humans to describe the flesh hosts of any djinn born of the shatek and the wurde. When the war between djinn and ur-humans intensified, the former adopted the term in defiance and proved, victory by victory, its superiority in every way to ur-human flesh.

FIRST INSURRECTION

The First Insurrection began with two terrorist attacks upon humans by the djinn. The first was an attempt upon the life of the Empress, which failed. The second was an attack upon the Imperial Academy, in which over a hundred lives were lost, including that of the High Adept. The djinn rebellion was eventually put down by the employment of the gramagandar, the weapon which dissolves false flesh.

GAMBLING HOUSE

The gambling agents (sometimes known as 'touts') accept wagers on behalf of the three large gambling houses which underpin the economy of Midgard. From their profits fees are paid to combatants who fight from the mag position. Only min combatants are allowed to bet upon themselves – but only to win.

Bets offered to Arena 13 gallery spectators are often very complex. Many aficionados attempt to predict the actual time of a victory and use accumulators, where winnings are placed upon the outcome of succeeding contests. Red tickets are sold, and these bets are made on the likelihood of a contestant suffering injury or death.

GINDEEN

This is the only city of Midgard, although there are some small towns and hamlets. Gindeen consists largely of wooden buildings, with roads that are just mud tracks. Its main land-marks are the Wheel, the large cube-shaped slaughterhouse, and the citadel of Hob, which casts its shadow over the city.

GORESTAD

Gorestad is the 'high mind' usually operative in all high djinn with more than one self. But despite this group consciousness, which makes a djinni with many selves just one entity, there is always some individual awareness particular to each self. Both asscka and shalatan can control the awareness of their selves, even denying particular selves access to gorestad.

GRAMAGANDAR

An ancient weapon, also known as the Breath of the Wolf, the fire of which is capable of dissolving all false flesh. This weapon is anathema to all djinn and its use is forbidden. It was created and deployed by the last ur-humans, and for this crime they were destroyed, their fallen and debased descendants, the barbarian humans, banished for all time to Midgard, the place within the Barrier.

GUNGARA

Gungara form the third component of all high djinn. These gungara are winged and are used to devour and absorb the mind and tissue of enemies or other creatures in need of study and/or reanimation by means of the wurde and the shatek. Gungara were not created by ur-humans and are a prime example of djinn self-directed evolution.

HOB

It is believed that Hob is a rogue djinn who remained within the Barrier when barbarian humans were sealed within it. He preys upon humans, taking their blood and sometimes their minds. He occasionally fights within Arena 13 from the mag position.

HUMANS

Humans are the ur-race of creatures that created the language called Nym, thus constructing the first djinn and preparing the way for those which would supersede them. Outside the wurde, they are termed ur-humans, whereas their fallen and debased descendants are called barbarian humans. These latter are closest in form to the type of singletons known as lacs, though without their strength, speed and coordination. Their strength comes from their ability to cooperate and combine forces for a common purpose. It may also spring from the fear of death, having only one self which can easily be snuffed out in battle.

INDEX

The catalogue of lacs, souls bound within false flesh, and wurdes offered by the Trader on his twice-yearly visits to Midgard. The Index exists only within the mind of the Trader and there is no written record of its contents.

KRANSIN

This is a substance used to coat the blades of lacs for contests in Arena 13. It is a combined coagulant and an intensifier of pain. Thus the ritual cut suffered by the loser is agonizing.

That pain must be faced with courage, as the spectators watching from the gallery judge how the losing combatant conducts himself.

LAC

This is an abbreviated form of **simulacrum**. Lacs are born of a shatek for the purposes of arena combat of various types. Although shaped to resemble barbarian humans, they have a throat-slit which, once penetrated by a blade, brings instant unconsciousness, the state called by the wurde endoff. They also have long arms to aid fighting in Arena 13.

LUDUSA

A type of binary djinn who share a gorestad equally. Sometimes, having no apparent connection in either appearance or role, they were created by ur-humans for the purpose of espionage.

LUPINA

A category of djinn which take on a variety of wolf shapes. Werewights are a debased and fallen form of this djinn category; they are instinctual rather than rational. However, true Lupina are the most intelligent of all djinn.

MANUAL OF NYM, THE

A detailed guide to the patterning language known as Nym and of the wurdes contained in its two dictionaries (known as *Fat Nym* and *Slim Nym*). The latter is a basic reduced version of the former, which is continually extending.

MAORI

These are the ancestor gods of the Genthai, who are believed to live in the sky on a long white cloud.

MEDIE

The Medie is a small river that flows out of the Genthai lands and meets the sea not far north of the Sea Gate.

MIDGARD

From Norse mythology, it means the Place Where Men Dwell or the Battlefield of Men. It is the zone allocated to the barbarian humans, the survivors of the fallen empire.

MUSEUM OF LIGHTS

This museum is reputed to hold a record of images and items from the human civilization that preceded the Fall. Its location is unknown but some believe it is to be found within the Protector's palace.

NEWT

An analytical wurde-tool used by an artificer to explore a wurde-matrix and, if necessary, penetrate defences set up by the original creator of that system. It is far more sophisticated than either **poke** or **peek**.

NYM

Nym evolved from a primitive patterning language called FORTH. It is the language that enabled the creation of the first djinn. All djinn are the wurde made flesh.

OBUTAYER

The Obutayer is the matriarch who rules the Genthai in times of peace. When the tribe are on a war-footing their leader is a male warrior.

OMPHALOS

This is the centre post of the Wheel. Cut from a tree of great height and girth, it is considered by some to be the very centre of Midgard and the hub of the Wolf Wheel.

OTHER

The 'Other' is the term used by djinn for those not numbered amongst its own selves. Only by protocol can djinn achieve cooperation. Only by combat can they know their position.

PEEK

A basic Nym wurde-tool which is used to read elements of patterns and work out how they are linked.

POKE

A basic Nym wurde-tool which is used to insert other wurdes or primitives into a pattern.

PRIMITIVES

Primitives are the building blocks from which a wurde is constructed.

PROTECTOR, THE

The ruler of Midgard. He was placed there by the djinn from beyond the Barrier and is answerable to them. His role is to keep order, and for this he has an armed guard of several thousand men who mainly confine themselves to the city of Gindeen and the surrounding area.

Some believe that the Protector is the same one who was appointed when the Human Empire fell and the remnants were placed within the Barrier. Others believe that he is a djinni.

PROTOCOL
Protocol is the name for the rituals, both physical and of the wurde, by means of which djinn coexist without constant bloodletting. Protocol, once completed successfully, is known as a handshake.

QUEUE
This is a long sequence of wurdes held within the mind of a lac. Called by a single wurde, this can result in highly complex behaviour which has been determined in advance by the patterner.

RASIRE
A type of low-level singleton, approximately human in shape, used by other djinn as beasts of burden. Having offensive capabilities, they are also used in battle, but mostly held in reserve. They are difficult to control and are inclined to rebel against authority.

RECARDA
Recarda are warrior djinn developed by ur-humans for combat in cold climes. They have six legs and can run on ice or

snow at great speed. Their triple-hinged jaws are capable of extreme leverage so that no armour is proof against them.

ROMANA

This is the name given to the Second Epoch of the Human Empire. Gladiatorial combat between djinn became the chief form of mass entertainment, and it became fashionable to associate it with the forms, names and behaviour of an ancient primitive human nation called Rome which spoke a language known as Latin. Thus many high-born families adopted Roman names. The terms Trigladius and Gladius are typical Latinate constructs.

SECOND INSURRECTION

The Second Insurrection was a co-ordinated surprise attack upon humans by all djinn. Human civilization fell, but a few thousand survivors were allowed to live and breed within a specially designated area surrounded by a Barrier. This reserve was designated Midgard.

SELF

A sentient component of a djinni; it is a host of false flesh born of a shatek.

SHALATAN

A second-rank djinni just below an asscka. The number of a shalatan is 713 and it has only one large shatek. Consequently, it takes time to regenerate selves slain in battle. This military djinni, created to wage war, is always ruled by a self which takes the human female form. If favoured, such a ruler becomes the concubine of an asscka. A shalatan has great skill in generating selves to perform particular tasks. One such self is known as a peri, which functions as ambassador to other djinn. A peri is skilled in understanding the 'Other' and is proficient in languages.

SHAPE-SHIFTERS

This is a category to which all high djinn belong. To change the form of a self takes time, ranging from hours to weeks depending upon the degree of change required. Preceding this process, high intakes of food are necessary, the most useful being blood taken directly from living creatures. The more usual method of shape-shifting is through use of the wurde and the shatek to generate selves for particular tasks.

SHATEK

A shatek is the mother of a djinni. The midwife is a Nym artificer who shapes the offspring using wurdes of Nym.

SINGLETON

A singleton is a djinni with only one self. This is the lowest form, a being superior to the barbarian human only in speed, strength and reflexes. Yet some singletons have great intellectual capacity and can, by disciplined study of the wurde elevate themselves to higher forms. A sub-form of singleton is known as a **lac**.

STACK

The stack is a defensive tri-glad tactic in which the human

combatant is sandwiched between two defending lacs which rotate like a wheel according to the dictates of combat.

The stack is also the term for a sequence of Nym code to which a patterner might add or subtract. New code is always placed at the summit of a stack.

SYCODA

These are djinn with multiple selves but a limited capacity to generate more. They are shape-shifters and have skills which make them good interrogators. Spying and torture are their main functions. Hob belongs to this category.

TASSELS

This is the name given to those who dwell on the fringes of Hob's citadel and sometimes within it, serving his needs. Some are related to Hob's victims and serve him hoping for news of their loved ones; some belong to a cult which worships Hob, hoping that one day he will return their wives, daughters or sons to them in perfect new bodies. Others are spies who scratch out a living by supplying Hob with information or acting as go-betweens in contacts with certain citizens of Gindeen.

It is the behaviour of this last group which resulted in the name tassels, which are fringed knots on the hem of Hob's cloak. The name was given in mockery because they are a fallen and degraded group, but the idea of knots is appropriate because they are also part of the tangle of conspiracy and counter-conspiracy as the various groups within Midgard struggle to achieve their goals.

TESTIMONY OF MATH, THE

A book written by Math, the hero of Arena 13. It documents his early training and deals at length with each of his contests against the djinni Hob.

TRADER

The Trader is Midgard's only source of lacs and new wurdes of Nym to enhance the patterning of lacs. He usually visits the Sea Gate twice a year: before the season begins and then halfway through it.

TRIGLADIUS

This is fought within Arena 13, the highest level of combat within the Wheel. Three lacs face a lone lac in a contest where victory results from the spilling of human blood. A human combatant stands behind the three in what is known as the 'mag' position; his opponent stands behind the lone lac in the 'min' position. They present themselves as targets for their opponent's lacs. Victory is marked by a ritual cut to the arm of the defeated combatant. Although the intention is not to kill, accidents do happen. In addition, grudge matches are fought which end in the decapitation of the loser.

ULUM

This is a sound-code used within the Trigladius Arena to communicate with and direct a lac, delivered by taps of the combatant's boots on the arena floor. Each combatant develops his own version of Ulum and keeps it a secret.

WEREWIGHT

This is a creature with four selves but a high mind. Three take the form of wolves, but the fourth stands upright and is a mixture of human and wolf. The Genthai fight this creature in ritual combat every thirteen years. Some believe it to be a type of fallen, degraded djinn. Others think this might well have been the origin of Trigladius combat in Arena 13.

WHEEL

The Wheel is situated in the barbarian human city of Gindeen, within the Barrier. It is a building where gladiatorial contests take place between lacs. It has thirteen combat zones, and the highest and most skilful of these is the Trigladius, which is also known as Arena 13.

WHEEL DIRECTORATE

The Directorate has a membership of five, composed of representatives of the gambling houses and headed by Pyncheon, the Chief Marshal. Its primary jurisdiction is over the Wheel, but it has wider legal powers. In the city of Gindeen it is second only to the Protector, but concentrates mostly on the business of the Wheel. For example, a killing in the streets in which a combatant or ex-combatant is involved would fall under its remit.

WURDE

The wurde is the basic unit within the ancient patterning language called Nym. Wurdes contain other wurdes, and to call one wurde is to call all that is embedded within it, both manifest and hidden.